# MURDER AT WHITBY ABBEY

# MURDER AT WHITBY ABBEY

## Cassandra Clark

**Severn House Large Print**
London & New York

This first large print edition published 2020
in Great Britain and the USA by
SEVERN HOUSE PUBLISHERS LTD of
Eardley House, 4 Uxbridge Street, London W8 7SY.
First world regular print edition published 2019 by
Severn House Publishers Ltd.

British Library Cataloguing in Publication Data
A CIP catalogue record for this title is available from the British Library.

ISBN-13: 9780727892553

Except where actual historical events and characters are being described
for the storyline of this novel, all situations in this publication are
fictitious and any resemblance to living persons is purely coincidental.

Severn House Publishers support the Forest Stewardship Council™
[FSC™], the leading international forest certification organisation. All
our titles that are printed on FSC certified paper carry the FSC logo.

Typeset by Palimpsest Book Production Ltd.,
Falkirk, Stirlingshire, Scotland.
Printed and bound in Great Britain by
T J International, Padstow, Cornwall.

# Prologue

*The fire pit in the middle of the small chamber glowed inside its metal basket. It was the only light. The man by the door was looking into the chamber with his hand on the latch as if preparing to leave. The woman sat on a box bed on the other side of the fire. A gold light softened the lines of anger on her face but left her eyes in shadow. Her hair was unbraided and fell in soft waves to her waist. Smoke coiled upwards and lingered under the beams. Rain battered angry fists against the door.*

*The man took a step forward and at the same time pulled his black cloak further round his shoulders as he prepared to leave. The fire sputtered.*

*Into the silence he said, 'So that's it then. I'll be back tomorrow. I'll bring you some apples.'*

*The woman gave a bark of laughter. 'Thank you, brother, thank you, thank you,' she mocked. 'Apples? Lord help me!' She dashed a hand towards him in a gesture of dismissal.*

*He hesitated. 'What else can I do?'*

*'Come to bed.'*

*'I can't . . . You know I can't.'*

*'Please?' In the middle of the pause that followed she rose and ran across the space that separated them to fling herself at his feet. She looked up into his face with her hands*

1

clasped. 'I'm abasing myself! I'm on my knees to you! I'm pleading with you! Look at me!'

A groan escaped his lips. 'Don't tempt me . . . I beg of you, don't . . . You know I love you with all my heart.'

'Do I?'

'You must do. I risk so much.'

'I feel I'd rather never see you again than go on like this. I may as well be a widow.'

'Don't say that.'

'It's true. If you were dead I'd have a memory of your body that would never show me coldness, instead of now – what? What do I have? This ache and longing for you? You'd be better for me dead! Have mercy on me. Don't put me through this hell.'

'I love you. I always will.' He looked helpless and took his hand off the door latch.

'Hollow words! You taunt me with them. You're dragging me down into the flames. I can't do this! Go away!'

A pause followed.

He made up his mind. His hand went to the latch. Rain blustered against the door, forcing it open. He pulled up his hood. 'I'll come back tomorrow.'

'Why risk it? So you can kill me with your cruelty?' She rose to her feet. 'I wish you dead!'

He opened the door and rain scudded inside. 'I'll bring you some apples when I come down again.'

# One

In the north of the country beyond the Humber, in the small Cistercian priory of Swyne by Beverley in the East Riding of Yorkshire, the prioress, a gaunt, ageless woman with a face criss-crossed as if with threads of gold filigree, was standing as usual in front of her personal altar within the chilly stone-built chamber she reserved for her private use.

Hildegard, her nun, entered.

'You know what this is about?' the prioress demanded as soon as the white-robed nun appeared. 'You are to go to Whitby Abbey! No' – she put up a hand – 'don't object! It is Abbot de Courcy's wish that you continue your penance until he is satisfied that you have repented and repined.' She softened her tone. 'You committed a grievous sin against him and against the Rule last autumn, Hildegard. It is only reasonable that you make amends. He could have had you whipped in front of everyone, or excommunicated as he threatened, or walled up the way they do in France! You're fortunate to be in England and to have escaped such an extreme punishment.'

Hildegard tightened her lips. It was true. Hubert de Courcy could do what he liked as

3

abbot. He could make her do anything. It was his right. He was lord at Meaux. She had nothing to say in her own defence. She had wronged him and broken the Rule and that was that.

A memory of the turbulent night alone with Ulf in the deep sea cave returned – the tide had ripped into the cleft between the rocks, cutting them both off from the outside world so that its disciplines and laws came to mean nothing. With a sudden and passionate force an image of her lover rose before her in momentary joy and shame, contrary flames of desire and regret obliterating all fear of hellfire in the hereafter.

In a barely audible voice she managed to say, '*Mea culpa*, my lady. I submit to the abbot's will.'

'He sees it as punishment to send you abroad at this time of year . . . which it is, of course. Who would want to be on the road in this dead month, with Christmas scarcely over and the Twelve Days turning the world upside-down in riot and feasting? And the weather, of course, even worse in the far north of the county to be sure.' She gave a mock shudder like one never able to feel the cold but aware that others did.

Hildegard felt chastened and, because it was a rhetorical question, did not answer.

'In my opinion,' the prioress continued, 'you are also the best woman to send up there.' She gave Hildegard an assessing glance. 'You won't be swayed by the Benedictines when they start to barter over the sale of their relic – unless you find a monk with excessive good looks and charm – most unlikely – but, if you do, that will

4

be part of your penance too and I trust you to keep a cool head on your shoulders in that case. There will certainly be no Sir Ulf of Langbar to lead you astray – or for you to lead astray either if it comes to that.' She rearranged the folds of her garments. 'It's a dour place, right for penance. From what I've heard those brothers eat, sleep and pray and not much else. You'll have a suitably hard time, as I reminded our lord abbot. And of course you'll have to take a priest with you for confession – Brother Luke will accompany you.'

'Brother Luke?'

'The same. He'll keep you on track. You wouldn't want to shock him, would you?'

Hildegard smiled wanly in response to the prioress's sudden chuckle of amusement. 'It takes little to shock dear Luke,' she replied. 'He's such a . . .' She searched for the right word and settled on the innocuous 'youngster' before continuing: 'He's had so little experience of the secular world that most things shock him. I'm sure my confession about my night with Ulf has already caused him his own sleepless nights.'

'Quite. It should also do him good to see how the Benedictines live, as I pointed out to Hubert.' A glint in the depths of the prioress's grey eyes offered a suggestion of complicity when she added, 'You may be wondering why our lord abbot smiles so on our desire for a relic of our own? I'll tell you why. He deems it useful to himself and the Abbey of Meaux to have a nearby priory with its own holy relic to complement the one he has on display. To complement it, mark you, not to compete with it. His Talking Crucifix is a great draw for pilgrims, but another relic with a different appeal would make the long journey to this remote part of the Riding a further incentive to pilgrimage. He hopes,' she added, 'that it will draw on the swarms of folk visiting St John's shrine at Beverley and thereby augment the number of pilgrims consulting the Crucifix. I understand his thinking without condoning it.'

'So I am definitely to set out for Whitby Abbey in order to obtain this relic?'

'At once.'

Hildegard opened her mouth to protest, then closed it and gave an audible sigh.

'Bear with him,' the prioress advised. 'You wounded our beloved abbot most grievously. He did not expect you to capitulate to any man, let alone Lord Roger's steward, a man famed as much for his martial skill as for his affable and attractive presence. Everyone loves Ulf and to believe he was condemned to death and that you would never see him again in this life was understandably too much for any compassionate woman to bear. Your surrender is no mystery to me. Hubert, however, is naturally bewildered. He's hurt and confused. Now you must complete your penance until he can reinstate you in his personal pantheon of saints again. If he has his way you will pay the price in humility and be better for it. It is not ended yet. Remember, he is not vindictive. I imagine the light punishment he is demanding has been discussed *ad nauseam* in Chapter. There are those who would encourage a far crueler penalty. A journey to Whitby at this time of year is nothing when you think about it. It's a charming place. You will suffer the weather. And you will return as pure as driven snow.'

'I stand in humility, my lady, and in gratitude, too, for the lightness of my punishment.' She guessed the prioress had spoken on her behalf – ever, as always, keen to defend her nuns against the encroachments, as she saw it, of the monks of Meaux. She lifted her head. 'And the holy relic I'm to barter for . . .? What exactly is it?'

A derisive aspect appeared in the prioress's demeanour, although she did not laugh out loud but merely allowed a twitch of her lips. 'It is no less than a lock of hair of our most holy sister Abbess Hild of Whitby.'

She held Hildegard's glance for one long, meaningful moment.

'Imagine it, if you will. It will be seven hundred years old by now. We might ask ourselves whether such a thing could survive from the time of the great Anglian foundation when Hild was abbess, to the present day. Holy though she undoubtedly was, without a miracle – which of course, we are told, may be possible – we might question whether something as fragile as a lock of hair can be preserved.' She raised her eyebrows.

'It might seem doubtful,' Hildegard ventured.

The prioress nodded. 'Given the violent assaults of the Northmen on the abbey, its burning to the ground, its rebuilding in stone by William the Bastard after the Harrowing of the North, and the turmoil that accompanies such events, is it likely such an object could survive? If so, may we ask how? Does it mean someone with

7

exceptional forethought hid it in a secret place which has only now come to light? How is it no-one has heard of such a miraculous find until now, in the days of the abbey's need? You can count on it, Hildegard, we would have heard of it, even down here in Swyne.'

'And if it is genuine, as is being claimed, why do the monks not keep it for their own benefit?' Hildegard ventured.

'Indeed.' The prioress shrugged her shoulders under the rough stamyn fabric of her habit. 'We must assume that their suddenly erupting need for gold can only to be assuaged by the sale of such a miraculous discovery. Maybe you will find answers, Hildegard. Perhaps you'll find a way of authenticating it – otherwise we have nothing to go on but the word of the lord abbot of Whitby.'

'A word I'm sure we can trust,' murmured Hildegard in a voice that showed she was not convinced.

'I'm sure we can,' agreed the prioress in a brisk tone that revealed she regarded the abbot's trustworthiness as of little consequence. 'The main thing is to get our hands on it. At any price.'

When Hildegard left the precinct and strode out into the crisp December morning with the blessings of her superior ringing in her ears, she was still feeling shocked. What had she commanded? Get it 'at any price'?

There had been no time to question such an injunction. That Hubert was behind the whole thing was not in doubt. And if this was the task he set, his price for her great sin against him, she would obey to the letter. She would wipe the slate clean. Her standing at Meaux, if not at Swyne, forced her to it. She would demonstrate her obedience to Abbot Hubert de Courcy's wishes, no matter how it irked.

But to bring back as a prize a possibly fraudulent artefact *at any price*? Would the lord abbot thank her for that?

*St Stephen's Day, late afternoon. The cliff path south of Whitby.*

Four riders appeared on the horizon. Swathed in flowing cloaks, hoods tied tight with linen strips, they urged their eager mounts northwards, up one rolling chalk hillside and down another, ever onwards, as light drained from the sky, and to the east, the cliff edge, the sea below, crashing on to the scaur, to the west the hills and dales of the North Riding, and further on, soon into disputed country and the beginnings of the raided lands of Northumberland.

The riders turned up a green lane that ran, it seemed, forever upwards in a steep gradient. Without pause, they continued their ascent.

Hildegard had been instructed to take with her not only the recently ordained Luke but, to her surprise, two monks as well. On Abbot de Courcy's orders they were assigned to the journey, whether as bodyguards for the long and treacherous ride through wildwood bristling with masterless men, or whether as warders, to show that she was still under a cloud for breaking the Rule and to prevent her from further straying, she did not know, nor had she asked them yet. They were old friends and allies, a cause for gratitude whether the abbot knew it or not.

Now she called to the rider in the lead. 'Halloo, Gregory! How much further? Can you see it yet?'

He reined in his great black horse as she rode alongside. 'Further yet, Hildegard. I see no sign of any abbey.'

'My palfrey is blowing somewhat, that's all. I think I may walk a little to save her.'

'We may as well take it at a slower pace. We can't be far away. We'll surely arrive by nightfall. The poor brutes have shown great willing since we left Meaux.' He hauled on the reins and soon enough slid down out of the saddle and stretched his long, taut body made muscular by years of physical endurance in the service of his Order in Outremer. Slapping his mount fondly on the neck, he said, 'They must be wondering what's happened to the flat earth of Holderness. I expect they're longing to be back there among the marshes. Are you going to walk for a while, Egbert?' he called out to the muffled rider following Hildegard.

A burly monk drew level. 'It surely can't be far?'

He peered up the steep slope where the lane ran between thick, leafless hedges of hawthorn and disappeared round a bend higher up. 'But for the moaning of the sea I'd believe we'd lost our way,' he remarked, slipping smoothly from the saddle. 'What say you, Luke?' He turned his head.

The fourth figure coming up slowly behind the others pulled his scarf from his face to reveal young, intelligent features, a wide, boyish mouth whose lips were now drawn back in a stoic grin as he caught up with them. 'My admiration for you two fellows increases by the day,' he replied, wincing in the saddle. 'How in the name of St Benet you rode all the way to Jerusalem, putting up a show against the Saracen as you went, amazes me. I'm lost in admiration. I bow down before you! I kiss your feet! At least I would if I could get down off this poor brute.' He chuckled. 'Since leaving Meaux we've ridden a fraction of the distance you fellows covered with such apparent ease but after this I doubt whether I'll be capable of even crawling across the garth. I'll have to be carried into church.'

'You've had life too easy, tucked up at Meaux, Luke,' observed Egbert with a teasing smile. 'Doubtless it's why your abbot has prised you out of your cell for a jaunt up-country to prove what you're made of.'

'Doubtless. I hope I don't disappoint him. But back me up in this, Hildegard. Do they set a cracking pace or not?'

'They do. I'm hard pressed to keep up. But we must surely be close by now.' She glanced at the sky. 'It looks like rain. Let's continue for a while on foot,' she encouraged. 'It would be best to arrive before dead of night if we can and not waste time resting when we must be close by.'

All afternoon clouds the colour of plate armour had been stacking in the east, shutting out what little light the December day had eked forth. Now as the light faded the day was uncannily still despite the restlessness of the unseen waves battering the shore. No wind penetrated the muffling tunnel of the lane. That, at least, was something to be thankful for, although the air still had a bite in it – an advantage, the ever optimistic Luke claimed, to prevent sweating, although their horses were steaming as if melting into the mist.

Dismounting, they began to walk on while Luke remained groaning in the saddle and came after.

The possibility that they might still have far to go brought a measure of uneasiness to Hildegard and she glanced warily into the thick hedges that closed them in. It was ideal ambush country, far from any visible habitation.

The leaves were gone from the branches at this late date in the year, leaving only blackened winter fruits, with a few rejected berries hanging motionless among the nest of twigs. Somewhere out of sight the piercing shrieks of sea birds sounded like cries for help.

Since leaving the last settlement they had passed no-one. Any traveller not driven by urgency would already be safely inside the walls of town, abbey or grange where the festivities would be continuing until Epiphany. It was a penance for all four to miss the one time in the year when feasting might take precedence over fasting and prayer.

The two Jerusalem monks did not seem bothered. Everything, in their eyes, was equal. Their experiences of bloody slaughter in the desert lands of Outremer had toughened them against horrors that would have had most people praying in terror for the deity's intercession. They seemed impervious to the fears of ordinary folk and merely thankful for every day of peace to befall them. They walked on until their horses seemed rested then got back into the saddle. The lane wound on higher still.

'I was at Handale priory to the north of here when I came back from Compostela,' Hildegard remarked in as normal a voice as she could muster to hide her uneasiness, 'but I've never been along these cliffs. It's wilder here than in Holderness, bleak though the marshland is at this time of year.'

The dark tunnel of the track was made more menacing by the constant melancholy thrashing of the sea. Concealing shadows lay across the track ahead. Hildegard tried to imagine spring when the blossom would be out. The scent would be ravishing but it suddenly reminded her of Hubert and she kicked her horse into a canter.

'Can any of you make sense of the country hidden beyond these hawthorn brakes?' she called over her shoulder. Occasional glimpses revealed only wide open grassland disappearing into low cloud.

'We're burrowing uphill like moles, that's for sure,' Egbert remarked, riding alongside. His right hand rested on the pommel of the sword under his cloak.

'It seems to be pasture hereabouts. It must be

where they run their sheep.' She matched his casual tone.

'I suspect we've been on Benedictine land for some time. What do you think, Greg?'

'I think that vill we passed – what was it called? Hawsker? – I believe it to be one of the abbey granges. We were told to look out for it.' Gregory drew a little ahead of the rest, his hand, too, Hildegard noticed, resting on the hilt of the sword concealed under his cloak.

Last of all came Luke, no sign of unease on his face. He seemed to be in a gentle dream of imminent arrival, as if already enjoying a winter fire and a beaker of mulled wine even as he suffered the unaccustomed toil of a three-day ride.

'We crossed a little stretch of John of Gaunt's hunting country when we entered the outreach of the Forest of Pickering,' Gregory announced, 'but this must be Northumberland's territory by now, so close to Whitby.'

'I wonder how their foresters get on,' Egbert wondered.

'No doubt well enough. No point in quarrelling with neighbours or you'd never get anything done.'

'I doubt their future venison knows well enough to keep behind their own lines!' Egbert grimaced. 'There must be plenty of occasions for disagreement.'

'Nothing to do with us,' Gregory rejoined with satisfaction.

As he spoke, it began to rain. Coming down without warning, it was a cloudburst, hard and vicious, halfway to being sleet already. They pulled their cloaks tighter, re-knotted the linen strips over their faces, and did not slow down but drove their mounts on into the full pitch of it.

Luke urged his horse forward and took the lead. 'I'll have a look up ahead,' he told them. 'See if I can spot anything.' He became a blur as he disappeared into the pelting rain.

When he reached the next bend some way ahead they heard him give a great shout. Egbert reached under his cloak for his sword but stayed his hand when he saw Luke stand up in the stirrups and punch the sky.

'He looks like a Compostela pilgrim!' Hildegard exclaimed.

But it wasn't the name of St James he bellowed. It was the name of the Whitby abbess, St Hild.

'Be praised! Huzzah for the Abbess!'

They quickened their pace to where the hawthorns opened out into a wide, rain-swept pasture. Beyond it, on the summit of the cliff, glittering and grey and even more massive than expected, rose a building of spires and roofs and one great east window set in the high wall facing them. It was a building erected so precipitously on the wild headland that it had nothing but sky behind it.

'Whitby Abbey!' breathed Hildegard.

'Amazing!' exclaimed Egbert. He gazed open-mouthed in the rain despite the many splendours he had seen on his travels.

'Impressive,' agreed Gregory with less emotion. 'Hail the master builders!'

Luke was exclaiming in awe as he rode back

a few paces down the slope to urge them on. His face was streaming with rain. 'Just look at that great east window. Isn't it glorious?'

Suddenly the entire edifice shone, brilliant and sinister, in a single splinter of light torn from the sun. The turrets spiking into the belly of the rain clouds glittered. Then, as the brief shaft of light died, the height and weight of stone acquired an aura of foreboding as it slipped back behind the rain.

They continued towards the summit. Sleet, borne on a bitter wind, began to slice into them. It obliterated the towers and roofs and allowed only a sense of the awesome authority of the church: its massive power stamped on the entire landscape, on the abbey pastures and the small, soft shapes of huddled sheep, on the thatched hovels, the distant outbuildings, the store sheds and the stables and on the large stone buildings that could be brewery or bake house attached to the grange. All of them were squat and diminished in the looming shadow of this symbol of power, the holy edifice of the abbey.

By now everything was streaming with rain and pricked by sleet – the horses, the four riders, everything in all directions was swamped and lashed by the sharp lances of the storm. Their cloaks flew in the wind like rags.

'We must find shelter!' Gregory shouted. He spurred his willing horse up the slope and, as it seemed, towards their fate.

'At least we shall be within the enclave before nightfall!' Hildegard exclaimed as she followed into the teeth of the storm.

Egbert urged his mount up the last remaining challenge until he overtook them both and began to canter across the pasture on a track that eventually skirted a long stretch of reed-fringed water. When he came to the margins he shouted something to the others, stood in his stirrups, and pointed: an image of the abbey was doubled in the rain-pleated surface as in a pocked looking glass.

For a moment, despite the weather, they were stopped, awed by the sight.

'Not one abbey but two!' Gregory exclaimed.

'It seems to be made of water and vapour. It's Undine's realm. It is not of our world of earth and stone and mud.' Luke furrowed his brow, and spoke in wonder. 'What alien realm are we about to enter?'

'Make haste!' Egbert called back. 'This storm is going to roll right over the headland. See!' He pointed towards the east. 'It's driving straight for us! Hurry, before it hurls us off the cliff to our doom.'

He didn't wait but whipped his streaming horse to a canter. After a brief, awed glance at the visible doubling of the abbey's image in the lake they hurried on to where the track bypassed the east end of the abbey church, skirted the unprotected north side and revealed the welcome shelter of the west gate.

Rain sliced across the foregate, turned to sleet and filled the tracks of their horses' hooves with pellets of ice as they hurried for shelter. Silence fell as soon as the constant roar of rain drumming on their waxed cloaks stopped.

17

'So here we are!' Hildegard said in a subdued voice as she pushed with the others further underneath the vault and out of the storm.

This was going to be a penance to satisfy even the Abbot of Meaux.

# Two

The porter was a bustling fellow, like many of his calling. He took a morose delight in welcoming them in 'out of this shower', as he put it.

'We'll soon have you people warm and dry,' he promised. 'Leave your mounts to our stablers. They'll be well stalled. You three brothers may go at once to the warming room where you'll find something to console your hearts, and when you're ready one of the brothers will show you to the dortoir where you may leave your saddle-bags. It's near on Vespers and if you hurry you'll have time to see to your comforts before the bell.'

Assured that Hildegard was in good hands, the monks from Meaux lunged through the sleet in the direction of the cloisters.

'As for you, my lady,' said the porter, turning to her, 'you're most welcome at Whitby. You'll find plenty of congenial company in the guest house. It's bursting at the seams for the duration of the Twelve Days, of course, but plenty of room for you. Here!' He grabbed a young lad by the scruff of the neck and dragged him before

18

her. 'This is Torold. Conduct this gracious lady to the guest house, lad. You can take one of them greased covers to protect her from the hail.'

The lad was about eight or nine, of an age to be given to the abbey to be taught the rudiments of reading and writing before turning to his chosen path. Bobbing his head, he gave her a sharp look that held in it something far beyond his years.

'You're drenched through, lady. Best follow me close as I know all the sheltered ways. Come.' Taking hold of the waterproofed cloth at the same time as he grasped the hand of a silent companion of about his own age lurking by his side, he beckoned for Hildegard to follow. Amused by his self-confidence she glanced after the horses as the grooms hurried them away, then followed her guide to where he waited in the doorway with his companion, the cloth held up ready like the roof of a tent between them.

His route to the guest house followed in the lee of a sandstone wall that enclosed the west end of the abbey precinct. On the other side of the path the cliff fell steeply away and, some distance below, the thatched roofs of many houses could be seen through a shimmering mist of sleet and smoke like a vision under the sea.

'Is that Whitby town down there?' she asked him, gesturing towards the fall of cliff.

'It is that. A bustling place, my lady, full of—' He broke off for a moment before saying, 'But maybe not a place for you.'

'So why is that?'

19

'Oh . . .' He pursed his mouth. 'They keep to themselves. It's a rough, irreligious port. We are up here,' he added sententiously, 'and they are down there. Abbey here, town below. As God wills it.'

They were almost at the doors of the guest house and before Hildegard could ask him to explain – it could surely be no worse than anywhere else she had visited – a monk in the black robes of a Benedictine came panting up the steep paved trod from that same direction. His hood protected his face from the driving sleet but he held it out in such a way that he could see a few feet ahead and where to set his foot on the uneven cobble stones. Even so he failed to notice the group huddling against the wall and was almost level when Torold shouted, 'Father! It's me!'

The monk stopped. He pushed his hood back a little to reveal sharp, hazel eyes in a face as pale as whey. He was good-looking despite that, no more than twenty-five or so, and now he gave a surprised laugh. 'You scamp! What are you doing out in all this?'

Then he noticed Hildegard underneath the waterproof. 'My lady, do forgive me . . .' He made an obeisance.

'I'm taking her to the guest house, Father. Running errands for the porter. She's that nun from the Abbey of Meaux. Her brothers are already headed for the warming room. You'll catch up with them if you get a move on.'

The monk's smile broadened. 'Will I indeed? I see you're well informed as usual.'

'I never fail,' replied the lad. 'They've come about the holy relic.'

The monk gave Hildegard a swift, enigmatic glance then, pulling his hood over his face again, he continued up towards the gatehouse and Torold, putting a friendly hand under Hildegard's elbow, urged her onwards. The priest strode away on rough wooden pattens, his bare red toes protruding and wet as he splashed headlong through the puddles, hurrying to be in time for Vespers, or maybe lured by the promise of a brief respite in the warmth.

'So what do you make of all this?' murmured Gregory when he saw Hildegard in the cloister after Vespers. Darkness had already fallen at this late point in the year and flaring cressets were ranged along the vault, making the shadows dance. Rain was falling with a constant drumming on the low roof. Gargoyles mounted under the guttering were spewing forth a never-ending stream of rainwater into the yard from their mouths.

'We were expected, that's clear, but so far I've been left to my own devices,' she replied. 'How about you?'

'I saw the prior and a couple of sub-priors from a distance near the high altar. No sign of the abbot. A crowd of choir monks were there, keeping themselves to themselves. When we met some of them in the warming room after we arrived they were not unfriendly but not forthcoming either.'

'They know why we're here. At least, if a young

novice like that one called Torold knows, I'm
sure everyone else does. Did you meet the priest
in the warming room?'

Gregory shook his head. 'None but monks
were present. They seemed to be reluctant to
refer to our purpose here, despite one or two
leading questions from Egbert to draw them out.
Maybe they've been given instructions not to
gossip in case it interferes with the abbot's
bartering strategy. How much do you think we
can get this relic for?'

Hildegard had already told him that the
prioress had instructed her to get it *at any price*.
His reply had been a mere raising of his eyebrows.
Now she said, 'I'm going to wait for their first
move. Let's see what they expect.'

'I'll be happy if we can do the business quickly
then get off back to Meaux. I must admit I find
it odd that nobody has bothered to approach us.
The porter was welcoming enough, doing his
job, but I feel a sense of hostility from everybody else, as if they have an opinion about us
we would not like. You'd imagine they'd want
to get on with the matter. Surely they're eager to
witness the transfer of our gold into their own
coffers?'

'Maybe it's because of the Twelve Days.
Everything is always topsy-turvy at this time.
Do they appoint a boy bishop here?'

'I expect so. Maybe you'll have to do your
bargaining with a ten year old!'

'If it's with the one who conducted me to the
guest house, I fear I might come off worst!'

They parted. Gregory returned to the monks'

refectory, Hildegard to the guest house. Given that it was supposed to be busy at this time, according to the porter, she had seen no-one else in the hall and when she returned it was to find only a few servants erecting the trestles for later.

Up in her chamber, small but thankfully for her sole use, she opened her travel bag and sighed over her damp clothes, the spare leggings and her shift, and after spreading them over a chest in the hope that they might dry out, she took something else from the bag. It was a small velvet pouch, a bursa, containing a wooden box. It was worked with Cistercian austerity and was an appropriate size for a lock of hair, holy or not. Skilfully fashioned from a single piece of oak, it was open on one side to enable its future contents to be visible and had an unadorned, closely fitting lid. A scent of beeswax rose up as she handled it.

Placing it back in the bursa she put it under her pillow – not because it was valuable in itself, but because it was a special thing, designed to acquire a new and holy significance. Next she took out a leather pouch with clever triple locks and buried it for safety deep inside her bag, stuffed the whole lot under her bed then went down to the hall again where at least there was a good fire and a warming mug of Rhenish waiting.

The hall was lit by floating candles set up in half a dozen wall brackets. The storm was still clattering sleet against the shutters. Lay servants began to bring in cloths to spread over the

23

trestles. A smell of cooking meat wafted from behind the screens, jugs of wine were set along the tables and bread was brought in on wooden platters.

A sound of horses and the shouts of a sudden influx of people entering the garth sent Hildegard to the door. A group of about a dozen riders in the turmoil of arrival were swarming on to the garth with cloaks, hoods and brightly decorated harnesses illuminated in the light of hissing torches. Covered in mud the horses backed and side-stepped as they were ridden in. Brindled hounds seethed between their legs. A cage of hawks was unloaded from a cart and whisked off towards the mews and amid the barking of the dogs and the neighing of horses impatient to be in the dry, the voices of the newcomers came, loud and confident, instructing the army of stable hands swarming into the rain to attend to their mounts.

A burly figure in a blue hood and shrouded in wet furs was conducted with much ceremony across the garth into the cloisters. A troop of monastics scurried in his wake through the puddles.

Was this the abbot? It was likely their indifferent reception was because he had been out hunting when the storm struck.

She watched from the doorway as some of the arrivals peeled off from the main group and, hunched against the squalls, rushed with boisterous shouts for the guest house. She stepped back as half a dozen strangers poured in. Seculars, she surmised, as she watched a crowd of servants bustle forward to attend them. The group comprised several men, one elderly, one young, and several others indistinguishable under the flickering light, with a young woman squealing and giggling about her wet hair and last of all, unexpectedly, a nun. Unlike Hildegard, this woman, when she shrugged off her cloak, revealed the black robes of a Benedictine.

The others were already flinging off wet furs for the servants to pick up while a pack of yapping table dogs ran about, smelling strongly of damp. The noise level rose to a deafening pitch.

The nun stood calmly to one side.

Hildegard went over to her. After an exchange of greetings she asked her directly if she had taken part in the abbot's hunting party.

'To my rue! It was a complete disaster!' She explained that it was too wet for the hawks to fly and they had to take shelter in a convenient manor house. 'Our host meanwhile complained about the weather the whole time as if it doesn't rain in his part of the world.'

Hildegard was puzzled. 'But this *is* his part of the world, isn't it?'

The nun shook her head. 'He comes from the soft south. Apparently the monks down there are so holy God never punishes them with bad weather.' She gave a placid shrug of the shoulders. 'So of course we all agreed that he was most fortunate to live in such virtue while we, poor northern sinners as we are, can only suffer the penalties for our wickedness. That seemed to staunch his plaints for a while.'

Hildegard smiled. 'But who is he? I thought it was the abbot of Whitby?'

'What? Him?' She adopted a cautious change of expression, little more than pulling back the corners of her mouth. 'The fellow you saw just now in the blue hood was no abbot. He's a Somerset manorial lord, here to do business on behalf of the abbot of Glastonbury, don't you know?' Her lips curled. 'To hear him you'd imagine he was second only to the Pope.'

'Glastonbury, did you say?'

'The same.'

'But—'

'Before you ask, he's here to take back the relic of our blessed St Hild for the further aggrandizement of his spiritual lord, the abbot.'

'I see.' Hildegard's expression gave nothing away, but she was stunned. It meant that the relic was to be the subject of competition. She wondered if her prioress had had any idea they were entering a bidding war. It would mean that the price would indeed be high, depending on how much this new contender desired to possess it.

The nun squinted up at Hildegard. 'I'm Sister Aveline,' she told her. 'I come from Yedingham. We're a small community with little to attract pilgrims. All we have are debts and discontented tenants and river tolls. It was to be our last chance. I'm saddened to think that I shall have to return empty-handed. It'll mean the end of us. We shall be dispersed – unless some rich baron steps in to save us.' She sighed. 'But despair is a sin and we can but hope and trust in God to see the justice of our cause. I expect you're here for the same purpose?' She raised thin eyebrows.

Hildegard nodded. 'And with a similar belief to yours, that the justice of our cause outweighs that of any other contender. I had no idea we were to compete for the privilege of owning a lock of hair! Nor, I doubt, did my prioress. It seems almost blasphemous to turn it into a merchant's auction. Maybe Whitby's need is more desperate than we know?' She frowned. 'But who are the others?' She glanced over her shoulder at the rowdy group already sitting at the table and making free with the wine.

'The elderly fellow with the grizzled beard is a minor baron, Sir Ranulph, from up country, and that's his new wife. Next to her is Sir Ranulph's son Darius from his first marriage. I'm not sure Sir Ranulph is after the relic. I can't see what he would want with it. I assume he has other business, or maybe he's merely here for entertainment during the Twelve Days? They only arrived yesterday.'

Hildegard frowned. 'From what I've heard of Glastonbury it's one of the wealthiest abbeys in the country. They must already be celebrating their victory.'

Before the Great Silence descended over the abbey between Compline and Matins, Hildegard let herself out on to the garth and went to find Brother Luke. He was pacing the cloisters with a shocked look on his face and when she appeared he went to her with a gasp of welcome.

'This is a strange place, Hildegard,' he muttered. 'Can you believe it, the monks are playing dice in the warming room! At least, those ones are who haven't disappeared on some errand into the town. It must be urgent business to make them brave the storm,' he added. 'I thought it might be a matter of some seriousness to force them out on such a night so I offered to go with them. All I got were odd looks!'

'The storm's beginning to abate a little. Would they not say why they were going down there?'

He shook his head. 'I mentioned it to Gregory and Egbert and they merely gave those world-weary smiles to suggest they've seen it all before and couldn't bear to talk about it. But what, Hildegard? What is it that I know nothing about?'

'No doubt someone will tell you later on. I'm more interested in why there's no abbot to greet us. Where is he?'

'I imagined he must be at prayer when we arrived, but he must let up some time. I suppose it is the Twelve Days when every sot-wit seems to take over.' Frowning, he added, 'Nobody seems to be in charge. I saw a group of novices playing bandy sticks in the north aisle earlier on! Nobody chided them. When they saw me they simply carried on around me. Can you imagine that happening at Meaux?'

With his habitual kindly expression and open, innocent face, he peered closely through the shadows. 'There they are, you see? Over there. Still playing. Are you shocked? I shudder to imagine what it must be like in the guest house.' He turned to her. 'Are you being made welcome? I hope they're showing you some respect. What's going on over there?'

'It's convivial,' she replied. 'A hunting party

came in not long ago. They couldn't fly the hawks so as far as I can make out they took shelter in some manor house and drank their cellar dry. But that's not all.' She told him about the Glastonbury visitor in the blue hood and his purpose in being here. 'For sure the prioress would not expect me to attempt to outbid their abbot's emissary. It would empty our coffers for years to come.'

'We could be back at Meaux by the end of the week if we left now,' he remarked with plaintive longing.

She gave him a candid look. 'Is that what you think we should do? Give up without even trying?'

'I feel uncomfortable here. They accuse we Cistercians of being austere – but when they say the Benedictines are becoming lax with their love of comfort, well, I never thought the accusation was to be taken so literally! It's not just game playing. You should have seen the amount of wine being drunk! And the food! Meat! Meat of every kind you can imagine. And not even eaten in the misericord, but there in the refectory for anybody to indulge in!'

'Be that as it may. One thing is certain, Luke. I can't return to Meaux without even trying to get hold of the relic. That's what we're here for. Hubert won't be pleased to see me trailing back without it. Nor will my prioress.'

Nor would it do anything for her redemption if she failed.

The Great Silence was to allow the monks time for rest before the night Offices, but it did not prevail in the guest house. Carousing by the unsuccessful huntsmen and their followers carried on until long after Matins itself.

Sister Aveline retired early and eventually Hildegard went in search of her own bed chamber where she tossed and turned for some hours within hearing of distant singing, sudden bursts of loud, male guffaws, and a deceiving silence that constantly erupted into more shouting and singing.

She lay with her eyes open calculating how many nights were to be endured like this. Perhaps Luke was right and they should cut off back to Meaux where they belonged. If, as he suggested, this was the usual pattern of behaviour, the criticism of Benedictine laxity seemed to be well earned. Worse, their chances of obtaining the relic seemed remote now she knew there were other contenders.

After revolving the matter in her mind for what seemed like hours she turned over for the hundredth time and buried her face in the unaccustomed softness of down. The novices Luke had encountered might only have been full of high spirits because of the celebrations taking place after the solemnity of Christmas. Boys will take advantage of any opportunity to kick over the traces. And as for the guests, seculars as they were, with no respect for the Silence, why should they not sing in celebration? Nobody expects them to get up and pray in the middle of the night. They can sleep when they choose.

She started to wonder about the guests again.

Sister Aveline had pointed out three corrodians who had joined the party. They were living in a row of almshouses outside the precinct under a permanent invitation to dine in the abbey. They could have no interest in the relic, even if they had possessed the means to purchase it. Had any others come to view it and put a price on it, or was it only Glastonbury and the little priory at Yedingham that Swyne had to compete against?

She began to drift towards sleep, lulled, surprisingly, by the sound of the seculars making merry and images of the last few hours . . . the seemingly endless to-ing and fro-ing of the servants with platters laden with flesh, fish and fowl . . . and the perpetual round of the wine jugs . . . and the heat from the fire with half a forest on it, roaring up the chimney . . . too tiring, coming after that long uphill ride to the abbey in the sudden violence of the storm . . . the rain . . . (she turned over again) oh, the rain . . . everything sodden, garments clinging, and the poor miserable horses, so valiant and obliging and that first sight of . . . that vision . . . even seen through sheets of driving rain . . . sleet really . . . rain first, drenching them all . . . then sleet . . . battering their capes with the sound of little pebbles being thrown at them . . . and must remember to get out the cures for coughs and sniffles tomorrow . . . should have thought of it . . . and will do that . . . yes . . . and how the rain, the sleet, had battered the surface of the lake, fracturing the reflected image of the abbey . . . and how she must pay attention to the guests . . . must do . . . must find out what they were willing to pay . . . how badly they wanted St Hild's hair . . . and it was impressive and glorious and sinister all at the same time . . . that first view of the abbey while far away . . . now . . . at this moment . . . far off in Meaux . . . he . . . aloof and irresistible . . . in the Abbey of Meaux where he would . . .

The bell for Prime woke Hildegard with a start. At first she had no idea where she was, but then the previous day's events came flooding back. After those first long, restless hours she had eventually slept the night through and missed Matins, and Lauds!

Vaguely she remembered being awake as the hall went quiet and stairs creaking as the guests came up to bed . . . and then, before she could drift off to sleep, came the sound of drumming from the direction of the town.

At first it was faint, scarcely enough to keep a mouse awake, and she had drifted in and out of sleep, the drumming fading then being taken up again, and a sound like Northumbrian pipes, far off, adding a tune to it and frail shouting, then all of it fading blessedly away until suddenly the bell tolled across the garth and roused everyone to prayer.

She stretched and yawned and realized she felt much better. Sleep had done her good. Today, no doubt, the abbot would bless them with his presence, they would be shown the holy relic and some overture would be made to enable them to assess their chances and secure it for their priory. As they must.

*Look at our claim*, she thought as she got out of bed.

St Hild was a woman. She was from Yorkshire. What better right to it did anyone have than themselves, a group of devout Yorkshire women? Certainly a house of monks from the south had no natural right to it.

Besides, Glastonbury had its Holy Thorn. They had their tomb of King Arthur. They had their tomb of Guinevere. What need had they of a mere lock of hair with all that in their possession?

Resolved to fight, she pulled up her woollen stockings to the thigh, adjusted the garters, pulled down her under shift, dragging over it her over-mantle and her habit, then stepped into her knee boots, pulling the laces tight. She plucked her cloak from its nail, wrapping her hair out of sight under its head covering, and determined to secure the relic for Swyne if she possibly could, she descended to the refectory to break her fast.

The son of the grizzle-bearded Sir Ranulph at table the night before, a man who ignored nuns or maybe women, or both, was fastidiously poking between his teeth with a splinter of wood and blinked his eyelids at her in greeting as soon as she sat down. Of Sister Aveline there was no sign. In fact, apart from the young lordling, busy with his teeth, the pristine state of the table suggested that no-one else had come down either.

To be certain she asked, 'Is everyone at Prime? I'm afraid I awoke too late to attend.'

'You'll be forgiven in heaven, sister. At least you're on your feet. Everybody else is still abed with throbbing headaches. I'm only here because I'm worried about my hawk. We had a devilish day yesterday and the creature wouldn't fly.'

'Too wet. They hate rain.'

'I'll get an eagle next. My saker is only useful in a desert, God blame her. I'll be sending her back if she doesn't buck up, useless creature – or have her baked in a pie.'

'You cannot expect a hawk to go against its nature.'

He grunted. 'For the amount I paid for her I expect more for my money. I expect her to do as I command.' With no further obeisance he pushed back the bench and strode out.

*If that was my son I'd teach him manners*, she thought as the door crashed behind him. Her son, sixteen next birthday, was serving in the palace of the Bishop of Norwich. It had been some time since she had been able to see him. The bishop and his army had not put in an appearance last summer at the battle of Otterburn. On one hand she was glad her beloved boy had been spared the danger of what turned out to be a deadly and vicious battle, but on the other hand she knew he would have been massively disappointed not to have had the chance to prove himself. He was still of an age, bless him, where chivalry was an enticing ideal. She was proud to say good manners were something he was born with.

*Later that morning. The cloisters.*

'Now, my dear brothers, Luke is of one opinion and I am of another but I doubt that we will stick so tenaciously to our different views should you go against us. I beg you, therefore, to let me have your honest opinion.' Luke made a murmur of agreement.

'What is it, Hildegard? This problem of whether we go or stay? Luke has already put it before us.'

The three of them had just come from Chapter and sought Hildegard where she was waiting for them.

Yesterday's storm had blown itself out leaving frost in the air, the garth grass glittering in its winter shade of green coated in silver and the grey walls of the buildings sparkling with quartz chips as if newly quarried.

The earlier gloom had been overtaken by an optimistic clarity that encouraged Hildegard to put a strong case for staying where they were until an answer to their proposition came from the mouth of the abbot himself. Privately she had decided that whatever the views of her companions she would stay to do her utmost to get her hands on the relic – but if they wanted to leave . . .

Gregory was adamant. 'I'm sure you, Luke, will accept that we cannot be so pusillanimous as to give up and go home quite yet. We've only just unpacked our bags! We came here to fulfil a mission and to ensure Hildegard's safety while she obeys her prioress and justifies our lord abbot's support for her errand. We can't give up merely on the grounds that we've not been properly welcomed!'

'Imagine Hubert's face if we returned not only empty-handed but without even a bloody nose to show for our efforts!' Egbert grinned. 'He'd never let us live it down. Besides, the news we bring from Chapter, Hildegard, is that the lord abbot of Whitby will receive you in his parlour before Nones. Only when we've heard what he has to say is it worth discussing whether we think we have a chance of obtaining this blessed relic or,' he punched Luke lightly on the shoulder, 'whether to saddle up and gallop back home to the safety of Meaux.'

'That's fair,' Luke agreed at once. 'My desire to leave as soon as we arrived was weakness. I felt overawed by the strangeness of the place. The weather, the unaccustomed hours in the saddle, the lack of welcome, an uncanny sense of doom – I don't mind admitting it! As soon as we set foot inside the precinct I felt a sense of evil, but it was fancy, nothing more. I plead momentary madness but am well again! Forgive me.'

'We do and always will.' Egbert thumped him again.

'I'm of a mind,' said Gregory, breaking in, 'to go down the cliff to stretch our legs. We can have a look at the town this morning while we have time. It'll clear our heads. What do you say? Are you coming with us, Hildi?'

'I am. I'm keen to find out what the pipes and drums meant last night. Did you hear them within the precinct?'

'Only faintly and then only when we crossed the garth. It sounded like the usual revels at this time of year, save them all!'

They set off with plenty of time before Hildegard's appointment with Abbot Richmond. It was a steep walk, almost a scramble down the cobbled trod that led past the parish church and came out near the first of a huddle of cottages at the bottom of the climb. A narrow street slewed out of sight behind a row of buildings parallel to the River Esk.

Egbert hailed a passerby carrying a bundle of nets. 'How far to the quayside, fellow?'

'Walk on,' the ship man explained, 'and where the estuary narrows you can get a coracle to t'other bank side. Or walk further on to t'wooden bridge at yon end o't harbour if you so wish.'

'He was friendly enough,' murmured Luke when they were out of earshot. As they followed the track down the rest of the incline Hildegard mentioned the priest she had encountered the previous day. 'He was friendly enough too. Soaked to the skin but smiling and attacking the climb with zest as he made his way back up to the abbey. My little guide, Torold, instructed him to seek you out in the warming room. I'm surprised you didn't see him. He certainly intended to join you.'

'One drenched fellow showed up,' Luke replied. 'No priest though. He was a Brother Aelwyn, another of those with matters in the town that needed his attention.'

'And as that friendly shipman has it,' Gregory broke in, 'we are now brought to the matter of fish.'

They were lower down the slope and appro-aching the end of the row of thatched hovels. There was a smell of smoke, acrid and strong, like one of last night's bonfires doused by rain.

'Why fish, Gregory?'

'I'll tell you why fish,' he continued. 'At Chapter this morning we had to sit through an extended diatribe that left us as the only ones largely unmoved. Isn't that so, brothers?' He turned to his companions.

'I'm mystified by it,' Egbert growled.

'What happened?'

'Nothing happened, as such, beyond the bursar urging the younger monks into a frenzy of indig-nation and the elder ones to strong grumbling. Apparently the abbey owns the beaches round here down to low water mark. The bursar takes it amiss that the fishermen land their boats on abbey property – as who wouldn't land on the beach, given that they sell their fish in the market here?'

'So what's the problem?'

'According to the lord bursar, an austere fellow called Peter Hertilpole, they're refusing to pay a suitable toll for the privilege. Armed men have been posted to maintain the abbey's rights—'

'What? Abbey men? Armed?' Hildegard was shocked.

'Mercenaries back from the border war and

paid for by the bursar, yes. The discussion centred on how much force should be used. Our Benedictine brothers,' he continued, in a dry, sceptical tone, 'are literally up in arms for another reason.'

'What's that?'

'The fishermen have assumed their ancient right to dry their nets on the said beaches.' Gregory shook his head. 'It amazes me that they cannot reach an accommodation over so trivial a matter.'

'What harm does it do to dry their nets there?'

'I don't think it's a question of harm – for what harm could there be? It's a question of revenue.'

'They have a high regard for rents and tolls,' added Luke, 'and they dare to accuse Cistercians of greed!'

'It sounds trivial as you say, but maybe that's only to such as we who give no thought to how the fish appears on our platters?' she suggested in an attempt to find something reasonable in the bursar's attitude.

'True,' Gregory agreed. 'But fishing happens to be the only source of livelihood for most of the men here. They naturally object to being taxed for every little necessity associated with it.'

'They're standing firm, despite the armed men?' she asked.

'And the bursar is not pleased.'

'He will not have it, it seems. Words like intransigent, profitable, theft, expedient and stronger ones I won't sully your ears with, Hildi, were uttered with much force—'

'Surprising force,' added Egbert, 'given that

39

they're monks espousing peace and universal love for mankind.'

'That is smoke, isn't it?' Luke interrupted, sniffing the air.

'Is it from the tar barrels last night?' Egbert, as usual well-informed, mentioned the custom of jumping over burning barrels that were pitched in flames down the sloping high street as a challenge to the local lads who showed their mettle by leaping over them, all part of the season's celebrations.

'I think it's coming from one of the cottages over there.' Gregory pointed down the street. 'Look!'

The thatched roofs hung low, a few feet above ground level. One of them had its straw partly burned off leaving the rest of the roof nothing but blackened thatch.

'Seems recent. The tar barrels must have been rolled down here last night and set the thatch alight! Let's go over and see if we can do anything to help.' Egbert set off and the others followed.

When they reached the cottage a figure was seen inside bending over a wooden bucket as if preparing to lift it. It was a woman dressed in a russet over-mantle with the white sleeves of her chemise tucked up to the elbows. As soon as she heard voices she straightened. 'Aelwyn?'

The one room, having no window, was dark. She stepped forward into the light and stillness fell.

Hildegard heard Luke, hovering beside her, give a quick breath. Gregory, after one glance, began

40

to peer intently at the damage to the thatch. It was Egbert who greeted the young woman.

She glanced steadily back at him with luminous eyes of an extraordinary blue, the colour of bluebells. They seemed to drink him in. Little more than twenty or so, she was fortunate to possess skin with the lustre of pearl and the faintest tinge of pink colouring her cheeks. Her brows were arched, her lips made a small perfect bow, and her hair, trailing from underneath a grubby head covering, was dark red, almost black, like polished rosewood.

After giving Egbert a thorough inspection with that blue gaze her lips parted slightly but she refused him a smile. Taking in his white habit, her face had fallen.

'I thought you were someone come to help.' She turned her head with a small but definite dismissal.

Egbert, hands folded inside his sleeves, inclined his head, not mocking as was his manner, but with an air of grave respect. 'And here we are. Help, should you desire, my lady. Ready and able to do your bidding.'

What is it that commands such respect from Egbert? Hildegard wondered in astonishment, watching the young woman watching Egbert, and aware that although Gregory appeared to be busy having a close look at the fire damage, he was attentive in a way that showed he was missing nothing. Luke was standing as if nailed to the ground.

The luminous eyes, having turned away and doused their light, returned in full flood to wash over Egbert's battle-scarred features with a hint of derision. 'Can you thatch? Are you a thatcher? As you can see my roof is ruined and I've had to catch rain in a bucket.'

'I can at least lift a bucket or two for you.' Gallantly, Egbert went to the door. 'May I enter?'

'If you so desire.' The woman gave him a side-long glance from beneath long eyelashes and followed him inside.

Hildegard nudged Luke in the ribs. 'What's the matter?'

The young monk turned with a dazed expression. 'She's beautiful, isn't she?' He spoke reverently. 'She's like – if it's not blasphemy to say so – she's like an image of the Madonna – or as I have always imagined her. How can such beauty exist here on earth in this . . .' He gave a disparaging glance at the one-room hovel, now ruined both by fire and yesterday's storm. Puddles of rainwater were visible on the earthen floor.

In a reverent tone he added, 'Does it not shame us to allow people to exist like this when we live in such comfort?' He stared inside the hovel from where the murmur of voices reached them.

Egbert reappeared, heaving a large wooden bucket filled to the brim with rainwater. He tipped it into the gulley at their feet then straightened. 'Are you just going to stand there, Luke?'

'What?' He did not move. It seemed as if he was incapable of doing or saying anything except in a dreamlike state.

'Come on, man, give us a hand in setting the place to rights.'

'What . . .? Oh, me?'

'Yes, you!'

'Don't forget we have a meeting with the abbot,' Hildegard reminded, 'unless you three want to stay down here? I can make my own way back and deal with him myself.'

Gregory came to stand beside her. 'I doubt whether even these two can help much here. It needs a master thatcher and someone who can work wood to do an adequate job. The fire has burned through to the timbers. The smoke must have been choking. She was lucky to get out alive.'

The woman made her appearance just then, looking as regal as if she lived in a palace. She opened her blue pools to Gregory and, as it were, invited him to drown.

'You were fortunate,' he repeated, holding her glance.

'Yes. I was forewarned. I heard the men who did this coming up from the quay in a gang.' Her eyes flooded over Gregory, noting that he was tall, raffish, good-looking and attentive. His Cistercian habit was clearly no bar to her interest. 'An old widow woman who lives at the bottom of the abbey path took me in. We barred the door against the fire-raisers. The storm doused the flames.'

'That was God and the saints watching over you.' Luke spoke in the tone of someone continuing a long and intimate conversation.

'There seems much to do.' Hildegard felt some sympathy for the woman despite any other thoughts she aroused. 'Will it help if we have someone sent down from the abbey to lend a hand?'

The woman gave an enigmatic smile that only seemed designed to increase her mystery. She drew back. 'I ask for no help – except just now with the bucket.' She nodded to Egbert. 'Most kind.'

With a languid gesture she wiped the back of one hand over her brow, drawing attention to the pearl and lustre of her features, the blue eyes already gazing past them up the path towards the abbey. With a small obeisance she stepped back inside the cottage but did not shut the door.

'Have you got a thatcher we can call?' Gregory put his head round the door.

'It's no use. They will not come.'

'Not come?'

'They are forbidden to help me.' She withdrew.

Clearly dismissed, they made their way down towards the river bank as they had been directed in what to Luke seemed to be a world made irrelevant by the realm he now inhabited.

'How can such a beautiful woman live in such vile circumstances?' he asked in a tone of wonder. 'Didn't you think she was beautiful, Hildegard?'

'Most striking, yes.' Her glance was sharp. 'Are you assailed by instant desire, Luke? You have all the symptoms.'

'I shall hasten to confession. I will make amends. But I'm quite knocked about in my feelings for her. Don't chastise me. Such beauty is God-given. It has its own holy power and speaks of celestial realms we can otherwise never know. She is Undine. She is like a holy being from angelic realms.'

Hildegard kept her thoughts to herself. He would

44

not hear them. Not in this dazed hour of his revelation. Poor Luke, she thought, this must be the first time love had brought out its arrows and pierced him to the heart. If, indeed, it was that organ that could so amaze and confuse his common sense by its love wound.

'She told me,' Egbert began when they were nearly at the top of the trod and, panting for breath, paused outside the parish church, 'that it was no accident, the fire. It was nothing to do with the tar barrel horse play – that was used as an excuse. The men who did it she knew by name. She said it was a deliberate attempt to frighten her out of her home.'

'What makes her say that?' asked Hildegard.

'She would not tell me. She seemed too frightened to say anything more. She kept looking over my shoulder all the time as if expecting someone.'

'Is that why she said a thatcher would not come, because it was deliberate?'

'It seems like it. The thatcher was warned away, she said. No man would work for her. Odd, isn't it?'

'Has she been to speak to the – who is it in charge down here?' Gregory furrowed his brow. 'Do they have a bailiff – or a provost?'

'It must be someone from the abbey. They own most things.'

'Well then, she must apply to the abbey for recompense. She must demand the services of a thatcher. And she must give the bursar the names of these men she mentioned so they can be fined.'

# Three

Abbot John of Richmond was waiting to receive Hildegard in the grand and substantial stone-built house reserved for his sole use set a little apart from the main abbey buildings. From its windows it had a spectacular panoramic view over the town and the undulating hills to the west. The sunsets would be magnificent. As was his right, he kept Hildegard waiting for some time in his hall before a servant was instructed to conduct her into his presence. She had decided to come alone.

The abbot remained seated when she entered, slippered feet resting on a padded footstool, and merely waved one hand towards a bench at some distance from the hearth. A fire roared up the chimney. Beside him sat a plump obedientiary with a satisfied expression and a goblet holding within it a dark, red liquid. The abbot did not admit to his identity. Hildegard made a guess and decided he was either the prior, John Allerton, or the bursar, Peter of Hertilpole. Either one would have an interest in the financial future of their relic.

'Welcome, domina,' the lord abbot began. 'I trust everything is as you would wish?'

'Certainly my lord – although . . .' Taking the bull by the horns, as it were, she added, 'I am somewhat surprised to find that our interest in the holy relic of Abbess Hild is shared by others.'

His smile was patient if lightly irritated. 'Your prioress cannot have imagined that so precious an object should be given gratis to the first comer?'

'That would be unreasonable,' she agreed.

'We have decided that the relic will be revealed to the interested parties one by one over the coming days. If you wish to make an offer for it this will be noted. A decision made by ourselves in full Chapter will be delivered at the Feast of Epiphany. That is all. Any other matters can be taken to the Guest Master. Feel at liberty to join us in our prayers and Holy Offices by attending in the screened area at the west end of the church. Or,' he added, and she was unsure whether this was intended as an insult or not, 'you may freely use the parish church of St Mary outside our gates along with the good folk of the town.'

At a sign the servant briskly held open the door to show that the interview was over.

'My feet scarcely touched the ground!' she admitted when she met up with Gregory and Egbert a little later. 'And I am honoured to learn that I may attend general worship with the seculars from the town . . . No chance of mentioning the poor woman in the burned cottage,' she added.

'Luke is all for going back down to see her. Indeed, he disappeared soon after Nones so maybe he's already busy with his sleeves rolled.'

47

Egbert chuckled. 'He's sorely smitten by a pair of blue eyes, poor lad. Still, he'll have plenty of time to amass a pile of penances if we're to remain here until Epiphany. That should cool his ardour. Did you get any idea whether we stand a chance of getting hold of this relic?'

'I've told you verbatim what he said to me. A man of few words and little warmth. We'll have to learn patience – as I'm always being told – and find solace while we wait for his verdict in what is offered to us as guests.'

'Plenty of wassail – that's what's offered,' Gregory broke in. 'At least they have a remarkable brew master and the refectory leaves little to be desired. Plenty of fish both salt and fresh. Their own produce from orchards and gardens. A skilled kitchen master. And we were offered the most delectable spiced apple pie and almond milk this morning. I hope the guest house is run on similar lines?'

'I've no complaints. I believe the monastery kitchens supply the guest house too. The guests were dining late last night after their day out with hawk and hound. My only complaint might be about the endless singing, but then, we must make allowances for the season. Soon we'll be in Lent. They naturally feel the need to celebrate, knowing that later they're going to be compelled to prayer and penance.' She sighed.

'And these guests, our competitors?'

'First, the Glastonbury faction, formidably wealthy, as we all know.'

'And then the nun you referred to as Sister

48

Aveline from a poor and obscure priory some-where in the Riding?'

'Yes. Thirdly an ambiguous lord from the north accompanied by his son.'

'Is that the full complement?'

'As far as I know. I'm not sure the northerner is after the same thing. He may have other business with the abbot. Why would a merchant or minor manorial lord, or whatever he is, want a holy relic? Trust me, Gregory, I will identify our competitors so we can decide how to deal with them.'

'We may as well find out how much they're willing to offer. Forewarned, and all that.'

The bell for the next Office, already tolling, drew the two monks away.

'Are you going in?' Hildegard nodded to where the last of the Benedictines were disappearing through a side door into the nave.

'Coming?'

'I'll be behind the screen at the west end. I know my place!' She grimaced. Gregory squeezed her arm. 'I'll listen out for your voice. We will survive, dear Hildi, and be better monastics for our patience.'

The mundane task of wondering how to dry her spare clothes, still damp after the storm, drew Hildegard to search out the laundry.

It was a noisy, echoing, steamy place, fragrant with the scent of lavender, everything pale and ghost-like as if in a dream, where the boiling vats of water bubbled in fury, belching steam. Shadowy figures laboured at their tasks and, after asking where she could hang her spare shift to dry, she was directed to a hot, dark chamber that backed on to the wall of the great kitchen fires to share its heat.

Dozens of wooden drying racks were hauled up to the ceiling, dangling with garments sent from the vats. Black Benedictine habits, cassocks, copes, cloaks, under shifts, the little surplices of the novices, laundered garments brought by the guests, head coverings, hosen, a kirtle or two, some dripping wet, others already crisply dry.

She hung up her own few damp garments and turned to leave, but just then Sir Ranulph's young lordling son, Darius, came storming into the outer chamber followed by a worried trail of launderers.

Hildegard went to the door and stared in astonishment as he huffed and puffed about the state of a fine linen shirt he was holding up. He berated the launderers in language that was soundly secular. Hildegard slipped out without being noticed.

*Later. The guest house.*

The guest house was seething with folk. Trestles had been set up and were once again laden with food of every description. Hildegard took a small portion of vegetables on a piece of wastel and sat at the end of the bench out of the way.

The northern baron, Sir Ranulph, assumed the right at the centre while beside him sat his wife, a pale, wispy yet pretty young woman half his age. In fact she was closer to his son's age and Hildegard wondered how that was working out. Sister Aveline sat quietly by her side. Darius was absent but to contribute to the noise and merriment there was the emissary from Glastonbury with a couple of his men.

Three strangers had appeared and raised the sound level with a heated debate about bread.

It was brought to a conclusion when one of them complained, 'I haven't had my dole yet. I don't know about you. How many loaves have you had this week, Ake?'

A long-faced man with noticeably thick, black eyebrows that gave him a saturnine aspect was sitting opposite and gave a shrug. 'The usual quota. *My* usual that is. I'm not honoured with more than one loaf per week, as you are aware.'

His companion chuckled. 'You're working for the wrong man then. The Pope would never hear of his people being at a disadvantage. How much ale are you allowed?'

'Again, you already know the answer,' replied the man addressed as Ake. He appeared unruffled but even so he half turned away as if to cut off contact with his interrogator. 'What's to do in the town this evening?' he asked a fellow sitting on his other side.

'Mayhem. Are you coming down with us?'

'I'll see how I feel.'

A commotion stopped this exchange as the doors were flung open to reveal Darius shrugging rain off his shoulders. By his side was a large deer-hound who came sniffing round the table, making mock attacks on a couple of yapping

51

table dogs that at once scuttled into the lap of Sir Ranulph's wife.

She raised her pretty face to Sir Ranulph. 'My dear husband, do tell your son to control that beast. You know he likes to tease *mes pauvres chiens*.'

'Down, Satan! You heard what Amabel said.' the youth growled before his father could censure him. 'Do you know,' he addressed the chamber at large, 'it's raining yet again! Are we going to let it stop us from going down into the town?'

'You go,' his father grunted. 'Amabel and I are content to celebrate in our own way.'

Darius cast a dark look in the direction of his forebear. 'I might do that. I'm told there's good entertainment down there for those who look for it.'

'You might find that monk that's gone missing,' his father growled. 'If so make sure there's a reward before you hand him over.'

'Do you imagine I wouldn't?' Sulkily the youth climbed on to a bench and reached for a hunk of meat which he started to hack with a long, bone-handled knife.

'What's that about a monk, my dear?' Ranulph's wife leaned forward.

'One of the brothers has absconded, or so the rumour goes.'

'Run off with some woman they call the Madonna of Grope Lane, I heard,' one of the Glastonbury men contributed.

'What? In this weather?' Amabel widened her eyes and everybody laughed.

Hildegard decided she would leave as soon as

she had eaten. Since returning to Meaux she had found herself less willing to participate in the secular concerns of the world. It did not satisfy the simplicity she craved since her disastrous return to face Abbot de Courcy's justified response following her affair with Ulf of Langbar.

Nowadays her vocation seemed like nothing more than a caprice, an arrogant folly, when she contemplated how far she had fallen from the Rule and how puny were her efforts to live up to its demands. Confession made no difference. Nothing could absolve her from what she had done. Abbot de Courcy, Hubert, had made an attempt, by exacting this penance, but it seemed there was no way she could really earn her way back into his esteem, no way to absolve the deep sadness that lay always at the back of her mind.

The shadow had briefly lifted when they set out to Whitby to buy the relic, but the cloud of hopelessness had re-descended almost as soon as she'd set eyes on the abbey as they came up out of the lane on to the headland.

The sheer magnitude and authority of the abbey put the events important to humankind into a proper perspective. *What are any of us, after all, with our trivial daily concerns, our desires, our ambitions? We are no more important than ants crawling about the surface of the earth. What is love? What is the havoc it causes with our peace of mind?*

'Domina . . .'

She glanced up. It was the man called Ake. He was smiling kindly down into her eyes, his little spat with his companion over loaves

53

apparently forgotten. 'I understand from the prior that you hale from the Abbey of Meaux?'

'From Swyne, yes.'

'And your prioress – I know her of old, a staunch and formidable woman. Still well, I hear?'

'She is.'

He glanced round in a furtive manner, all the while smiling should his glance happen to mesh with anyone else's, and continued with a meaningful lowering of his voice: 'Sister of Alexander Neville, lately Archbishop of York.' He lowered his voice still further. 'We will talk, domina. I shall regard it as an honour.'

Sliding away he sauntered over to the top end of the table and was soon part of the convivial group passing the wine flagon between them.

A few moments later Sister Aveline came down from the upper floor looking flushed and harried. As soon as she noticed young Darius speaking to his father she went over.

Hildegard watched her give a little curtsy. 'My lord Ranulph,' she purred, 'I shall be happy and delighted to accompany your dear wife to the midnight Office as you suggested.'

'Well, that's settled then.' He patted his wife's hand. 'I told you she would accompany you, Amabel.' He turned to the nun. 'She's fretting because we could not bring her maid with us. The woman fell ill two days before we set out. There, you see.' He smiled down at his wife. 'Everything works itself out.'

Amabel fingered a small gold and ruby crucifix in the cleft between her breasts and murmured, 'Thank you, husband.' To Sister Aveline she said,

'Most gracious of you, my dear. I'll send for you when I'm ready to go.' She tugged at her husband's arm. 'We have the rest of the evening's entertainment still to come.' She gave a sudden sideways glance at her stepson, who purported not to notice but turned his face away with a set mouth.

Hildegard rose to her feet. Wishing for nothing more than to go to her chamber, before she could venture two paces along the corridor outside, the fellow called Ake caught up with her. 'Domina, a moment.'

When she paused he stepped up to her, one eye on the door to the hall where servants carried in ever more platters, and said, 'Those two fellows you saw me talking to at table, do you know who they are?'

She shook her head. 'Forgive me. I did not catch their names.'

'Their names would have meant nothing to you. I know who they are. They make no secret of it. They are the Pope's men. Regarded as privileged guests here. Like me they are corrodians, though serving a different master. We all live eyeing each other up in that row of cottages near the west gate. I thought I should warn you of their presence in case the prioress of Swyne was in ignorance of the fact.'

As he headed back into the hall he threw a glance over his shoulder. 'For King Richard,' he murmured and before she could do more than open her lips to reply he vanished into the festive chamber whence storms of laughter were already sweeping.

* * *

The prioress's plans were often unfathomable until too late. Surely there was no doubt that she would know down to the last man who was who in the abbeys and priories up and down the coast? If there were the Pope's men here she would know it. She had her spies. As a loyal sister to the ex-Archbishop of York, who was at this very moment paying the price, banishment on pain of death, for the support he gave to young King Richard during the bloody dealings of the Lent Parliament, she would of course know where the Pope deployed his spies.

Was the task to purchase the relic nothing more than an excuse to conceal a deeper purpose? To place one of her nuns here at Whitby to spy out the land?

It would be a useful move.

The abbey was on the cusp of two territories as Gregory had already pointed out, the vast northernmost terrain of the earl of Northumberland stretching to the Scottish border and, south and west, the extensive domain of John of Gaunt and the house of Lancaster.

Until last summer's disastrous defeat when Northumberland's eldest son, Harry Percy, had been captured by the Scots and held ransom as a Marcher lord, appointed by the King's Council to keep the Scots out of England, Northumberland had been the dominant force in the North.

Meanwhile, ambitious John of Gaunt held Pickering Castle and the Royal Forest that stretched almost to the walls of York.

For the time being, with Gaunt himself in Castile, his son, Henry Bolingbroke, was in charge, but he was more often down in Monmouth, fathering a dynasty of his own. It was a given among those who followed such matters that Bolingbroke was as anxious as his father to obtain a royal crown in order to foster Lancastrian power for generations to come. Hadn't Gaunt already tried to establish himself overseas by being crowned King of Castile in the great cathedral of Santiago de Compostela?

Here in the north of England the thorn in the side of the Lancasters was Northumberland, and vice versa. At this low point in the year both earls had withdrawn behind their walls but it could be believed that the two dynasties continued to view each other with suspicion. The Pope himself, ever eager to maintain his authority in England and to keep on collecting his taxes, would be watching the two factions with a keen eye. Hence the placing of his men here.

But was that all? Was something else brewing? Not for the first time Hildegard wished she could be taken into the prioress's full confidence. But then, maybe that way danger lay?

What she did not know she could not confess, not even under torture.

# Four

Unable to ignore the bell summoning the monks to the midnight Office, Hildegard stepped out on to the foregate and hurried under the shadowy gatehouse arch on to the garth. The cloisters on four sides were equally dark so she cut across the turf to the south door of the church and on entering found a suitable pillar where she might join the congregation of monks who were even now filing in soft-footed down the night stairs from their dortoir.

Although their faces were shrouded beneath their cowls, Gregory was unmistakable, not only because of his height but by way of his athletic stride, what someone had once called, admiringly, his 'Jerusalem swagger'. The stocky figure by his side could only be Egbert. Did they know about the two corrodians spying for Pope Urban?

She turned her head.

The two men were standing by the far wall, recognizable by their dark red hoods. A third figure, face in shadow, stood not far off, watching everything they did.

None of the secular guests were present until a gust of wind rustled in through the west door and two women entered. One was Sister Aveline, the other the wife of Sir Ranulph. With the nun clearing a path for her the two of them made their way to the front, knelt, crossed themselves, then stood where they were in full view of everyone. A little troop of novices scurried behind the screen into the choir and Hildegard, having noted all this, let her thoughts drift back to the ritual of the night Office.

It was later, when the prior had made a stately exit and the monks began to return to their quarters, that she noticed a small figure lingering until the last of his fellows had disappeared from view before making a stealthy dash for the south door. Curious to know where he was going – and already feeling that she recognized him – she left the same way.

Slipping into the cloister he fled like a wraith to the far end, only the soft slap of his little boots on the stone flags giving him away. She followed the sound. Not much more than a flickering shadow speeding past the light shed by the cressets showed that he was going in her general direction. Curious to find out where he was heading at this time of night with such speed and stealth, she followed.

Without looking behind him he had already slipped through the night-door in the gatehouse by the time the porter glanced out of his chamber. Noticing Hildegard he called, 'I thought I heard someone. God be with you, domina.'

Murmuring a response she went out on to the foregate and looked about. That little will o' the wisp was Torold, creeping outside the precinct, of that she was sure! But where was he?

A movement at the top of the path leading down to the town caught her attention and, fearing that he was about to get himself into deep trouble, she increased her speed until she could call out. He was in such a hurry, sliding in his haste on the frosted cobblestones, that he failed to hear her until she called again.

With one frightened glance over his shoulder he began to scramble faster downhill, falling and picking himself up as he went.

'Wait, Torold! Where are you going?' She caught

59

up with him in a few long strides. 'Should you be out so late?'

'Leave me be!'

She managed to grasp him by the shoulder. 'Stop a moment; are you in trouble?'

He wriggled under her grasp.

'Well?' she insisted, increasing the pressure to show she demanded an answer.

'I'm not but someone else is.'

'Are you trying to help them?'

Realizing that her firm grip was for the moment inescapable he stared at the ground. A faint light from the cresset outside the gatehouse scarcely made it possible to see his expression but she had a strong feeling that a lower lip jutted and his expression was mutinous.

'I'm not here to chastise you but I am worried that you're going into the very town you warned me against. Do you remember?'

'It's different for me.'

'Why so?'

'I'm from here. You're an outsider and a nun.'

'So?'

'They don't rate Cistercians, these black monks. Nobody in the town does.'

'I fear we're getting off the point. Where are you going? Do you have permission from your novice master?'

He kicked a stone.

'I suppose that means no.'

He remained mute.

'Well,' she said, 'I'm mystified. What's so special down there?'

'You don't need to puzzle yourself,' he admitted.

'I'm only going to dash down to see my mother.' He lifted his face and the cresset-light made brief sense of his expression. Defiance, definitely. Untruth? And was that fear in his eyes?

Before she could react he gave a quick twist and was free from her restraint. In a moment he was sliding and skidding headlong down the path again.

She watched him disappear from sight and hesitated, wondering whether to go after him. It wasn't any of her business. It was for the novice master to keep a watch on his charges. Torold seemed to know what he was doing, if, indeed, it was his mother he really intended to visit, and why should it not be? But that shadow of a lie on his face mystified her.

Was he homesick for his mother's comforting embrace and ashamed to admit to a childish weakness? Boys had their pride. If that's all his midnight errand boiled down to, she should leave him to it. Frowning, and somewhat reluctantly, she turned back towards the guest house.

Tomorrow she would keep an eye on him to see if it was necessary to step in. The neat way he had slipped away from the other novices gave the impression that an escape from the confines of the precinct – from what must be like a prison to a young lad of spirit – was a normal occurrence.

The guest house was full of wassailing far after midnight. A couple of minstrels had been brought up and Sir Ranulph and his wife presided with their small retinue. Darius himself must have escaped the abbey confines for the dubious night-time entertainment offered in the town, as he said he would, but the Pope's men were present along with Master Ake, three or four strangers, and the burly fellow from Glastonbury, seen first as he was whisked from out of the sleet into the abbey when the hunting party had appeared.

Now, black-bearded, red of face, with fists like hams, he was holding out a wooden mazer to have it replenished and when it was filled to the brim he lifted it shakily to his lips, drank a solid measure, turned it round and handed the rest with lavish ceremony to Sir Ranulph's wife so she could drink from the same place.

'To lady Amabel, and all women everywhere!'

Hoping to remain unnoticed, Hildegard slid along the wall to take advantage of all the commotion, and was about to leave under cover of a trio of serving men when the main door was flung open again.

It was the guest master himself, accompanied by half a dozen servants.

'Friends!' He marched confidently into the hall. 'I beg your attention. There is some dismay among the brothers. You may have heard it rumoured that one of their number is missing. May I plead your indulgence and ask you to remain here while my men search the building? If you wish to send your servants to accompany them when they enter your personal chambers we shall indulge you.'

'This is something of an outrage, isn't it?' objected one of the Pope's men. 'Why would the fellow be loitering in a guest chamber?'

Gales of male laughter greeted this remark and he joined in with an elegant, self-abasing gesture of his hands.

'Do not worry, my lord. When your quarters are inspected you can go along with the search party to lay your hands on him should he be hiding under your bed. This incursion is only to set the abbot's mind at ease. He would not want to be considered lax in his efforts to apprehend the fellow.'

'Have you any idea why he might have gone missing?' asked Sir Ranulph.

'Run off with a lady love,' one of the strangers suggested.

The guest master frowned. Turning to his escorts waiting in the doorway, he called, 'Enter! You know what to do.'

Hildegard went over to him. 'I have no servant to send up with them. May I attend with the members of your search party?'

The guest master puffed out his chest. 'You may, domina, although I hardly think it likely that he will hide himself in the chamber of a blessed religious such as yourself. He might deem that to be too obvious a hiding place because so unlikely.'

His confidence was deflated when Hildegard made a mild remark along the lines of hoping it was unlikely he had a knife with him too.

'He's a monk, dear lady. He would indeed be unlikely to go armed.'

'As unlikely as disappearing no-one knows where?'

He gave her a look and moved off.

She was sick of him, sick of them all. Tired after so little sleep. Tired of the raucous assumption that everyone wanted to celebrate in the same drunken manner. She wanted the tranquility of Meaux. The peace and order of her own house.

Above all she desired the joy of seeing Hubert about the place. Treading the precinct with that thoughtful, austere deliberation as he attended to the material and spiritual welfare of his monks. Nothing else would suffice to improve her spirits or the deep sorrow lodged in her heart.

She stepped back as the search party, having swarmed about the hall, next thundered upstairs, their wooden pattens on the plank floors making enough din to drown out the two minstrels who, rolling their eyes at each other, put down their instruments and waited until silence would fall again and they could hear themselves play. The searchers soon hammered down again, shrugging their shoulders, and as soon as they poured outside the roistering started over.

How many nights left before Epiphany? Lying in bed a little later Hildegard counted them off on her fingers. Too many. Tomorrow she would crave an audience with the abbot to try to persuade him to allow her an early sight of the relic. After that she would decide whether it was worth staying on to counter Glastonbury's offer.

*The cloister. Next morning.*

Egbert tugged at Hildegard's sleeve. 'You know the monk who went missing?'

She yawned. 'What about him?'

'They found him.'

'Is he well? He'll be in for trouble, causing such uproar.'

Egbert looked sombre. He led her to their private corner. 'You said you met him the night we arrived – climbing up from the town in the middle of the storm.'

'Did I?'

'It was the fellow called Brother Aelwyn.'

'What was he doing, causing such turmoil?'

Egbert shook his head. 'He was found in the apple store.'

'Found?'

'Found by one of the kitcheners shortly before Prime.'

'I don't understand.'

'His body was found.'

Hildegard was shocked. She said what many people say when confronted by a sudden death. 'But he was so full of life!'

'Be that as it may . . .'

'Poor fellow. I thought him pleasant and . . . But how did it happen?' She remembered the way he had greeted Torold and the boy's cheerful reply. 'He'll be sorely missed.'

'And not just by his fellow brethren either. Do you remember the young woman in the burned cottage? He was helping her set things to rights. She'll be lost without him. At least . . .' He gave an odd smile. 'That's Luke's view this morning. He's cutting the next Office and already on his way down there to see what comfort he can offer.'

'Luke . . .?'

65

'Gregory and I thought it might help if you went to look after him. He might need a chaperone.'

So it was that Hildegard found herself scrambling down the cliff side again until she came to the cobbled stretch where the houses began. A few beggars were waiting at the bottom and she dropped some small coins into their open palms as she passed before knocking on the door of the cottage with the burned thatch.

A head appeared at a window from a house across the street. 'You won't find her there. She's left.'

'My gratitude, mistress. When did she leave?'

A grey-haired old woman, bent almost double over a stick, shuffled outside. 'That monk has been down already.'

'Which monk is this?' she asked, feeling she knew the answer.

'Not him, not the one that was causing all the to-do up top. One of yours.' She eyed Hildegard's white habit.

'I know who you mean. Do you happen to know where they've gone?'

'Not I. It's nowt to do wi' me.'

Hildegard fished in her scrip for a coin to hold up to the woman.

She peered at it with suspicion. Then reached for it. 'Try Grope Lane. That's where she started. That's where she's ending up.'

Not wishing to lay herself or her Order open to ribaldry by asking for such a place among the passersby, she wended her way down Church

Street towards the quay, following the route they had taken the day before. If she remembered rightly the men had exchanged pointed glances as they passed the end of a small alley near the waterside. That must be Grope Lane. It was a slightly more polite name than some of the ones she knew. Every town and port had one. But why on earth was the woman Luke was so determined to befriend retreating to a place like that? More to the point, what was Luke doing accompanying her? He was such an innocent. Did he know what he was getting into?

She reached the turn-off and hesitated. A passing carter shouted some comment as he ambled by, which she ignored. *Here goes*, she thought. At least it was not as busy at this time of the morning as it would be later that night.

Ducking her head under the lines of washing strung across from house to house, she was halfway along when she noticed an open door. She poked her head round it. What was the woman called? Luke had mentioned a name but she had forgotten it. She gave a general call then had to step back as a jaunty young fellow came hurrying out into the street pulling his capuchin over to conceal his face as he set off back towards Church Street, joshing, 'I hope that's a mummer's guise and not the real thing! *Mea culpa*, sister!'

A shifty-looking fellow with a shiny waxed cap on the back of his head materialized in the doorway as if to bar her way. She demanded to know whether he had seen a Cistercian and a young woman pass by.

'Who are they representing?' he queried.

'Themselves.'

Light dawned. 'I thought you meant a couple of mummers,' he replied. 'What you want with 'im?'

'Just to warn him his abbot will be on his trail if he doesn't show up,' she invented, not altogether dishonestly.

'Oh I get it.' He leered at her, showing stumps of black teeth, then turned and bellowed to someone inside, 'Roke! Where did that monk go with Sabine?'

An indistinct voice echoed from somewhere deep within the building and the man turned back. 'She'll be down with Master Selby.' He came helpfully out into the street. 'See yon two-storey house on the corner? He'll be in there with her.'

At least he didn't have his hand out for passing on this information. With a nod of thanks she went on until she was standing outside a substantial brick-built merchant's house with people lounging around outside and one or two others hesitating about going in. To her relief Luke appeared in the doorway. A woman in one of the inner chambers was laughing in a high, false-sounding squawk. Luke's expression was grim. When he noticed Hildegard he came straight outside.

'This is a terrible business. Let's get away.' He took her by the elbow and guided her to the corner of the alley. 'They tell me there's a path leading from the end here straight up to the abbey. It's the one the monks use, if you can believe it.

We'll take that. On the way I'll tell you what's been going on. Come on.'

Briskly he led the way to a path at the end of the lane and only when they were halfway up the steep climb to the top did he stop to throw himself down on a rock. He put his head in his hands.

'What has happened, Luke?' She went to sit beside him.

'You have heard the terrible news about Brother Aelwyn and what a calamity has befallen Sabine?'

'Who?' she asked, to slow him down a little. He looked frantic with worry and was breathing rapidly as if he had recently been in an argument and needed to catch his breath.

'That beautiful woman we met yesterday. The one whose cottage was set alight.' He leaned forward, fixing his glance searchingly on hers. 'Can you believe it was deliberate?'

'She said as much.'

'Yes, but did any of us take it seriously? It turns out it was true. She rents that little hovel from the abbey but the rest of the nearby ones have been bought up by a fellow who rents them out on short leases at a price few locals can afford. His intention is to force Sabine out so he can put in an offer to the abbey to buy her place. It'll mean he owns the whole row. His eventual purpose is to knock them down and build two large houses on the site which he can rent out to the abbey when important visitors and their retinues are summoned. So far she has refused to budge. Brother Aelwyn was giving her advice and persuading her to stand firm.'

'Against the wishes of this landlord fellow?'

'Presumably so.'

'Acting from the goodness of his heart?'

'Naturally.'

'And now?'

'She's distraught. She heard what had happened early this morning. It's terrible for her. Her only friend and ally, dead . . . Is the news all around the abbey? I imagine that's why you're here.'

'Yes. But Luke, why is she seeking refuge in the stews?'

'It's quite innocent. She happens to know someone here who might help her. Someone from long ago, a maid servant I believe. One who is now a servant to the merchant in that house you saw.'

Her glance was undisguised scepticism, but Luke didn't seem to notice. All his concern was centred on the young woman who had cozened his heart with one look from her guileful blue eyes.

'What do you intend to do now?'

'I've made sure she's safe with Master Selby and his wife—'

'His wife?'

'Oh, it's a good thing you didn't meet her. I doubt whether you would have approved. Unfortunately she's one of these big blowsy women dressed quite inappropriately, on account of the festive season, and as loud of mouth as extravagant of empty gestures. But I'm told she has a good heart. She and her husband, a well-set-up sort of fellow, were keen to offer Sabine a room.'

'Perhaps we should go back up to the abbey. It's terrible news about Brother Aelwyn,' she reminded him. To herself she wondered how Sabine viewed it, apart from the inconvenience it was causing her, and was tempted to ask, 'What did she say when she heard about Aelwyn?'

'I don't know. She was over the first shock by the time I managed to get down to help, but she's quite distraught, sobbing and tearing her hair the minute I mentioned his name. Her grief was such she was unable to speak to me in a way that made sense.'

'Let's go up, Luke.'

She took his arm gently and pulled him to his feet. He would get a dreadful shock when certain truths would be revealed. Why on earth did he think Sabine had gone to live in Grope Lane? All Hildegard could do was hope she was wrong.

# Five

*Cloister garth. A little later.*

As soon as they entered, Egbert noticed them, detached himself from a group of Benedictines and came over. After a brief greeting he told them that Gregory had gone down to the apple store where Aelwyn's body had been found. The infirmarer and several monks, including the prior, had invited him to go with them.

71

'They're there now,' he added. 'I think we might go over ourselves – only in the cause of Christian charity and because we met him and found him a most congenial fellow.' He glanced from one to the other. 'Yes?'

'Tell us what you really think,' Hildegard invited.

'I do really think that. It is the right thing to think. What you may mean, Hildegard, is what do I think in addition?'

'You clearly have other thoughts about the matter.'

'Let's go over first and then I'll tell you if it seems relevant.'

He gave one of his close smiles.

Without further discussion the three of them set off through the gatehouse to where, behind a low wall, orchards of apple and pear trees were planted on terraces overlooking the harbour. Clipped trees, leafless at this time of year, stretched in row after row under the shelter of the headland. At the far end on rising ground was a long stone-built store shed. When he was within hailing distance Egbert announced them and one of the abbey servants appeared from inside.

'Welcome, brother.'

An elderly monk with a flushed face and streaming nose appeared behind him. 'Brother, most timely. I am back to my bed now. I trust I may leave this matter in Cistercian hands. We have been won over by Brother Gregory's argument.'

Gregory stooped under the lintel to come

72

outside. 'The infirmarer, Brother Dunstan, is suffering with a fever and will fare best in bed with a cure. I've told him that as outsiders we are well placed to attend to matters. The prior has given us free rein to do what we need to. Pray enter, all of you.'

The infirmarer nodded his gratitude and, accompanied by his servant, stumbled back down the terrace towards the precinct. Several others, apparently after having already discussed their usefulness, followed in melancholy order.

'Come,' Gregory gestured. 'This is a strange business. There's no sign of violence on the body. The monks are at a loss to explain why a hale and hearty fellow like Aelwyn should drop dead for no apparent reason.'

The interior of the store was pitch dark. Fortunately for the task of examining the body, Aelwyn lay in a shaft of light that came through the inward-opening doorway. His body had been pushed back by the force that had to be exerted to open the door, but that aside there seemed to be no further marks on the body other than ones usual in a monk going peacefully about his day.

'Who found him?'

'We did.' A voice came from deeper within the store.

A frightened young fellow of about fifteen with a blaze of red hair tied back with a green tie stepped forward. He was shadowed by another lad with hair cut in a pudding bowl style like a mercenary. The first one said, 'We were sent to fetch apples before Prime—'

'They're kitcheners,' explained Gregory. 'They

73

fetch and carry. This morning was the first time they've been up here since yesterday when all was well.'

The red-haired lad nodded. 'And the door had its beam down on the outside as always. I lifted it up and Will pushed the door to open it.'

'But it wouldn't open,' added his companion. 'Something was wedging it shut.'

'So we put our boots to it.' The red-head looked pleased at their obvious initiative.

'And bit by bit,' interrupted Will in a voice dark with foreboding, 'we were able to force it open.'

'And when it was open wide enough to put our heads inside—'

'We saw him!'

'Lying there behind the door!'

'Stiff as death.'

'But peaceful, like, as if he'd fallen asleep.'

The two youths folded their arms and looked solemn, waiting for judgement.

'See for yourselves,' Gregory invited.

Hildegard stepped round the door and peered down at the body. It was the same monk she and Torold had met coming up through the rain from the town on their arrival. Poor Aelwyn. He did, indeed, look peaceful. 'No sign of violence?' she asked, to make sure.

'None, domina,' the elder of the two boys replied. 'He's just as we found him.'

Gregory nodded agreement.

'We ran like the Devil,' Will, the younger one, admitted. His friend nudged him and he looked shamed.

'I'm sure anyone would run if they found a dead man behind a door,' murmured Hildegard. 'How did you know he was dead and not just sleeping?'

'Cos I touched him, thinking exactly that, but he was stiff and his cheek, which I also touched, was right cold, just like stone.'

'You gave a big yelp and grabbed my arm . . .' Will piped up.

'And of course you had to shake free and come back to have another look and then you ran, yourself, if you're being honest, it was not only me, and we finished up with the Master Kitchener telling us not to be such right sot-wits and where was this so-called dead man.'

'And he came up with a couple of fellows all ready to beat the daylights out of us until they saw for themselves we were telling the truth.'

'Then all hell broke loose,' added the red-haired youth. 'The lord prior had to be sent for.'

'It's not our fault,' said Will.

He went pale at the sudden thought that they might be blamed and it was clear that the horror of potential retribution had only at that moment occurred to him.

'Of course it's not your fault, if what you say is true,' Hildegard reassured him. 'He must have been lying here all night. Why would he come up here?'

'Same as us. To get apples for the kitchens.'

'We know who sent him and when.' Gregory looked down at the body. 'Poor, sad fellow.'

'Not so sad, an' all,' one of the boys said, then clamped his lips shut.

'What do you mean?' asked Hildegard.

'Nothing much . . . only that it must be a nice life, being a monk and being waited on and that.' A sidelong glance from under his thatch of red hair was ostentatiously ignored by his companion, as if to avoid any accusation of complicity after this obvious extemporization. Now was not the time, thought Hildegard, to follow up that out-of-place remark.

She bent down and took a closer look at the way Aelwyn was lying. A few apples lay next to him, neatly placed as if he had put them to one side while he had a nap. A bluish tinge lingered round his mouth and his knuckles, she noticed, were raw and bloodied.

Standing up, she peered at the inside of the door where someone might have reached out to batter on it, to draw attention to the fact that they were trapped. Some dark lines like dried blood were caught between the splinters of planking. Evidently Aelwyn had tried to attract attention but no-one had heard him. That was no puzzle. The store was set well out of range of any of the abbey buildings.

But why had it ended in death? Finding that someone had accidentally dropped the beam without realizing that there was still someone inside the store, he might have settled down for the night, an uncomfortable one without doubt, but with a few sacks pulled over him from the pile near the door he might have slept safely until the morning when someone could be expected to appear and release him.

Egbert had been silent for a while and now

went deeper into the store to look round. On dozens of wooden shelves stretching far back into the darkness the summer fruits lay neatly arranged to feed the monks throughout the winter. It had been a good harvest and the shelves were still almost full. Hildegard followed him. There was nothing much else to see. She turned back with the ripe, sweet scent of apples filling the air. The deeper inside the store the stronger the scent became. Egbert gave a cough and followed her into the light.

'We shall not move the body yet,' Gregory told the boys. 'Will one of you run down and find a couple of men to stand guard over him?'

Both boys jostled to be the one to get away from this tainted place and in the end they were both told to go together.

'Sot-wits,' murmured Egbert when they were out of earshot. 'Is it the first time they've seen somebody dead?'

'It could well be,' Hildegard suggested. 'They're kitchen lads. Probably the only thing they've seen dead is a shoal of herring and some venison.'

Gregory was puckering his brow. 'He came up here after midday, apparently. The kitcheners were pleased with the reception their spiced apple concoction received and decided to make a special one for the abbot and a guest he was entertaining at his own table last night. It must have been that fellow from Glastonbury. Brother Aelwyn was present and offered to walk down to bring a few back as everybody was busy preparing the feast. He said he needed to clear his head.'

'Was he not feeling well?' Hildegard asked.

'They say he often came out here for solitude but there was something to do with an argument he said he'd had and he needed to calm himself before going into the next Office—'

'Which was Nones?' Gregory nodded.

'Who did you get this from?' she asked.

'The head kitchener himself. And no, he didn't say what the argument was about because we did not then suspect that foul play was a possibility.'

'And do we now?' Egbert scratched his head. 'I know I do. I've heard the monks gossiping. He was regarded by some with great suspicion, if not with fear for the possibility that he had the power to conjure the Devil.'

Gregory shrugged. 'It didn't do him much good then, did it? The important point is, somebody barred the door with him inside.'

'And when the door was shut and he was plunged into darkness the natural thing would be to batter on the door and yell to be let out,' added Hildegard.

'A plea that was clearly ignored,' Gregory affirmed.

'Maybe it was shut carelessly, whoever did it hurried off and didn't hear his shouts, and he died from shock?' suggested Hildegard. Even she sounded unconvinced by this argument and added, 'There's sure to be at least one deaf monk in the abbey – or a serving man.'

'I suppose it's a possibility. And yet the infirmarer was in a position to know whether Aelwyn had any physical weakness, and he was adamant that he was known for his vitality – "fit as a flea up and down that cliff side," he told me when I put the question to him.' Gregory frowned.

Two burly servants were making their way towards the store and when they presented themselves were instructed to stop anybody going inside until the body was moved. 'Shall we be here all day and night?' one of them asked. 'Only it's feast time and we're missing out.'

'What are you missing?' Egbert wanted to know.

'Events in the town,' he admitted. 'The usual sort of thing.'

Egbert gave him a look as if he knew exactly what sort of thing the fellow was alluding to and, in a comradely fashion, told him he would come up himself after Compline if they would do him the favour of hanging on until then, and he would himself take over from them until the night Office. 'Then we'll have to think again.'

'Does that mean we have to trail back up before midnight?' the man persisted.

'Not at all. You stay down there if you so wish. My brother Cistercians will come to my aid.' He clapped him on the shoulder. 'Worry not, friend. Be thankful, merely, that it is not you lying dead on the cold, hard earth.'

Shamefacedly the man nodded his thanks. 'It's not that we don't want to look out for him, but after all, he lived off the fat in every way, so why should we be put out for a fellow who lived so well? This is our only chance to see what it's like.'

His companion shook his head. 'Come on, he

79

was a good lad when you take all into account. Better than most, considering.'

Before they could get into a discussion about Aelwyn's merits and demerits Gregory moved briskly off. 'Settled then. Until shortly after Compline. Give my brother here time to walk up from the refectory.'

The two were settling themselves on the ground outside the store by the time Egbert closed the door and dropped the bar back into place.

'Till later then,' he said, following the others.

All this time Luke had been silent. Now Gregory turned to him. 'So what did the lady Sabine tell you about him?'

Luke stuck his lip out and muttered about Gregory being too sarcastic for his own good. 'The Wheel of Fortune turns as it will and the ones at the top may be brought low and the lowly, as we are enjoined to believe, may rise through piety and the will of God . . . All right, then,' he conceded when this brought no response, 'maybe there is something odd about seeking refuge in the stews. I'm not a sot-wit. I know what you're thinking.' He was reluctant to say much more but finally seemed forced to explain. 'She admitted she knew about Aelwyn already, before I even saw her after Prime. She said somebody from the abbey had come down specially to tell her but would not say who it was. She shook her head and avoided my glance.'

Gregory was puzzled. 'Why would anyone think to tell her? Was something going on between those two? He seemed to take a great interest in her.'

'And who wouldn't?' Luke remarked.

It was left like that with no further comment.

The bell summoning the monks to the Holy Offices was as powerful as an iron chain drawing them back every few hours to their obligations. Feeling no requirement to stand humbly behind the screen at the west end of the church, Hildegard made her way thoughtfully down the cliff path towards the town with the music of the choir fading as she went. When she drew level with the parish church she paused and decided in a moment to go inside.

It was already full of people from the town. As she slipped in at the back and stood among them she realized the whispers were for Aelwyn. Anger was almost palpable until the rector climbed into the pulpit and spread both palms in blessing.

It was soon over. With sideways glances the congregation began to leave, knots of gossips lingering in the graveyard, a few tears being shed. For a monk, leading a relatively cloistered life, Aelwyn seemed to have endeared himself to many in the town.

A woman's voice came to her clearly from one of the groups as she continued on her way down the path. It was a complaint. 'Evil eye my arse,' she was declaiming. 'He didn't deserve it, monk or not. Somebody must have done it!'

'What does her down there think . . .?'

The reply was lost on the air. Unobtrusively

81

Hildegard moved near enough without drawing attention to herself. When she had a chance she asked the woman standing nearest, 'Poor fellow, how did it happen? Was it a seizure?'

'He's done for him just as he feared he would . . .' The woman bit her tongue and gave Hildegard a sudden wary grimace. 'Hold on, who are you when you're at home? Are you one of them?' She gestured up towards the abbey.

'I'm a guest,' Hildegard replied honestly.

On hearing this the woman eyed her with outright suspicion. 'Oh aye? Spying for the abbot, are you?'

'Not at all. I hardly know him.'

The woman turned a defensive shoulder. 'Come on, you lot. Keep your lips buttoned or it'll be us next. There's a spy among us!'

In a hostile group they went out on to the path and Hildegard had no choice but to let them go.

Hildegard scrambled the rest of the way down the cliff and when she reached the burned hovel she found it in the same sad state as before. The congregation had dispersed. With no-one around except the same neighbour peering out of her doorway, she paused to give her time to come over. This time, however, the neighbour bobbed out of sight thinking she hadn't been noticed.

By the look of things Sabine had abandoned her cottage in some haste. Its desolation looked final. The door, blown by the wind, creaked on its hinges. Whatever sticks of furniture had been there – the bed in the corner, a rough table – had been taken away, leaving only a broken crock on the packed earthen floor and a pile of ashes in the fire pit.

A sharp prick of conscience reminded Hildegard of the conditions up at the abbey and, more, the polished but austere comfort of her own abbot's house at Meaux.

Intending to go on down the hill towards the quay, she turned the corner on to Church Street.

# Six

The town was busy, the shutters of the traders let down to display their wares, purchasers fingering what was on offer, banter of a rough kind flying back and forth. Hildegard had gone no more than a few paces, however, when she saw a gang of men marching resolutely up the street from the direction of the quay. They were armed. The long-bladed gutting knives the fisher folk used glittered in every hand and a few men wielded boat hooks as if they were pikes.

She stepped back into the lee of the nearest building to let them pass. The men were marching with a shared sense of purpose and when they reached the turn up to the abbey, instead of starting the climb they carried on where the street narrowed and became a lane with crabbed houses on both sides running along beside the Esk towards the mouth of the harbour.

Breaking into a jog to the cheers of the shoppers they were soon out of sight between the houses but almost at once she heard jeering, followed by a kind of shouted challenge and a sudden cacophony of curses. People in the street began to run towards the sound as an abrupt clash of steel on steel broke out. Yelps of pain quickly followed accompanied by the screams of women and children caught in the affray.

Swept along in the crowd, Hildegard reached the corner to discover two gangs of men fighting right there in the street. No quarter was given by either side as boat hooks and knives were pitted against broadswords and bucklers. It seemed the fishermen would have little chance against their better-armed opponents. She guessed they must be abbey men sent down to exact fines and tolls.

The two gangs surged back and forth with neither one gaining ground. Over-confident because of their superior arms, the abbey men reckoned without the rage of the less well-armed town's folk. By means of sheer will, the group armed only with the tools of their trade began to beat the others back up the street yard by hard-fought yard. Jeers and catcalls issued from the houses on both sides. Pots and pans rained down from upstairs windows on the abbey's hired men.

Apparently regretting the lack of caution that had led them into the conflict without any particular plan, their captain ordered a swift retreat up the cliff side. It was accompanied by the triumphant yells of the knife-wielding mariners.

As soon as they had been beaten off, scrambling back up the cliff side to the abbey, the fishermen vanished from the street with surprising speed, as if they expected immediate retribution.

A few returned innocently to their marketing as the shutters were flung open again while the rest crowded into the houses with new ale on offer. Making sure her cloak was securely concealing her habit, Hildegard mingled with them and soon found herself swept inside one with a bough hanging above its lintel where everyone was crammed shoulder to shoulder.

She was thinking something must surely be very wrong if the abbey could set about its own tenants with armed men, when she felt somebody grab her roughly by one shoulder.

'Here, you! Who are you?'

'Who wants to know?' she asked, taken aback by the abruptness of the question.

'Me.' A finger was jabbed towards the man's companion, an equally bearded fellow in the garb of his trade. 'And 'im.'

Both men were glowering at her through the thickets of their beards. One had a fresh gash on his cheek. Both carried knives.

'Tell me if you will, what was all that about?' she asked evenly. 'You certainly saw them off.'

'If you were from round here you wouldn't be asking.'

'I'm not from round here.'

He gave her a sardonic look. 'We know that.'

Deliberately and slowly he hooked a finger under the cord round her neck and pulled out her small wooden crucifix.

'So, what are you doing being a nun?'

Both men crowded in even closer, preventing her making a move towards the door. A group of strangers, some already the worse for drink, turned their heads. She steadied herself.

'I know of no law that says such a profession is closed to me.'

The second man moved in to support his comrade. 'Don't get clever with us, nun.' He jabbed a finger into her shoulder. 'Sing us a hymn if you're so holy.'

'Yes! Sing! Sing!' Shouts of encouragement followed from the crowd who had quickly guessed that something was up.

Guessing that they were feeling thwarted by the swiftness and inconclusive street fight and were out for more action, Hildegard bunched her fists inside her sleeves and was preparing to take them by surprise and fight her way out when a voice from the doorway called, 'Now hold off, fellows, I know her.'

A robust-looking figure in the russet garments of a mendicant order forced a path through the crowd. He grinned at her. Robust and confident, with a small, careful black beard on his chin, he held her glance. 'Remember me, domina?'

'What? She really is a nun?' One of the men gave a jeering chuckle. 'So we were right! I knew it as soon as we saw her up at St Mary's, asking questions. She's working for them abbey men.'

The word 'spy' hissed round the crowd. The first fellow grabbed her by the arm and she was about to bring her knee to his groin when a large hand came down on her assailant's shoulder and pulled him off. 'Calm it, Utred, I can vouch for her. I've told you that!'

The mendicant bestowed another confident smile on Hildegard. 'Remember, domina? The Abbey of Meaux not two months since?'

She peered through the gloom at the speaker, wondering whether he was friend or foe despite his words. Meaux had been anything but a safe haven last autumn.

He pushed his hood right back. 'For King Richard,' the stranger said to her, watching her closely with a calm smile playing round his lips.

'And the true Commons,' she replied with relief.

The first two ruffians moved back as a sign of respect.

The stranger slapped them both on the back as if they were old mates. 'If I were a mason,' he smiled, 'I'd tell you she was on the level. As it is all I'll say is we have an understanding.'

This seemed to mean something to the two bearded fellows and they turned to the group still pressing round in the hope of further excitement and growled, 'You heard what the friar said. Back off.'

Friar? Of course. Meaux. The body in the locked chamber. And, as ever, the Prioress of Swyne mixed up in it somehow. The long and short of it meant she had a protector.

Glancing at the ambiguous expressions on the faces surrounding them she saw that the air of menace had dispersed.

'Come,' said the friar, 'let's sit on a bench by

the fire and take a drink together and you can tell me how you come to be on such good terms with my friends here.'

His status among the ruffians in the ale house was such that a kerfuffle ensued when a bench was dragged forth, tipping off its occupants to everyone's hilarity, and placed so that the friar and Hildegard could sit down in privacy. In a moment two jars of ale were thrust into their hands.

'You were caught up in that fracas in the street?' the friar asked, with a shooing gesture to send away anyone who thought they had a right to listen in.

'I'd just turned on to Church Street when I met the men marching up. Who are they, fishermen I take it?'

'And a rough corps of abbey men, no better than mercenaries, albeit on a negligible scale.' His sudden smile, world-weary, keeping to itself more than it gave away, brought his name to mind. Of course she had seen him before, but the context had been so different.

'You're Friar John! You've grown a beard. I did not recognize you. I owe you my gratitude, John. Those fellows over by the ale barrels,' she nodded across the chamber, 'were in an ill temper when they saw my cross. What's been going on?'

He told her what she had more or less already discovered – that the abbey was trying to enforce its demand for higher tolls on anyone using what they deemed to be abbey property, in this case the beaches.

'It seems unfair. Where else can they dry their nets?'

'If the fishermen give in, the abbey will be able to cite a precedent should they decide to take them to court for any infringement of their so-called rights in the future. I've seen it happen over and over in different parts of the county. Scarborough, and down to Bridlington with the Augustinians. It's not just Cistercians who are rapacious in their dealings with the laity.' He bowed his head in apology. 'I except the abbot of Meaux from my criticism.'

'I hope so. I cannot imagine Abbot de Courcy wishing to take unfair advantage of anyone. I suppose,' she added, 'the abbey regards the people down here as tenants?'

'As indeed they are. One or two fellows think to challenge them by buying up property when it falls vacant but I doubt their eventual success if they think to take on the Benedictines. The monastic orders are too powerful, too rich. Their resources make most challenges futile. But of course you'll be aware of this.'

She nodded, remembering Sabine and how she was being harassed by her landlord. 'Neither side seems to have the welfare of their tenants at heart. It looks as if everything is being brought down to financial gain.'

'That's true. So it goes. May I ask what brings you to Whitby?'

She told him briefly about the relic.

'A valuable addition to entice any pilgrim,' he remarked, adding with honest cynicism, 'whether clipped from Abbess Hild's hair or not. The abbey appears to be in dire straits. Desperate measures for desperate needs?'

'I fear so.'

'This is a place where it's difficult to guess who is friend and who foe. Conflicting interests are like the weave in a bagman's cloak.'

'The conflicts are unexpected. I'm sent here as a penance.'

'In fact?'

She nodded. 'By Abbot de Courcy.'

'I remember the scandal you caused.' He chuckled.

She saw no harm in adding, 'I came down into the town just now for another reason. Someone died last night at the abbey. One of the fraternity. A monk called Aelwyn.'

The expression on the friar's face did not change. He gave no sign that he knew about it and she watched him as she said, 'I heard some interesting comments from the congregation at St Mary's earlier. They believe it was not a natural death nor an accident.' She turned a puzzled glance towards him.

'And I can tell you why,' he said, interpreting her expression. 'It's because he alone of his fraternity made a stand against the exploitation of the tenants by the cartel of masons I've just mentioned. It aroused great enmity in some quarters. Much gainsaying. Of course, as you no doubt know, he had a personal interest in the matter, but I believe he was also acting from a sense of justice and a compassionate regard for what is right. He was someone worthy of our regard.' He gave her a meaningful glance.

She lowered her voice. 'What was his personal interest?'

He rose to his feet, handed their two empty ale beakers to a hand that reached for them, and said, 'I'll walk with you as far as the bottom of the steps.' Not waiting for an answer he carved a way for them into the street. A chorus of blessings followed him out.

He warned, 'There will be repercussions for the fishing community after this fracas. The bursar and the lord prior, who I'm sure you know run the abbey as they please, are relentless in their exactions. Despite the Great Rising in the south eight years ago, they seem not to have learned the lessons from it. Taxes unwillingly exacted will not be paid without bloodshed. People must feed their children. The fruit can be squeezed only until its juice is gone; after that it is folly to persist.' He turned sharp eyes on her. 'Have you seen how they live?'

'A little. Yesterday we saw inside the young woman's house, the one with its burned thatch.'

'Ah, Mistress Sabine. The cartel were sure they could push her around. A lone woman? Easy prey, or so they thought. They may have to think again.'

He said no more and when she tentatively asked him to explain, he merely shook his head and she was left with the feeling that her question was considered to be crass.

'What is it I don't understand about this place?' she asked as they came to the steps leading back to the abbey.

He merely made a small obeisance and murmured,

'Some things you do not need to understand, domina. You do not live here. Fulfil the terms of your penance and watch your step. One innocent man is dead. Let us pray there will be no others.'

'But John . . .' she called after him as he turned quickly and began to stride away, but either he did not hear or had said all he wanted to say.

She began the long climb up to the abbey and while trying to shake off the feeling that the friar had been unnecessarily cautious she corrected herself with the thought that what she had wanted to ask him was probably something he could not answer anyway – because how could he know how or why Aelwyn had died?

If it was foul play, as it was rumoured down here, it was beginning to look as if he had come up against the cartel that was trying to bully Sabine out of her home. How far would they go to further their interests? As far as murder?

# Seven

Hildegard decided to search out Gregory and Egbert, but when she entered the guest house to find a bite to eat she was met by solemn faces from the few servants in the hall.

One of them approached her. 'The body is to be brought down after the next Office, domina.'

Thanking him for the information, she went across to the church before the bell began its summons and was straight away taken aside by Sister Aveline who was hovering in the entrance. 'News about the monk who died,' she whispered. 'Gold has gone missing from the bursar's coffers. Now they're out on another search party.'

'Are the two things linked?' Hildegard frowned.

'They are saying he embezzled the gold to give to someone in the town. A woman, it is rumoured.'

She thought at once of Sabine. 'But why would he need to do that?'

'These fellows run up debts in the stews and eventually their debtors find them out.' Sister Aveline gave a sanctimonious pursing of her lips.

'That's monstrous!' Hildegard exclaimed.

'Isn't it!'

'I mean, if it's untrue it's a slur on a good man.' She could not believe she was wrong about Aelwyn, although how could she know after one glimpse of the fellow? Friar John's reticence in the matter suggested that there was more to him than she knew.

Sister Aveline adjusted her veil. 'Now we have a requiem mass to sit through after the next Office.' She gave a heavy sigh. 'More delays.'

Hildegard wondered for a moment what she meant. Then it dawned. 'You mean before we can view the relic?'

The nun nodded.

'If the abbot will not make his decision before Epiphany there's plenty of time for us all to have a look at it,' Hildegard pointed out.

'Do you believe he has not made up his mind already?' Aveline trilled and added a light, irritating laugh full of knowingness. 'And do you also believe it is the abbot's decision? I think not!'

Hildegard remembered the prior sitting beside the abbot at her interview with him. Is that who Aveline was referring to? He did not have the air of a plotter nor a decision-maker. Now the choir struck up and all chance of continuing the conversation was drowned out in the ethereal chant that followed.

By the time Hildegard lifted her head after praying for peace and for the safe journey of Aelwyn's soul, Aveline had already slipped away. She went outside and paced the north cloister. In a moment Gregory and Egbert would appear and she had plenty to ask them.

'So, how fares it in the town?' Egbert greeted her. 'We saw a few men-at-arms returning in some disarray. Apparently they were maliciously set upon by mariners armed to the teeth and twice their number and had no alternative but to flee back to sanctuary to discuss future punishment.' He was smiling and clearly did not believe a word of what they claimed.

'There was a bit of a fracas, soon over, and it turned into a rout more by the determination of the mariners than by the strength of their armed opponents. The abbey men were wielding broadswords, for heaven's sake. What sort of men are they?'

'Felons, in short.' Egbert turned. 'Here's Gregory.'

'We were worried about you,' he called. 'Then Torold came dragging back and told us you were in the thick of it, talking calmly to a friar.'

She told them what had happened. 'I can't help feeling that the abbey is being unduly aggressive over these nets,' she concluded.

'It's not just nets but the fact of being opposed. They run sheep on their land and they want to run the people in the same way. They don't want individuals to stand up for their rights.' Gregory shook his head. 'The history of our own Order is not unblemished, is it? When Rievaulx and Fountains were established I understand whole villages were razed to the ground to allow the flocks free pasture.'

'Enough breast-beating for what happened before our time. We cannot help that. We were not involved. We would not behave in the same way either. It's what is happening now that we have to deal with. A man dead in mysterious circumstances. Let's deal with that.' Egbert swung impatiently away. 'I'm going across to the apple store now. We need to have another look round before they bring the body down. Coming?'

The two guards rose reluctantly from their dicing when Egbert strode up. 'All right, men. Has anyone been up here since we left you?'

The men glanced at each other then shook their heads.

'Who was it?' demanded Egbert.

One of them grimaced. Despite his monk's habit, Egbert looked as if he could take on anyone, and would, if thwarted. 'We thought you meant anybody who shouldn't have been here,' he defended. 'It was only the bursar come up with his man.'

95

Egbert made no reply but went to the wooden beam that barred the door and lifted it off.

'Did he go inside?' he asked. 'This bursar.'

The men nodded. 'Only for a second to view the body. He deemed it ripe for taking back to the mortuary.'

Hildegard winced at the callous way he referred to Aelwyn's remains and bent her head to follow the two monks inside.

'Why is it so pitch dark in here?' she asked when she joined them. 'Is there no way of letting in light? How could anyone see what they were doing?'

Egbert was coughing and choking again and went outside. When she went deeper into the store she could understand why – the strong, sickly sweet fumes rising from the rows of apples was overwhelming.

Gregory came in and looked about him with a puzzled frown. 'What is it about this place?' he was asking. The body lay where it had lain last time they were here, a sleeping man, his chosen fruit lying in a neat, methodical row beside him. 'There's something not right. Why are there no window slits to let in the light? You're right, Hildi, they could not see what they were doing at the back of the store. Is there something there we missed?'

He roamed about, going right inside, looking under shelves, reaching out into the darkness at the back but finding nothing.

Hildegard went over to the long wall running the length of the store. It was difficult to make much out, but trailing her hands over the stones in case there was something they had missed, she eventually found a nook where a rag of some sort was bundled between the worked sandstone blocks. She pulled it out. It brought a cry to her lips as light flooded in as soon as the blockage was removed. She held up what she had found.

Gregory reached out. 'A garment of some sort?' He rubbed the coarse cloth between his fingers.

Now there was more light he peered along the wall and noticed something similar wedged between the stones. He went over and gave it a tug. 'And another?' He held it up.

Hildegard was puzzled. 'But aren't they the little surplices the novices wear?'

'What on earth is going on?' He went along the wall and at intervals pulled out more block-ages until they held four little garments and the store was filled with light. 'Why do that?'

It was not only light that flooded in, but air too. A wind from the east rustled a few dead leaves still attached to the apple stalks.

Hildegard's eyes were round with astonishment. 'They would know . . . whoever did this . . . would know . . . they must have known that stored apples in large quantities give off noxious fumes . . .? Don't you see? Anyone trapped inside the store and unable to get out would, over several hours . . .' She glanced at Aelwyn's body. 'The slight blue tinge round his mouth and nose makes sense now. They're signs of asphyxiation. Now we know why . . . Oh, poor Aelwyn . . .'

It was deliberate. The words spoken in anger

by the woman outside St Mary's came back to her: *They've done for him.*

'I think,' she said, turning to Gregory, 'we have to accept that we're faced with a plain case of murder.'

The three of them walked slowly back towards the abbey precinct but did not at once go within.

'It is assumed,' Gregory began, 'that we can be safely left in charge of any inquiries into Aelwyn's death because we are strangers in ignorance of the factions here within the abbey.' He looked affronted. 'And perhaps because we are deemed to be blind as well as stupid.'

'On which view they were nearly right,' added Egbert, but he was looking grim rather than amused. 'We cannot rely on chance any longer. Who?' he asked. 'And why?'

It was close to the question that had bothered Hildegard enough to seek them out. 'I was going to ask why and how,' she told them. 'Now we have our answer to the latter, but as to the former . . . Why Aelwyn?' Then she recalled the words of Friar John. She explained. 'But I cannot believe,' she concluded, 'that Aelwyn's support for one poor townswoman could lead to actual murder by someone in the cartel they mentioned. It's so . . . it's so extreme . . . it makes no sense.'

'Is the profit this landlord fellow will make from putting up the abbey guests be so much he's willing to risk hellfire for it?'

'There's more to this place than meets the eye,' Egbert muttered somewhat superfluously. 'A

98

monk murdered, a coffer of gold gone missing, armed men sent into the town, and now garments belonging to the novices crammed into the air vents.' He paused. 'Well, I suppose it might have been a prank and we should get the novices out of the way first before we seek out more likely suspects. Shall we do it now?'

Hildegard left the two monks to use their advantage in being able to go where they chose within the precinct and went to sit in the part of the cloister where guests were allowed.

It was not long before Torold made an appearance. He was looking thoughtfully at the ground when she called to him and had evidently just left the church where the rest of them were being put through their paces in readiness for the requiem mass and, no doubt, discreetly questioned by now about their missing garments.

When he saw who had called him he took one look and ran back towards the church. She got to her feet. He glanced over his shoulder and slipped hurriedly through the west door. *Now why* . . . she asked herself, sprinting after him. He had the look of a hunted animal but it was a mistake to try to hide in the church because with its screens separating the laity from the monastics he would have nowhere to hide. By the time she burst in through the door he was backed against the far wall.

'Torold,' she began. 'I just want to—'

But he was off again, dodging round one of the big columns of stone before making a run for the small door to the tower steps. She could hear the scuffing of his boots as he ran pell-mell inside and started to climb.

*He can certainly run*, she thought as she hurled herself up the steps after him, *but he's got himself into a sure trap. There's no way out up here.* When she reached the top, however, where there was nothing more than a window slit giving a view of the ocean and a closed door on to the walkway between the towers, there was no sign of him.

From outside came the piercing shriek of gulls. It continued deafeningly in a crescendo of avian rage.

In sudden fright she guessed what it meant: he must have gone outside. The builders, Master Buckingham's men, off celebrating the Twelve Days like everybody else, had left buckets and a short ladder tightly tied down for their return. Climbing over these, Hildegard pushed open the door and stepped out on to the narrow stone ledge running along the inside of the north wall. The only problem, if Torold imagined finding refuge here, was that the wall between here and the tower on the corner of the north transept had not yet been finished. After a few paces it simply stopped.

Gulls with predatory beaks letting forth their outrage at being disturbed swirled about her head as she stepped outside. A glance along the parapet showed that it was empty so she shouted, 'Torold! Where are you?'

The wind whined between the unfinished crenellations. The gulls stormed and shrieked. But Torold seemed to have vanished like a wraith.

She called again.

Then waited without moving.

The gulls swooped and slid savagely down the air currents, circling and returning, avid for prey.

Far below lay the pavers round the Anglian burial ground.

The wind out here was strong enough to make her fear being tugged from her perch. Carefully she forced herself not to look down again. Close at hand, underneath the high-pitched screams of the gulls, she could hear a sound, almost less than a sound, a breath, no more. It was coming from somewhere above – to the left just above her head where the gulls were circling.

And then she caught a glimpse of the smallest movement. He was on the leads covering the roof directly overhead.

'Torold,' she called more encouragingly. 'There's nothing to be afraid of. Why are you hiding?' It was the second time he had run away, she recalled.

No reply.

'I know you're there. And you'll know how dangerous it is. The builders haven't finished work. You could fall to your death. Please now, be a sensible boy and come down. You have nothing to fear from me. If you tell me what's frightened you I can help.'

There was still no answer and she continued to talk, edging closer to where she could get a glimpse of him by moving cautiously along the parapet. All that was visible were his hands and the edge of a cuff. He was gripping on to the calmes between the lengths of lead that had already been put in place and she saw his knuckles whitening with the strain. *He must be terrified,* she thought. *He could slip at any moment.*

Quietly she told him about her son Bertram, keeping her voice level, reassuring him that she understood and that he could trust her. She saw the fingers relax and shift position. However, it was not to lower himself down to safety but to edge further away. The gulls did not let up.

She asked, 'Are you frightened of being punished? I promise you I will never let that happen.'

A croak, a clearing of the voice, then firmly, 'I did not steal anything, neither garments nor gold. I will not be accused of it.'

'They cannot accuse you of it. There is no proof. Who accuses you?'

'The bursar's clerk.'

'Let me tell you that I and my brothers from Meaux are in charge over the matter of the garments. We thought it might have been a prank. We think no ill of you. We were appointed by the prior himself to look into this—'

'That's what I mean!' Torold exclaimed. 'You are all in league!'

'I can assure you we are only in league with God and the truth. The garments are a part of the matter concerning our aim to find out how Brother Aelwyn was murdered.'

A choking cry came from above. A voice like one she did not recognize croaked, 'Is that true?'

'Yes. We found them in the apple-store—'

'I mean about him being murdered?'

'Yes, we think that's how it must have been—'

'He was going to come and play bandy-sticks with us. And he didn't come. And he was nowhere around. And then they started to look for him and I went down to tell . . .' He changed direction. 'Who murdered him?'

'We don't know that yet. All I can say is that we shall discover the truth if it's humanly possible. I promise you that.'

'Are you sure he was murdered?' he demanded urgently. 'Is there proof?'

'If there is we shall find it. And it will lead us to his murderer. Why do you ask? Do you have something to tell me?'

In answer she heard a scrabbling sound and, alarmed, she saw him edging higher up towards the roof ridge. By now the gulls were beginning to circle off in search of easier prey. There was nothing for it.

She had no choice but to climb out and try to coax him back, face to face, or at least get a firm hold of him to prevent him climbing further.

Taller than he was, she found it easy to swing out over the edge of the guttering and hoist herself on to the sloping leads. When she lifted her head he was sitting on the ridge staring down at her, white-faced but determined to remain there as she edged towards him. The wind blustered over the roof top and, afraid it would whisk him from his perch, she stretched out a hand.

'Torold, come down, I beg you. It is not safe here and I'm afraid you'll fall and that would be a waste of your precious life.'

He remained mute and immobile.

'There is no need for this. Whatever is wrong can be put right if we trust in God's mercy.'

She risked reaching out her hand again to entice him down, but she could not quite touch him. His face was streaming with tears.

'What is it, my dear child? Whatever it is can surely be put right—'

'It never can. Never, never!' He began to sob.

'Trust me. Such grief can be assuaged. Forgiveness for transgressions can be granted. No-one is ever so far out of God's grace that they cannot be redeemed.'

'How can you say that?' he gulped between sobs.

'It is my firm hope and belief—'

'It's not true!' he yelled in sudden defiance. 'His murderer can never be redeemed! Never! Never! Never! He shall burn in hell for all eternity! I shall pray to God to make him suffer!'

Alarmed at the strength of his rage, she stretched for his hand but could not reach. 'Please, child, I beg you come down—'

'Never!' he shouted again. 'You say he is murdered! How can that be put right? He is gone forever.' He lifted his face to the sky and began to howl. 'I am bereft! I want him back. I want him! He was my father!'

He started to cry, passionately and unrestrained, and she realized how young he was despite his usual jaunty adult manner. In reality he was no more than a babe in arms.

But his *father*?

She gazed up at him in wonder. 'Brother Aelwyn . . .?'

'He was my beloved father! Everyone knows that. They have killed him!' As his grief took over he loosened his hold on the calmes and began to slip down the roof. Realizing what he had done, he tried to grab on to something but the lead was as smooth as silk and his fall became a headlong slide. Hildegard, horror-stricken, could only watch and brace her feet against the edge of the gutter and reach out both arms as he hurtled helplessly towards her.

# Eight

The infirmarer was sitting in his bed, propped up on a stack of pillows, between his hands a bowl of steaming liquid, his eyes watering. The vile aroma of this beverage filled the entire chamber but the two elderly patients playing a fierce game of chess at the far end and the one or two corrodians lying in the beds opposite and suffering the general discomforts of old age seemed unbothered.

'I am a living exemplum of the advice given us by the great Hippocrates,' the infirmarer was saying with a comfortable smile. 'Physician heal thyself!' He drained the liquid in the bowl with apparent relish. 'Elecampane, white hore-hound, thyme – and one or two other things obtained more expensively than the home-grown cures we are fortunate to be able to lay our hands on.' He set the bowl down beside his bed. 'I am feeling sounder by the hour. I especially wanted to speak to you on the matter of one or two observations I made yesterday when I was feeling as if I was living out my last day.'

He called across the chamber to where Torold was sitting, white-faced, on a stool by the door. 'Dear lad, I'm going to ask you to run and fetch a flagon of water and wine from the kitchens in a moment. Enough for me and my visitor. And get yourself one of the kitchener's pastries at the same time. But first I want to ask you something. Come closer.'

Torold, self-consciously tear-stained and suddenly wary, stepped closer to the infirmarer's bed. 'What is it, Brother Dunstan?'

'I'm puzzling my poor old head about why you should do such a wild thing as climb on to the roof. Now you're feeling calmer can you tell us why you did it? Were you in thrall to some demon of self-destruction?'

Torold shrugged.

'Come now, lad, what set it off? Did somebody say something untoward that made you think it would be a good idea to do such a thing?'

Torold pursed his lips and seemed to struggle with himself.

'I believe I may have frightened him,' suggested Hildegard softly. 'He thought I wanted to reprove him, perhaps?'

Torold, still biting his lip, nodded and stared at the floor.

'I've often wanted to run and hide from people,' Brother Dunstan announced with a rueful smile.

'Sometimes it's the only way. Other times it can make matters worse.'

'I'll tell you what somebody said,' Torold burst out. 'When the two Cistercian monks appeared somebody whispered that they were come to find a thief. I said, "What thief?" And my friend said, "Everybody knows some gold has gone missing from the bursar's chamber or wherever he keeps it and they think we did it." I said, "I never did it. Did you?" And my friend shakes his head and says, "No, but if they say we did, we did, and that's that. Punishment will follow whatever we might say." "I'm not staying to be punished for something I never did," say I and that's when I got out into the garth and the domina sees me and I think it best to escape but she follows. And I never expected her to follow me up the tower. And,' he shrugged his thin shoulders again, 'at the top there was nowhere else to go but on the roof.'

'You might,' suggested Brother Dunstan gently, 'have stopped to find out what Sister Hildegard wished to ask you. Just think, if you had slipped, it would have been for nothing.'

Torold gazed intently at the toe of one of his boots.

'Go on then, lad, about your errand. And if the pastry cook demurs over the pastry say I order you to have one.'

As Torold shut the door of the infirmary behind him, the old man leaned forward. 'It is distressing to him. His father. The disapproval some show because of the misfortune of his birth. It's good that you brought him to me. I'll see what I can find to occupy him until he has survived the first days of his grief. Poor lad,' he continued, 'he is quite bereft – as he informed us and every hearing creature within a dozen leagues!'

'He can certainly shout. But it's best, in my opinion, that he gets the pain out of him while it's still raw.'

'Quite right.'

'I had no idea his father was Brother Aelwyn,' Hildegard admitted. 'It was a shock to me – and then to have him nearly tumble to his death . . .'

'He will be more cautious in his climbing about in future, I doubt not.' He offered a complicit smile. 'And you will want to know how it came about that he is a son of the monastery?'

'I suppose Aelwyn fathered him before joining the Order?'

The infirmarer shook his head. 'Alas, no. I believe he had no experience of a carnal nature when he became a novice, he was a mere child, but like all the young ones as they find themselves growing to manhood he would betake himself down to the stews with the others to assuage his ignorance. The trod they ascribe to the great poet Caedmon of our dearly beloved Abbess Hild's day fetches up at the end of the lane where, I'm told, such business is carried on by whore-master Selby.' He brought his lower lip over his upper one and paused for a moment. 'It was there Brother Aelwyn met Sabine,' he resumed, 'the Madonna of Grope Lane as she became known . . . a genuine Magdalen as dear Aelwyn believed. When he knew she was with child he persuaded the abbot at that time to allow her a rented cottage at the foot of the steps and in all but daily practice fulfilled the role of father. He could not renounce his vocation but neither could he renounce his Madonna and child.'

'This is sacrilegious if not blasphemous to use the word Madonna in such a context,' Hildegard murmured in astonishment. The old fellow was talking as freely as a Lollard and she feared for him.

He was aware of what he was saying but remained quite calm. 'We do things pragmatically here, as you may have observed. No stigma attached to him and whatever stigma Sabine acquired is entirely her own doing. She has confessed and sinned and confessed again. She will not change. I can tell you in confidence she has been secretly to me several times for cures for the inevitable results of her way of life. She cannot help herself. Perhaps she is led astray by her beauty and what it brings her?' His glance meshed with Hildegard's. 'Men find her irresistible but do not know how to revere such God-given physical grace without trying to possess it. Aelwyn was simply happy to worship her. That is not to excuse her, or him, but merely to explain the danger of vanity.'

'And did Brother Aelwyn condone . . .' She hesitated, deciding how to put it. 'Did he condone her visits to you?'

'He would not know of them. In his innocence he would not imagine such a thing. And I doubt whether her honesty would take her so far as to tell him. He is not a priest, he is not her confessor.

Why should he know? I am not her confessor either.'

'If there is no other purpose in inviting me here other than to pass on gossip—' Hildegard began but Dunstan forestalled her.

'Forgive me. I thought only to clear the ground for what else I have to say.' He hesitated. 'I was not myself yesterday, suffering this wretched bout of the rheum, and at first I doubted my own eyes at what I saw. After further thought I decided to speak out. You and your Cistercian brothers will see events more clearly than we who are embroiled in them morning, noon and night. There are undercurrents here of which, sad to say, our abbot John of Richmond appears to be unaware – or too weak to counter. What rules this precinct is ambition, greed and a lust for personal power instead of – as it should be – compassion and love of God. It is a common criticism of our Order – and of yours too, domina, if I may presume to remind you. The Church as it is leads men blindly down paths that can only take them deeper into the realms of Satan . . . I cast no stones. We are all human and we are all capable of folly. However,' he leaned back into his pillows, 'there is something rotten here that must be rooted out.'

He looked weary and Hildegard reminded herself that he was still suffering from the affliction that had brought him to his bed yesterday.

'You have already spoken to my brothers?'

'That is why I invited you here, domina. I have something to tell you that you may pass on to

110

them, as they have the prior's permission to intercede.'

'Is it about something you noticed in the apple store?'

'What I observed yesterday,' he said at last, 'was what you yourselves have already seen – the blockages in the air vents, the door barred from the outside and, what almost passed me by, the signs of asphyxiation on that poor fellow. What you can do is find out who set up Brother Aelwyn for death.'

He sighed and closed his eyes. 'I cannot summon the strength to leave my bed. If I could I would want to know who barred the door and who, if anyone, gave the order to do so.'

'That's a long matter when we know so little about the conflicts that thrive here. No-one has admitted to being even near the door, nor do we know how the little surplices were stolen and put in the air vents. Without knowing more it's difficult to find a place to start.'

'Then let me tell you something of how things are.' He settled more deeply into his pillows. 'You may learn over time that we possess property both down there in the town and along the coast, many farms and parishes throughout the county. You might imagine the rents and produce would satisfy all our material needs and, indeed, make us wealthy?'

'I would. But then, your abbot is offering us a priceless relic because, we are told, of the straitened circumstances of the abbey.'

'True. That is the reason being given to all and sundry. You will also soon learn that we have been in contention with the fishing fleet at Scarborough over the landing of their catch on our beaches, and vice versa, that our tenants in the town are harried not only by us in the matter of tolls, but by ambitious men intent on buying up any property they can obtain by fair means or foul, and intent also on building new properties in order to rake in more rents. They are building on the other side of the Esk now and own the means to cross from one side to the other. They are a challenge to us. Our wealth is being chipped away by deliberate attempts to impoverish us. That is the view of our bursar, Brother Peter of Hertilpole, and of our lord prior, John Allerton. Our lord abbot appears to have no opinion, his mind,' he added dryly, 'being set on more spiritual matters.'

'Hertilpole and Allerton will no doubt say in their defence that it is their duty to protect the interests of the abbey?'

'Indeed they will.'

'I see no wrong in that – beyond the misgiving that monastics are vowed to poverty and their desire to fill the coffers of the abbey seems to take them beyond immediate needs—'

'Instead of trusting in God like the lilies of the field?' He gave an impatient shake of the head. 'But if the filling of our coffers can be justified, what about the method by which we do so? What about that? What about bribery? What about blackmail? What about abduction? What about outright theft? I put these accusations in no order of heinousness. Each brings its own special misery to the victim. There is, domina, always a victim.'

'And Brother Aelwyn?'

'What has he to do with this, you ask? I believe he felt that Brother Hertilpole went far beyond the bounds of what a promised religious should do. I believe he felt that he should be stopped in his vicious attempt to bring in gold regardless of legality and justice. I also believe that he felt himself to be alone in thinking so.'

'Was he alone?' It was a blunt question and Dunstan gave an equally blunt answer.

'He feared to be seen as a Lollard. In truth he had few allies here. The way things are run satisfies the vanity, greed, and complacency of our fraternity. He was one man against a corrupt system. Except for . . .' He looked thoughtful, as if a sudden idea had come into his head.

'Except for?' Hildegard prompted.

'Except for one to whom the wrath of the abbey hierarchy would mean nothing . . . a lay assistant to the bursar.' He pondered the matter and then suggested, 'For a fuller picture of what is going on here you might talk to Master Edred. He goes freely between the monastery and the town. Indeed, to some here he is persona non grata for his familiarity with certain men down there, although deemed useful in our dealings with them.'

'Why do they look askance?'

'They fear his views. Lollards are greatly respected outside the precinct as elsewhere throughout the country. Their honest poverty appeals to those forced into it by the caprice of fortune. They see themselves sharing a similar fate. People respect the plain dealing of Wycliffe's preachers, especially when they witness the

113

wilful extravagance of their betters who only pay lip service to the demands of their Order. Wycliffe's views fascinated Aelwyn as a child of the monastery. Perhaps he was of a rebellious nature and it shows up clearly in his son? Edred and Aelwyn were often in discussion on such matters, Brother Aelwyn being a reader and Edred encouraged, indeed driven, to learn.'

Dunstan lifted one hand wearily and let it drop. 'All for now, domina. Talk to your brothers. Tell them what I have said. Talk to Edred. Be discreet. Root out this evil before Whitby Abbey is overrun by the ungodly.'

This time when he closed his eyes Hildegard was confident he would sleep and she tiptoed towards the door, noticing that one of the ancient corrodians was now sitting up in bed. He watched with unblinking eyes as she left.

Torold was already waiting outside the door with crumbs round his mouth. As soon as he saw Hildegard he said, 'I peeped in and saw you with Brother Dunstan and thought it best to leave you to talk. Does he still want his wine?' He had set the flagon and beakers in a niche by the door and gestured towards them.

'I think it best to leave it by his bed for when he wakes. He will deem it an honour if you will wait on him later.'

'I'll do so. He's the best here. Even though,' he added, 'he cannot bring my dear father back to life.'

The falcons were kept in cages in a dark shed, each on its own separate perch. They were hooded.

The little jessies on their legs made a soft and constant tinkling. The falconer stopped what he was doing and came to the door when Hildegard put her question to him from the yard.

'Edred? He hasn't been near today. Guests still at table, no doubt, those who are out of bed. There they'll stay if they've any sense. Last thing on their minds at present is hawking. Weather like this.' He grinned as he mentioned the weather.

'It looks fine to me.' Hildegard glanced up at the blue dome above their heads.

'Mark me, it'll be snow later.'

'So do you have any idea where I might find him?'

'Try yon stables. He might be giving that merchant fellow's horse a work-out, as his master won't be out to do it himself. It's a big brute, needs plenty of exercise.'

'I'll do that.'

She found the stables but no Edred.

'He's taken yon black devil out for Sir Ranulph,' a stable lad mentioned, over-hearing her question as he staggered by with a bale of hay.

'It's like looking for a needle in a haystack itself,' she said as she left. The weather changed within an hour. The wind got up and swept like razored steel over the headland. The clouds heaped along the horizon. The sea was dun-coloured one minute then covered with glittering surf the next. The falconer as weather prophet gained her respect.

A file of monks in black habits was beginning to leave by the south door as she approached the church and, sheltering in the lee of a wall, she watched for the white garments of Gregory and Egbert. Like surf on the sea of Benedictine black, she thought as they soon appeared at the tail end and she waited until she could go over without drawing too much attention to herself. 'Nobody knows how the surplices were stolen,' Egbert began at once when they met halfway down the cloister. 'Have you had any luck?'

She shook her head. 'Did you find out anything else?'

'The spare ones were kept in an aumbry in the boys' dortoir. Anybody could have got in and snatched a few. The lads themselves came up with some original ideas about how they could have been taken. A great bird with eagle-like talons was top suggestion, followed by suspicions about the guests, although why a guest would want a surplice too small to wear they could not determine. Maybe it was a gift for a small boy who has been sadly left at home, was one little chap's belief.'

'Older fellows are tight-lipped about who was last seen up there yesterday,' Gregory added. 'We inquired of the kitchener who sent Aelwyn up to fetch some apples for the Abbot's dish and a few for himself but he could only say that he usually took a stroll up to the orchards at around the same time most days.'

'He was blaming himself, saying he wished he'd bitten off his own tongue rather than to have caused what happened.'

Hildegard told them about her meeting with

Brother Dunstan. 'I was on my way to find Edred to see if he can throw any light on the unseen currents swirling about the place.' She lowered her voice. 'He's something of a Lollard, that Brother Dunstan. Do you believe there's a clue there? Edred and Aelwyn were close apparently, and all three seem to share the same views. As you can imagine, John Wycliffe and his preachers don't go down well among the rest of the brotherhood.'

'They wouldn't!' Egbert grimaced. 'Some of them even resent the screening off of the west end for people like you to use for prayer, Hildegard. They'd much rather keep the church for the exclusive use of themselves.'

'That sounds like Hertilpole,' said Luke. 'He wants to clear away the beggars at the bottom of the cliff as well: *They take and they do not give.*'

'Apparently he's not so choosy when it comes to raking in the rents and fines,' she replied. 'Taking and not giving.'

'So I've been hearing.' Gregory was impatient. 'But why does Dunstan believe Edred knows something?' he demanded.

'I'm not sure he does. I think he only suggested him as somebody who knows how the various factions hold power and to try and find out who might have resented Aelwyn so much that they wanted rid of him. In the town the view is that the cartel of masons wanted him out of the way because of his support for Sabine.'

'And here?'

'No idea, unless they agreed with the idea of another bigger guest house down there.'

'Doesn't Abbot Richmond himself have anything to say about that?'

'Apparently not. He believes the art of delegation is a skill to be fostered.'

'I can't imagine Hubert de Courcy sitting back while we brought Meaux into faction,' Egbert remarked.

'You do that anyway,' Gregory quipped, 'reprobate that you are.'

'Look here, this is getting us nowhere. I was off to find Edred as it's the only lead we seem to have, but I thought I'd check with you two as he's still out exercising Sir Ranulph's horse. In the meantime, what's this about a theft of gold?'

'I don't doubt that while we were at our prayers all our belongings were given a good going over. And look, here come the solemn faces.'

They glanced across to where Egbert indicated and watched as several monks appeared in the garth.

Head and shoulders above everyone else was the bursar, his already saturnine face darker still as he said something to the prior. A tubby fellow Gregory identified for Hildegard as the sacristan was waving his arms in explanation, and a fourth monk was recognized as Roger of Pykering, Master of the Blessed Virgin's altar, who came up with a flotilla of servants attending him.

One of them, the sacristan, flourished something between finger and thumb. The others stepped back either in horror or to disassociate themselves from it. The bursar reached out. As if coming to a sudden decision he swung on his

118

heels and marched off across the garth towards the gatehouse, indicating that the servants should follow.

Gregory decided to drift along in their wake.

'What's that they've found?' muttered Egbert. 'Was it a coin? I couldn't tell from this distance.'

'It looked like it.'

'I wonder where it turned up.' He gave Hildegard a long glance. 'I don't like the way this is going. Can it be connected to this business with Aelwyn?'

'Gregory will find out if there is anything.'

Some instructions were being given to the porter and he brought another fellow out to speak to the bursar. Together the two men stood before their superior with respectful expressions. A crowd began to gather made up of a handful of passing servants engaged on other business, the couple of corrodians, the Pope's men, and one or two guests including Sister Aveline and Darius. The latter approached the prior when he had completed his instructions, if that is what they were, and appeared to be demanding an explanation about what was going on.

'But are our goods safe?' they heard him demand in his loud voice after listening to the bursar with a scowl on his face. Assurances seemed to be given. He flung his cloak over his shoulder and stamped away.

The bursar and his entourage eventually headed back across the garth to the path that led to the abbot's lodge. The servants spread out in a desultory kind of way, peering at the ground with

119

their hands in their belts for want of anything to carry, and were seen to make a clean sweep of the garth. Clearly their hearts were not in it.

Gregory strolled back. 'Some gold pieces have been found, one near the altar of the Blessed Virgin, another in the garth. The belief is that the thief dropped them in his haste to find a suitable hiding place.'

'What would he be doing at the altar?' asked Egbert, adding, 'In their opinion.'

Hildegard gave him a sharp glance. 'You sound sceptical, Egbert.'

'It takes everybody's attention away from the main issue, which, as I see it, is the death of a man on abbey property – and not just a man but a respected monk.' He sighed with impatience. 'And they're bothered about a few pieces of gold.'

'It's more than that, so the bursar was telling them. It could make the difference between the life they're used to and what some might regard as penury. The entire year's rents have been stolen!'

'The Pope's men won't be happy to hear that. Nothing to send home to Il Papa!'

'We'll soon find the brothers down at the bottom of the steps begging for alms,' Egbert grinned. 'But he cannot be serious? The entire year?'

'That's what he said, and with sufficient force to have us all believe him as the words fell from his lips . . .' A roguish smile twitched across his face.

'What is the conclusion then, Greg? Are they throwing suspicion on anybody yet?'

'No name was mentioned.'

'They'll find it difficult to pin it on anyone, surely? Who has access to the bursar's coffers?'

Hildegard's eyes sharpened and she put a hand on Gregory's arm. 'Look over there. Towards the gatehouse. See? It's some of the abbey guard who were thrashed earlier today by the mariners.'

'Come for their pay or for more orders?' Egbert followed her glance. 'Bad timing if the former.'

One of the men left the others and followed the bursar and his group. He caught up with them as they let themselves through the gate into the abbot's garden. It looked as if they invited him to join them because he continued along the path and disappeared round the side of the lodge in their wake.

'So that's that. Let's go and pay our respects to Aelwyn. They brought his body up earlier.'

The three of them, still puzzling over the matter of the gold coins, moved off.

The body was resting in one of the side chapels and Aelwyn looked at peace, no matter in what manner he had met his death. After a prayer for his journeying soul towards its hoped-for redemption there was little more they could do. The bluish tinge around his nostrils looked less prominent. His hands, with their grazed knuckles, were folded on his chest. Silver coins rested on his eyelids.

'And they found a gold coin in here?' asked Hildegard.

'So they say.'

'What? Fallen from Aelwyn's garments?'

'I didn't hear anyone suggest that.' Gregory frowned. 'What are you suggesting?'

'Nothing much. It brings the two crimes together, that's all. When did the rents go missing?'

'This morning. At least, that's when the loss was first noticed.'

Gregory wrinkled his brow. 'I can't fathom what they're thinking at present.'

'Do many use the side chapels?'

'They're in constant use. The master is always in attendance, and when he's not there an acolyte is instructed to tend the flame.'

Gregory gazed up at the coloured glass in the window with its golden-haired Virgin dressed in blue. The thrusting bones of his strong features softened and the lids closed over his dark eyes for a moment. There was a pause, but when he turned he was himself again. 'Let's go up to the store to see if there's anything else we missed.'

# Nine

The long grass in the orchard was crisp with frost. The falconer must have been confounded by the weather because the clouds had been driven back out to sea and sunlight shimmered over the crooked shapes of the wintering trees. At the lowest end they were half-hidden under a gauze of mist. It seemed impossible to believe in rain on such a day.

'How fine it is out here,' murmured Hildegard.

'I can understand why Aelwyn saw it as a private place for contemplation. There at his back is the abbey.' She turned to look up the slope. 'His home since childhood and his security, and down here in the orchard something free, natural and beautiful, bringing him close to reverence by a different path. I wish we had had the chance to know him.'

In silence Egbert lifted the beam from across the door. The two guards, sitting at a distance, barely glanced up after they registered their arrival. They looked bored and ill-tempered, one whistling through his teeth while he threw pebbles at an irregular turf of grass, the other whittling a piece of wood into a rough animal shape with his eating knife.

As Hildegard entered the store she noticed how fresh the air was now the blockages had been removed. Nothing else had changed. The earthen floor was scuffed where the body had been removed. Many feet had trampled about near the doorway. Deep inside, ranged along the length of the building, rows of apples waited to be collected for the kitchens.

Turning, she noticed that something else had not changed – the six apples chosen by Aelwyn and placed in a row where his hand had lain. 'They're still there,' she remarked to the others.

'Nobody would want to scrump apples in a dead house.' Egbert stood looking down at them. 'The kitchener was complaining that his great piece of culinary art is now out of favour. People won't go near it. He's going to have to invent something new that doesn't involve apples.'

Gregory stood looking out through the door to where their footprints had left a trail of darker coloured grass as the frost melted under their tread.

Hildegard glanced at the apples then walked slowly along the shelves built from floor to eye level where the remainder rested on slats of wood. When she came to a space in the rows she stopped. This must be where Aelwyn had made his choice. There was not enough room for six; enough, maybe, for two. Close by was another space and, above that, room for the rest of the apples.

Sunlight streaked in through the gap between the stone blocks. It lit up the slats at eye level. The separate fruit ranged there shone in colours of russet, amber, ruby, and jade, brought to glowing light, like jewels in a crown, in the final flaring of their beauty. She peered more closely at a glimpse of gold, noticing a fine thread shining in the shaft of light. When she moved her head it vanished into shadow. She edged out of her own light and, free of shadows, the thread glinted again, as frail as air.

Carefully she felt around in her scrip for something to put the thread in. Then, holding her breath so the air around it was not disturbed, she pulled the thread from between the grains of wood where it was trapped and held it up.

'What have you got there?' Gregory asked from behind her.

'It looks like a piece of gold thread.'

With her free hand, she passed him a small glass phial used for seed-collecting and asked him to remove the linen stopper from it. He held it steady while she inserted the thread and replaced the stopper.

'Look at this, Egbert.' Gregory indicated the phial Hildegard was holding up. 'What do you make of that?'

As was their right as guests, the monks were free to enter the guest house and the Cistercians made use of this privilege by returning with Hildegard to find a private place in the hall where they could discuss their find.

'Clearly no monastic in rough woollen garments could leave such a betraying thread.'

Hildegard gave Egbert a quick glance. 'That's true . . .'

He raised his eyebrows but she didn't explain. 'Who else has access to the store? Surely only servants, kitcheners, and an occasional helpful and apple-loving monk like Aelwyn?'

'That's what we're told.'

The two monks had no suggestions to make and they looked up expectantly when the great doors opened and someone entered.

'That's Sister Aveline,' Hildegard murmured.

The nun, in plain black wool, was sharp-eyed. She at once spotted the two tonsured monks and, despite their dark worsted cloaks and the alien robes of unbleached stamyn their cloaks only partly concealed, she came over and spent a moment or two in pleasantries before setting off in the direction of her chamber.

Darius soon followed. He was sweating and red-faced when he strode in. For one so young he was, judged Hildegard, too irascible. Why was he always so agitated? It cannot surely have been anything to do with pressure from his father who, on the whole, seemed a genial, easy-going sort, interested only in enjoying his young wife's company to the full in this season of pre-Lenten festivity.

Gregory noticed him at once and called over. 'Out with the hounds today, my lord?'

Darius, creaking in *cuir bouilli*, came over. 'Not much chance of that, brother. The guests are too slothful and full of Christmas cheer to stir themselves. Too many sore heads around after last night's entertainment to join me! I thought to take my father's horse out for exercise but it was already out. Instead I took my hawk up to the fish pond to see what we could raise.'

'Any luck?'

'Not much.'

'If it's any solace, for our entertainment we were forced to our knees on the stone floor of the church most of the night, praying for your sins.' Before Darius could think up a riposte, Gregory added, 'I hear the town band were up here. Any good?'

'Passable.' Darius took this as an invitation to join them. He flung one leather-clad leg over the bench opposite Hildegard and gave her a nod in greeting. 'The variety of guests is somewhat restricted this year – apologies, domina. I mean there are few laity here. I'm having to amuse myself in the town most of the time.'

'I understand the Pope's men do the same,' she rejoined.

Darius laughed. 'They can afford to, the amount of tax they gather for His Holiness. The bursar reeled off the figures for me. It's astonishing that the abbey has anything left.'

'So the supporters of King Richard would say,' agreed Gregory. 'The Court is down to its last shilling, to hear them talk. Or so we are given to understand,' he added, with a flash of humility. 'We poor monks must be keeping Rome afloat with the amount of taxes the Pope extracts from our flocks. What line are you in yourself?' He put the question casually, as man to man.

'My father is lord of several manors up near Berwick,' Darius admitted. 'The greater part of our income comes from our farms, but I'd prefer to go into wool, as you do. I don't like the idea of dependence on one source. Father does not agree with me.' He hesitated but then decided not to continue.

'Are you much bothered by the Scots invasions?' asked Egbert, coming to life. 'I hear there was a bit of a skirmish last summer.'

Darius's face turned to stone. 'They waste our crops, steal our sheep, burn our vills. I wish them in Hell.'

'Surely the Earl of Northumberland is a stout protector?'

'Of his own!' Darius shifted angrily, soon roused again, Hildegard observed. 'It's a question of defending ourselves and to hell with the latest Marcher Lord or bowing before the reivers. We'll only be free from attack when we're adequately armed. Northumberland can raise an army when he wants but he only wants when it

127

suits his own interests. We small men need to form our own defence. And I don't mean by getting into endless treaties, broken as soon as sealed. I mean by the use of hard steel.'

'Wielded by private armies? Mercenaries? Beyond the usual levies?'

'Definitely, despite the barons. They'd have apoplexy if they knew what we were planning once Percy's ransom has been paid.' Darius gave a humourless smile. 'You must have noticed even here in Whitby that the monks believe they have to use armed force to protect their interests? A poor lot their muster turned out to be! Were you down there yesterday?'

Both monks shook their heads. 'What happened?' asked Gregory, although he very well knew.

'A gang of cut-throat fishermen consider themselves robbed of a valuable liberty and refuse to pay their dues. The bursar sent down half a dozen men with broadswords to persuade them otherwise. It turned into a rout. The whole town supported their own men and chased the abbey guards back up the cliff. Of course,' he added, 'they won't get away with it for long. The bursar and his friends will make sure of that.'

'They want what's theirs?' commented Gregory dryly.

'Indeed they do.'

He got up. 'Interesting talking to you, brothers. I've always had a regard for Cistercians. You seem to know what you're about. Maybe we can exchange ideas sometime on how best to protect our wealth? I understand you run things to your great advantage down in the East Riding.'

128

'We endeavour to run things to the advantage of all,' Egbert corrected with a genial smile to soften his words.

Darius was impervious to nuance. 'I expect the way you put the fear of God and hellfire into your tenants is enough to keep them tame. I wish I could do the same with mine, the godless losels.' Almost smiling, he went through into the kitchen, calling out for a flagon of wine to be sent up to Sir Ranulph's solar.

'Do you have a solar, Hildegard?' Gregory teased.

'Sot-wit! Do you imagine so? I'm lucky to have a small sleeping chamber to myself. I wouldn't know what to do with a solar.'

'I expect that young fellow could teach you. Does he not have a wife?'

'It appears not. And I'm not sure he's in the market for a wife at present. His interests seem to lie closer to home than his father might relish.'

Gregory lowered his head. 'Those two fellows in black who came in while we were sporting with young Darius—'

'They're the Pope's men he was referring to.'

'Soberly attired in plain velvet.'

Egbert sighed. 'Not a thread of gold in the entire place,' he concluded, summing up the purpose of their visit.

'Are we reduced to inspecting the wardrobe of the lady Amabel to find our gold thread?' Gregory asked Hildegard as they walked across the garth towards the church some time later.

'I doubt whether she had any quarrel with Brother Aelwyn!'

They reached the west door. 'Is this where you leave us?'

She rested her hand on the latch. 'Amabel is usually at one Office or another. If she's there now, Greg, I'll save you the inconvenience of going through her under shifts by making an inventory of every garment she's wearing.'

Gregory slanted her a smile as he left. Not for the first time Hildegard registered with surprise how good-looking he was in a haunted, world-weary way that touched her heart. His smile was like the sun breaking through clouds of serious-ness and was both disarming and dangerous. But then Egbert, bluff and foursquare, stalwart in his integrity and loyalty to those to whom he felt he owed allegiance, was attractive for that very sense of moral strength, and was all male, despite his spiritual calling.

With a shock she realized that she would prob-ably be expected to confess such wayward thoughts – but she had not seen Luke, who had to listen to her catalogue of sins, for some time. Dear Luke. No-one had mentioned him.

'Where is Luke?' she called after them now.

'Where do you think?' Egbert looked disgusted when he turned back for a moment.

'Our dear brother is engaged in physical labour on behalf of the widow Sabine,' Gregory called as he too turned.

'"The poor girl must have somewhere to live other than down that wretched alley," says he.' Egbert shook his head in wonder. 'I applaud his compassion but not his judgement.'

They parted, finally, the monks to their privileged

position behind the screen in the choir, Hildegard to her more ignominious place with the laity.

*The nave at the west end.*

Master Buckingham's unfinished building works were much in evidence. His men had done their best to give as little inconvenience as possible to the worshippers when they knocked off. Scaffolding was erected against the west wall where the roof was awaiting completion. It was too distant for Torold to have made any use of during his grand escape attempt.

Now, as everyone waited for the service to begin, a stiff breeze winkled its way under the waxed covers over the highest walkway and was making them flap with a sound like a constant slap in the face. A bucket rolled from one end of the platform to the other. A rope or two worked loose.

People glanced up and edged away from the structure. Someone hurried outside, to return a few moments later with one of the servants who was instructed to uncouple the ladder from where it was tidied away and climb up to secure anything that was not tied down.

He went up like a shot then struggled for some time to catch the end of the flapping waterproof. When he eventually did so, standing on tiptoe, there was subdued applause from the watchers below.

He returned to ground level with a wide grin. Hildegard, standing against the door, heard him say to the man who had called him in, 'I could

131

have dropped that bucket on the heads of you lot and there'd have been nowt you could do about it!'

'Good job you didn't with Master standing by.' They both glanced furtively at a tall, broad-featured fellow in an ochre capuchon with a fur slung over one shoulder before they snuck outside.

Master? *So that's Master Buckingham,* Hildegard surmised. Chief figure in the Guild of Masons, he was renowned throughout the county for his building works and Whitby Abbey was the latest venture to add to his fame.

Commissioned to build extra bays, his major innovation was the style of the windows, slender perpendiculars, and the massive columns that held up the extension to the roof. Although work had started with an energetic flourish, it had stalled somewhat of late due to an argument about payment.

'I want paying on the nail,' Buckingham was supposed to have said. 'My men can't live on fresh air and promises. They have mouths to feed.'

Now it looked as if he was back and prepared to continue the work he had begun. Someone must have paid him, Hildegard decided, because he did not look like a man who would concede anything once he had made up his mind. From past experience, recalling her old acquaintance Master Sueno de Schockwynde, in charge of building works at Durham, she guessed Buckingham would have a similar desire to keep his builders happy. The times were such that it would always be possible for a man or woman to find work elsewhere if their current conditions did not suit them. She remembered the imager, too, the talented daughter of a master mason and her team of masons making additions to Handale Priory. A close-knit group as she had discovered, as close and secretive and self-protective of the mysteries of their guild as any fraternity of monks. Or nuns, come to that.

The man she assumed to be Master Buckingham looked up as Sir Ranulph entered. It seemed to Hildegard that something passed between them, nothing tangible, a too hurried lowering of the eyes, no more. Sir Ranulph turned his back and went to lean against the opposite wall. After a moment his wife, accompanied by Darius, followed him in, just as the monks on the other side of the screen started the first chant. They went to join Ranulph and Amabel slipped her hand inside one of his sleeves and looked up at him with a little smile.

Hildegard moved closer. It was a *jeu d'esprit* of Gregory's to suggest that Amabel might have been inside the apple store, but, loathe to leave any stone unturned, she gave her garments a surreptitious stare. No sign of gold there either.

A whisper in her ear startled her. She turned her head. A stranger was smiling into her eyes, his own a sharp hazel in a healthy brown face. He was clean shaven and his dark hair was tied back in a leather thong. His rough woollen garments showed he was a servant of some kind.

'Domina? Forgive me for interrupting your

prayers but I hear you would like to speak to me about our dearly beloved brother Aelwyn and some related business?'

'And you are . . .?'

'Edred,' he confirmed. 'Assistant to our lord bursar, Peter Hertilpole.'

Hildegard eyed him as carefully as he was eyeing her. If she had understood Brother Dunstan aright, this was the fixer between abbey and town for all things non-secular. Whatever his role, so far she approved of what she saw.

He seemed to come to a similar judgement because he whispered, 'I'm busy until after Compline. Can you meet me then?'

'Where?'

'I'll be in the lane outside the guest house.'

She nodded. 'I'll be there.'

# Ten

Brother Luke had evidently returned to the abbey in time for Vespers and when Hildegard emerged he was making his way across the garth to intercept her. 'Domina, I need a word of advice.'

They stood under the shelter of the south cloister. It was already dark this far north. Single flakes of snow were beginning to drop out of the velvety dark sky.

'What's the problem, Luke?'

'I regret having to bother you with this, but I am, to put it frankly, at my wits' end.'

'What on earth has happened?'

'You must remember the beautiful young woman . . .' Words seemed to choke him and he struggled to continue.

'Sabine, you mean?'

He nodded.

'I understand you're helping restore her cottage to rights?'

He swallowed. 'That was my intention. I imagined it was what anyone would do – I mean, I couldn't understand why no-one else offered to help. To leave someone in those conditions – so alone, so courageous – it is beyond my understanding. Her neighbours – where were they in her time of need?' He bit his bottom lip. A struggle was clearly going on and eventually he burst out: 'She is the victim of this cartel we've heard about. No man will work for her. The landlord of that wretched cottage has made threats to break the legs of anybody who lifts a finger to help.' He beat the fist of one hand into the other. 'Can you believe anything so diabolical?'

'I know it does happen. I've heard that maybe the abbey sees him as a challenge too, buying up property and depleting the rents anciently due to them.'

'It cannot be borne. That she should be a victim of such heartless greed!'

'I fear it is not our problem, Luke. We are here for such a short time and the abbey and the town must sort things out between themselves.'

'That's not the worst of it.'

'Oh?'

135

'I went to speak to this fellow, this rapacious landlord. Do you know what? He had the effrontery to threaten me!' He gave her an astonished look. 'I'm a monk! Can he not see that?'

'I fear our standing in the town is not what we would hope for. They do not trust the monastics here. They see them, in fact all of us, as people encroaching on their freedom.'

'I've heard all about that. It's why I felt I should step in and do something, to show that some of us have good intentions. There's an old quarrel between the abbey and a family called Brek going back seventy years about rights and grievances . . .' He bent his head. 'Shall I tell you about it?'

'Briefly. I haven't eaten yet. But look . . .' She put a hand on his arm, for he sounded desolate. 'Why not come into the refectory and have something yourself while you explain?'

Everyone seemed to be present in the time between Vespers and Compline and the guest hall was full in expectation of the entertainment later on. They managed to find a space at a corner of one of the long tables where they could talk in private.

Luke could not hold back the words. He began even before he sat down. 'When this dispute started all that while ago, nearly seventy years since, if you can believe it, it came down to a quarrel about ownership of a piece of land in Eskdale. The matter was taken to court and the abbot won. Since then the family involved – feeling that they've been thrown off land they'd always regarded as their own – have held a grudge against the abbey. You may feel that's understandable. Recently, because they deemed Abbot Richmond more lenient than his predecessor, the Breks and a number of their allies decided they would rectify the situation.'

'What could they do?'

'What indeed! They broke into his enclosures, cut down his trees, removed the underwood, dug up his turbaries and stole his goods and chattels to the value of twenty pounds! They then let their cattle in to eat his corn and grass and all the saplings he'd recently had planted. Naturally, they were hauled before a jury on a charge of trespass. This is where it becomes complicated because several of the accused were fined but others were let off and the interesting thing is that the fines themselves were later cancelled by Abbot Richmond himself. You would think, wouldn't you, that this made the abbey seem like the friend of its tenants, but it isn't working out like that because there's a schism here.' He glanced round and lowered his voice. 'I have it on good authority that the prior and the bursar deem Abbot Richmond too lax with regard to profit and loss. They are determined to claw back the disputed acres and are even demanding rent going far back over the decades to the original dispute.'

'That's going far.'

'But don't you see? Sabine, poor, lovely woman, is caught in the middle because she has a family connection to the Breks, but the abbey, out of grace and special favour, allow her to rent that hovel from them. You see how she's caught between the two?'

'Luke, I don't think we can do anything about this. It's for the law men and the justices to sort out.'

He ran his hand over his hair. 'I know that. I know . . .' He looked agonized. 'But Sabine is so lovely and I long to relieve her suffering . . .'

His misery was so palpable that she could only place a hand on his arm and ask, 'So how is she embroiled? It's not her fault she's related to the Breks.'

'True, but she's being dragged into it against her will and told to take sides.'

'And it's this that's causing you such distress?'

'It's more than that. The fact is . . . she does not want my help.' His voice held all the misery of a broken-heart. 'She rejects me. She does not want anything to do with me.' He put his head in his hands.

She indicated to one of the servants that they would like food and drink then turned back to Luke. 'It's painful when we're rejected,' she murmured. 'We have to learn to accept that we cannot control everything. Our sincerest wishes can be thwarted and we have to learn to accept that. Not every problem is our own to be solved by our efforts either. Give to God what belongs to God. And trust in that.'

'You see me as taking too much on myself? Maybe you think I lack humility?' He looked confused. 'It's true I would lie down under her feet and let her walk all over me if it would make her happy.'

'That is not humility, Luke. It is something else . . .'

'What do you mean?' When she did not reply, he said, 'I worship her. She is my star in heaven.'

'Luke, do you realize what you're saying?'

He stared at her. Tears welled in his eyes. 'This feeling – this power driving me to . . . Look, I'm ready to face any threat from those who want to harm her. I would die for her, for one smile.'

He pressed his knuckles into his eye sockets.

Hildegard's expression was thoughtful. He was young. She could remember what it was like and also how the feeling of wildness was never entirely extinguished.

'Have you asked yourself what might be behind your determination to . . .' She searched for the right word, aware that much would hang on it. 'Let's look at it like this. By burning her out of her cottage there's a financial advantage to the landlord because, as I hear, he wishes to pull down that row of cottages and build a bigger, more expensive house there to cater for the pilgrims wanting to visit the abbey and unable to find accommodation in the guest house. At the same time,' she paused, speaking carefully, 'Sabine herself has gone to live elsewhere.'

'With Master Selby and his wife.'

'A couple who happen to live comfortably in a large house in the stews.'

He looked affronted for a moment. 'She can't choose where she lives,' he muttered. 'You cannot blame her for living down there under their protection. It is not a free choice.'

139

'Is it not?' She gave him a steady glance. 'Ask yourself honestly, Luke, is it not a free choice?' To forestall a likely objection she added, 'Is she not free insofar as any of us are free to do anything she chooses?'

'I am in Hell,' he muttered after a pause.

When Luke eventually got up to go, having picked at his food and left most of it, he opened the doors to a swirl of snowflakes. They flew inside as if to put the final seal on the prophetic skill of the falconer.

Hildegard watched him pull up his hood as he stepped outside. It must be the first time he had been beguiled by a beautiful woman. It was misfortune that he had been committed to celibacy before he had reached the age where he understood what it meant. *Heaven knows, it's difficult enough even so*, she thought, despite all the knowledge in the world. An image of her beloved Hubert swam before her eyes. Like Luke she might weep with longing for a forbidden and unattainable love if she had not hardened herself against the wilful desires of her heart.

Steeling herself once more, she thrust the image of Hubert de Courcy aside and decided there was little else but to go out into the growing blizzard for the purpose of Compline. Sister Aveline was making herself agreeable to Sir Ranulph this evening and looked indifferent to the bell calling them forth. Hildegard resolutely pulled on her cloak and followed Luke into the snow.

It was already piling thickly across the path to the very edge where the ground fell away down the cliff to the town. The jumble of roofs of the cheek-by-jowl cottages facing the direction of the wind racing along the quay were already smothered and looked like great boulders scattered along the waterfront. Even in the darkness of the winter evening the River Esk could still be seen where it wound like a sheet of gleaming grey ice between its banks. Far out beyond the estuary a light bobbed and winked as it was lifted by the waves and dropped back into the heaving void.

Turning away, Hildegard trudged through the snow towards the gatehouse. Seen through the partly opened shutters, the porter's lodge looked inviting, a fire blazing in a little hearth and the porter and his assistant warm inside with their feet up. He poked his head out when he heard the night door creak again to let her in under the arch and she returned the friendly lift of his hand as he watched her pass beneath the light shed from the cresset.

The bell was still tolling over the garth as she crossed to the church, her footprints briefly visible before being covered over. One or two people were stamping about in the doorway to clear snow off their boots before entering. Hildegard did the same, then pushed back her hood and went inside the chilly vault.

A few candles flickered here and there, nothing, she guessed, like the lavish display behind the screen to light the monks to heaven. On this side of the abbey servants made up most of the

141

worshippers, an assortment of kitcheners, fetchers and carriers, a few outdoors men but not, she believed, peering through the shadows, Edred. Busy with his chores, she supposed. The ethereal singing of the choir closed around her and she gave herself up to different thoughts.

Afterwards, with the words of the evening Office still echoing in her ears, she approached the guest house expecting to find Edred sheltering under the lee of the wall, but there was no sign of anyone. The snow was untrodden, her own prints covered. She looked about to make sure he wasn't sheltering anywhere else before hurrying inside to wait.

A narrow window loop beside the main doors let in draughts when its shutter was opened so, not wishing to cause any discomfort to those within, she took one quick look outside at the still bleakly empty foregate and the lane running down the cliff, then went to sit at a nearby table where she could wait. Three large trestles had been pushed back to make space for some planned event. An air of expectancy filled the place.

'What's on?' she asked a passing wine servant.

'Mummers sent up from the town,' he replied. 'Some acrobats. A stilt walker.' He smiled with pleasure at the prospect.

Impatiently Hildegard went back to the shutter and peered out. The snow was still coming down but it seemed to be easing off. Maybe Edred was waiting for it to stop. His cloak had been somewhat thin. It must be hard to face the weather in so slight a garment.

The hall was quickly filling with guests and their retinues, platters of sweetmeats were being carried in, wine flagons refilled, the musicians struck up, and the mummers, six or seven of them, garbed in outlandish costumes, eventually burst in to the tumult of knackers and pipes.

It was true. There was a stilt walker. It was a young woman with streaming false locks who paced about like a stork looking down on the guests and doing feats of rare balance for the price of a few thrown coins and the shattering crescendo of the kettle drums.

An assistant, a very small man, was eagerly picking up the coins by scrambling between the legs of the guests which were adorned in well-turned-out coloured hosen. They also wore a variety of fancy indoor footwear, and as he stuffed every clinking piece into a leather pouch, he tugged playfully at feather and fur and jewel. Every so often he rose on his short legs and shook the pouch to make it jingle, showing the stilt walker what they had earned, and she would mime extravagant signs of gratitude which she quickly turned to tears as it was not enough. Urged to extract more from the onlookers, the little man hopped about to continue his cozening. And so it went.

Hildegard had waited with enough patience. Suddenly snapping, she dragged on her cloak and slipped quickly through the doors on to the foregate. Still no sign of Edred. Still none! The snow was untrodden, an unbroken crust, carved by the knifing wind into undulating ripples. It was bereft of life.

143

Pulling up her hood and tramping through the drifts as far as the gatehouse, she tapped on the shutter. The sound of voices inside stopped on the instant. She could tell that those inside were listening.

'It's Hildegard of Meaux. Open up!'

The porter imposed a bleary-eyed face in her line of vision.

When she asked him if he had seen Edred he shook his head. 'Only fiends and fairies out on a night like this, domina. You're not thinking of going far, are you?'

'Only back to my bed. If you see him tell him to get them to wake me, will you?' Thanking him, she trudged back.

Later, wearied by the fruitless wait and the necessity to keep on smiling at the tricks and treats taking place, she thought as she climbed into bed: *So, he did not come!*

Maybe he had decided there was little he could tell her, despite Dunstan's view, or little enough to make it worth an outing in such weather.

# Eleven

There was an element of similarity in the way the rumour began to circulate next morning after Prime.

Edred was missing.

He had not returned to his wife in their eyrie above the stables that night. No-one made any

144

suggestion that he had gone down to Grope Lane or anywhere else in the town and might be sleeping it off. He was a man known to be faithful to his wife.

She turned out to be a stocky, frizzy-haired practical-looking woman with a child on one hip, another clinging to her knees, and one playing in the snow.

'He said he was coming up to see you, domina, at the guest house, he said. After Compline. Just for a few minutes, he said. To tell you something. I'd poured him his ale and got his dry boots ready for when he came back in.'

'Did he set out to see me?'

'Yes, that's what I'm saying. He finished his chores and set off back to meet you at the guest house.'

'When was this?'

'Straight after Compline. I've just said.'

'I'm trying to get it straight. Did anyone else know he was coming?'

'Everybody, probably. He had chores to rush through. With the snow and that he said he didn't want to be out late.'

'Do you know what he wanted to tell me?'

She shook her head.

'And after he left home, did anybody else see him?'

The woman, Anna, eyes darting helplessly about the precinct, allowed only a tremor to shake her bottom lip. 'I know nothing about that. How could I?'

The search parties set out once more. Some even searched the apple store but came back with shrugs and defeated expressions. The snow-covered cliff side was inspected but as there were no footsteps except on the town path, going down and coming back, they left the cliffs as being an unlikely spot for anyone to fall without leaving the trail of a great avalanche behind them. The cloisters, the stables, the mews, every nook and cranny had someone peering into it or under it.

It was the same as when Aelwyn had gone missing. Or almost the same.

This time the body was found in the fish pond.

Dead all night by the look of the snow crusted on his frozen face, the rest of his body was lying under the surface of the water, held in the doubly frozen clasp of ice and death.

Hildegard and the three monks from Meaux were among the first on the scene. Gregory at once appointed men to keep everyone back.

Two sets of footprints went to the waterside and only one set made the return journey. Not that they were clear. Snow had partly filled them in but by a trick of the ice forming later, the footprints, vague though they were, had been carved as in a block of marble.

Edred's thin cloak was frozen in the ice too. It lay in stiff, motionless billows under the water, sculpted just so at the moment of being frozen.

After a good look at all this they made a final inventory. Hildegard gazed out across the ice. It was already beginning to thaw in the middle where a large hole like a flaw in a mirror was attracting the sharp beaks of gulls hungry for fish.

'We'd better get him out.' Gregory was terse. His hands had gone to the back of the dead man's head and he glanced up at the other two. 'Is there a weapon of any kind in the water?'

Egbert broke the thin lens of ice and lifted it like someone peeling back the silvering of an eyeball to reveal an empty cavity beneath. He rolled up a sleeve and as the weeds swayed in the disturbed water his pale hand groped around in the brackish depths but failed to find anything. 'Maybe we can have a better look once the body is out of the way.'

Edred lay between two small promontories made by the twisted roots of a thicket of tall reeds growing round the margin of the water. It was a perfect place to throw out nets, pegging them into the soft bank and waiting with every likelihood of success for the supper that would eventually swim inside.

Egbert groped under the water again but although it reached his elbow he could not find anything. 'It's relatively shallow here. He must have been knocked unconscious. Is that what you suggest? If he'd slipped he could easily have floundered back to shore.'

'They've probably taken the weapon away.'

Drying his arm on his cloak and pulling down his sleeve, Egbert helped Gregory drag the body on to the bank. 'I'll get some of the fellows to fetch a board to carry him on.'

'Straight to the mortuary, I think.' Gregory was grim-faced.

Hildegard found Luke's arm round her shoulders. He was weeping. His tear-stained face

147

rested against her shoulder as he stooped his head to hide his tears.

'I'm sorry, I'm sorry,' he was muttering. 'Life is sometimes too sad to bear. What use am I? What use? Forgive me, Hildegard.'

Black-robed figures were stationed at the four corners of the slab on which the body of Edred was lying, their prayers the only sound while the body was stripped of its clothing by a lay servant. His leather belt, his woollen smock, his undershirt, his boots tugged free, and leggings rolled down and dropped on to the tiles with a brief sound as soft as the snow falling outside.

'A man comes down to so little stripped of his clothing,' Luke whispered. 'Underneath that, what are we, after all?' He bestowed his bleak gaze on the body. He could have been looking at a man sleeping. Any man. No man.

He would not be comforted. Hildegard saw him lift one arm and pull at the edge of his own Cistercian sleeve and murmur, 'We come from nothing and to nothing we return. Is that not the truth?'

She met his glance. Pressed a hand against his arm. 'Pray for him. And for us all.'

'As well as for the devil who did this to him,' suggested Egbert, his manner brusquely purposeful, adding, 'He'll need your prayers, Luke, when he reaches the gates of Hell.'

The tapping of a wooden stick on the tiles alerted them to the entrance of the infirmarer, old Brother Dunstan. When he stepped from the shadows into the light of the two candles at each end of the bier his wrinkled face was full of sorrow.

'I liked him,' he said in a voice hoarse with loss. 'He brought light to our sometimes dour existence. Everyone liked him. Even though some did not agree with his views on certain matters – nothing,' he concluded, 'should have brought him to this.'

Brother Dunstan followed them out into the side chapel and, detaining them for a moment, asked a question. 'It is certainly foul play?'

'A bruise on the back of his head we found when we dragged him from the water almost certainly proves it.'

'But I don't understand why he would be out near the fish pond during a blizzard.'

'Nor do we.' Gregory raised his eyebrows as if inviting Dunstan's speculations.

'He often walked with a falcon up there, to limit the theft of our fish by the gulls. But in a snow storm? What could have lured him forth?'

'He was supposed to meet me near the guest house,' Hildegard told him. 'He had something to tell me about Aelwyn.'

'Ah, Aelwyn, yes. The link between them. Who is it?' Dunstan shook his head. 'Edred was a man who went among all kinds of folk both lay and monastic. His dealings were often secret though always, as far as I know, for the benefit of our abbey.'

'In what way secret?' Hildegard asked.

'Regarding the price of fish, mostly!' He gave a slight smile. 'He paid a good price to the sea fishers, believing that as they risked their lives for us we should help maintain their lives for them. He was always in trouble with our lord bursar for overspending. But he was a tactical man. He knew that if we did not pay them fair and square their catch would be sent off to the towns across the Moors and eventually we should be the worse off.'

Pondering the mystery of a link Hildegard asked, 'The bursar, Peter Hertilpole, does he ever go down to the apple store?'

'That would be too incriminating. Crime solved! There was no love lost between him and Brother Aelwyn. Everyone knew it. But no, I doubt he even knows where the store is. Far too important a figure to bother himself with the mere necessities of life – if indeed apples are necessities and not merely pleasures which would put them even further outside his boundary of attention.'

'The apple, an eternal cause of strife,' Brother Luke remarked in a doleful tone but a theological discussion about Eve was not uppermost in anybody's mind at that moment.

'Let's take this problem where it belongs, to the abbot and his obedientiaries.' Gregory was ready to go in search of the abbot at once. 'In his lodge as usual, Brother?'

Dunstan gave a rueful smile. 'Where else? To forestall criticism we might ask ourselves which is best, hands grasping tightly on to the reins or ones that hold them with a gentler touch?'

Egbert remarked with a wry smile, 'I'd choose the latter even so. We can light our own way to

Hell . . . I prefer that to the feeling that I'm being ridden by the Devil's cohorts.'

Dunstan told them that he would not come with them, pleading the after-effects of his brief fever, but begged them to find him in the infirmary afterwards if they discovered anything new.

In a group the rest of them moved off towards the abbot's lodge. The only time Hildegard had been there before was when she had been told about the arrangements for purchasing the holy relic of Abbess Hild. That item now seemed a distant concern.

The same servant opened the door. He looked surprised to see them and placed a foot behind the door. Gregory was in no mood for prevarication but adopted his smoothest manner and, after a frightened glance over his shoulder, the servant gave way. And who could not, Hildegard thought, as Gregory swept in ahead of them, stamping snow off his boots and only stepping back for a moment to allow the servant to lead the way to the abbot's chamber. The moment the door opened the servant scurried off.

The abbot was not alone. The elongated and somewhat saturnine figure of Peter Hertilpole was standing with his back to the window. Through its leaded panes falling snow could be seen. It lent a pale-blue light to the interior where Abbot Richmond was at that moment lifting a chased silver goblet to his lips in front of the fire. When four newcomers entered without warning he gave a start and a drop of dark red wine spilled on to the previously spotless cuff of his undershirt.

Hertilpole became as alert as a fox.

His clerk, sitting unobtrusively in a corner, inspected the point of his quill.

Gregory made a deep and obsequious bow. 'My lord abbot,' he murmured in his smoothest courtroom voice. 'We crave and beg indulgence for entering so precipitately into your presence, but we have an urgent matter that requires your attention and we beg and desire leave to offer the facts for your consideration. May I continue?'

Abbot Richmond stuttered some kind of agreement but Hertilpole glided forward from his seat on the window embrasure. 'Our lord abbot is already engaged with the important business of the abbey accounts – I fear you will need to make an appointment to speak to him and I shall be—'

'No, no, Peter. They are here now. Let them tell us what they will. Please – where is that servant of mine? Find seats, brothers, and the lady Hildegard, please.'

He did not rise from his own chair but gestured vaguely round the chamber. Brother Luke quietly and obediently read his mind and shifted a bench a few inches from the wall for his brothers and placed both hands on the back of a wooden upright chair to invite Hildegard to sit.

Gregory leaned towards Richmond, not ignoring Hertilpole, but showing that he knew where power should lie, whether it did or not. The bursar

152

took the hint and returned to his seat on the window ledge where, with the light behind him, his expression became unreadable.

After a few pleasantries Gregory mentioned Edred and paused only for a moment while Hertilpole briefly explained to his abbot who he was.

Richmond crossed himself. 'Pray continue.'

'It is our belief that the man was killed deliberately—'

'What? Murdered? Within the abbey precinct?' Hertilpole rose to his feet. 'This is preposterous!'

The clerk beside him mirrored his movement so that it might have been read as protest too.

'We have proof of a sort,' Gregory proceeded cautiously, not glancing at the bursar. 'There was a wound on the back of his head as if he had received a blow.'

'An accident when he threw himself into the water,' Hertilpole pronounced.

'Please, Peter. Let Brother Gregory say what he has to say.'

Hertilpole sat down again with deliberate non-chalance to await his turn. The clerk went back to contemplating his writing instruments although he did not pick them up.

'The wound could not, in our opinion, have been caused by a fall into the lake. He would have had to fall backwards on to some hard object, like a rock for instance. But after a search we found no such thing. The sides and bottom are smooth mud.'

'Did you find the instrument used for this crime?' Hertilpole's voice dripped scorn and he made a slight obeisance towards his abbot at having interrupted again.

'It's a fair question,' Richmond said.

'Unfortunately the answer is no. The attacker had probably taken it away with him.'

'Or thrown it into the snow where it lies buried,' suggested Egbert. Hertilpole turned to gaze out of the window.

'I understand that my prior has given you permission to look into the accidental death of Brother Aelwyn. As this seems to be an area of interest for you, while you are here might you set your minds on to tracking down the cause of this second strange death?' His button eyes were of a bright though pale blue and they suddenly pierced their faces like an attempt to see every dark secret in their souls. 'It would be a most kind and compassionate way of showing amity between our two Orders.' He smiled at them again and was suddenly a kind old man, saddened by the folly of the world and eager to return to more spiritual matters.

Hertilpole had turned to survey the chamber and his silence, thought Hildegard, was audible – if that were possible. He was poised like a hawk waiting to stoop to the prey.

'As for the matter of the relic,' the abbot continued, 'I shall be most happy if our dear lady of Meaux would attend at the shrine to give the relic her most reverent attention tomorrow after Chapter. I believe she will be in awe of such a blessed relic and it seems appropriate that a nun, albeit a Cistercian, should have sight of the precious lock of hair that once belonged to

154

another nun, one of the greatest Benedictines of her time . . . renowned throughout the Christian world for her diplomacy and subtle reasoning.'

If a sting was intended, he inclined his head to bestow a gentle smile on Hildegard who could only acquiesce with grateful thanks for the honour of being allowed to see the object she had travelled the length of the county to behold.

Gregory said something and made as if to shepherd his oddly silent flock from the chamber, but the bursar suddenly rose to his feet. 'My lord abbot.' He turned to Richmond. 'May I beg leave to add something?'

'You may, Peter, of course, say on.'

'I find it an outrage; it is quite beyond words.' Despite that he continued in tones of ever-rising anger. 'A monk of this abbey is found dead, having suffered an accident as honest men know and believe, and now, again, a man is found dead in circumstances that can easily be explained by men of good will. But no! The imputation is that someone here – here! Within the Abbey of Whitby! – is responsible for his death! It is clear, is it not, that this man, Edred, killed himself? And my proof is this—'

He drew from his sleeve a gold coin. 'Ever aware of the value of everything, and, I have to tell you this, long under suspicion for his double-dealing over the rents and fines accruing, his eye ever on profit, as I say, he stole from my chamber, from my locked coffer, with its key in a place he had seen me use many times under the impression that I could trust a servant of the abbey, he stole, I say, stole from the abbey, from you, my lord abbot, from me and from my brothers, the very gold he had earlier extracted from the good folk of the town.'

He moved rapidly towards the door, black robes flapping, more like the wings of an angry crow than an eagle now, and turned with his hand on the door ring. 'I am sorrowed, most profoundly, to hear our visitors impugn our honesty.' He gave them all a black look and, bowing to Richmond, went out. The clerk snapped his portable writing desk shut and hurried after him.

'Oh dear,' remarked the abbot in an unexpectedly mild voice. 'You see how things are here?'

Gregory, halfway to leaving, said, 'We make no accusations, my lord. We merely place the facts before you.'

'Two accidental deaths in succession are unlikely. Or is it possible you may have misinterpreted them?'

Egbert stirred himself. 'Possible, my lord, but unlikely. We are not people to jump to conclusions. Neither man could have killed himself. It follows, therefore, that someone else did.'

The abbot reached for a small hand bell and rang it sharply. His servant, looking frightened, reappeared.

'Bring the bursar back here. And let's have my prior present too.' When the servant hurried away he indulged in an easy resettling in his gilded chair with its stack of velvet cushions. 'We cannot have rumours running the rounds of the precinct. If they can offer proof of what they say and you can do likewise then we shall have to use some other method for teasing out the truth.'

He offered wine from a silver flagon whose workmanship, thought Hildegard, Abbot de Courcy would have admired but thought improperly fine for his personal use.

In a short time, while Luke was still searching for enough goblets, the bursar reappeared. He and his clerk must have been waiting quite close by, Hildegard decided, and had not even got as far as the outer door as their boots were quite dry. The visitors were blessed with another black scowl and Hertilpole murmured something about having informed the servant where he could find the prior.

They settled to wait and Abbot Richmond engaged Luke in some mild repartee on a theological topic that had Luke's eyes lighting up for a moment. But before the elegance of a conclusion could be reached, the door opened and Prior Allerton entered.

He made his obeisance to the abbot and in lifting his head exchanged a swift telling glance with Hertilpole.

'My lord?' He addressed Richmond.

'Find a seat, John. I am being told extraordinary things this morning. Tell me, what is your opinion of Master Edred? You know him – the fellow who brings us our sea fish?'

'Faultless in his care for us, my lord, but with some lingering doubt over his honesty.'

'Is he a man likely to kill himself?'

'Himself?' Allerton looked with an appalled expression at the abbot. Hastily crossing himself

157

he struggled for a moment and then pressed his lips together before speaking in a considered tone. 'In theory any man might be pushed far enough to contemplate such an action. But to do it?' He gave a slight shrug. 'It is not for me to make such a statement about any man. It is an inconceivable act; it flouts God's law. He would know that.'

'And was he attentive to the law of God?'

'Sad to say, no more than any superstitious peasant.'

'Peasant? But he was a free man?'

Allerton acquiesced with an inclination of his head.

'So . . .' Settling back in the mode of a theologian weighing the pros and cons of an abstract argument concerning angels and their dancing, the abbot invited his bursar and his prior to state their case.

'It is no light accusation,' Hertilpole began. 'My coffer was opened and gold to the value of one year's income was taken from it. We have found three coins already, one in the shrine to our Blessed Virgin, one dropped at random in the garth as if by someone in a hurry, and one in the fish pond near the place where Edred threw himself, in contrition, perhaps, and under the stress of the great shame he felt for his heinous ingratitude to us.'

Gregory put up a hand. 'If I may so say, you are insinuating details into your story which have not been ascertained as fact.'

'Yes, you are rather begging the question, Peter.' Richmond settled back again. 'Proceed.'

'I think I've said enough to show that Edred was dishonest. He was seen at the shrine before Prime where the first coin was found. He could have crossed the garth as he did many times a day and thus lost the second coin, and the third find is quite conclusive.'

'It does appear that despite his alleged care for money, he was quite careless once he got his hands on it. However, I will not prejudge. What say you to this, Brother Gregory?'

'I say, my lord abbot, that anyone could have dropped three gold coins in strategic places – should they have wanted a reason to cast doubt on a man's honesty.'

'Anyone? Do you mean anyone in this abbey?'

'Certainly, Prior.'

Allerton looked shocked. 'But we are holy men, not a gang of peasant rogues and cut-throats!'

'I did not say any monk was involved; only that anyone could have dropped them, any person with access to the abbey precinct.'

The Prior was slightly mollified but his glance searched out that of Hertilpole. 'What do you think, Peter?'

'I still think it's outrageous. That anyone could risk hellfire and eternal damnation for the murder of two men for no good reason is beyond my comprehension and for strangers, guests in our abbey, to make such a claim is . . . Words fail me!'

*Words fail him again*, thought Hildegard, and waited for him to continue but this time they did, indeed, fail him, or at least, Gregory prevented him from continuing in the same vein by breaking in with a gentle reminder that as they did not yet know the advantages to anyone for two such deaths, they were in no position to make assumptions that it was for no good reason.

'For all we know there might be something important at issue – indeed, some, as you say, good reason, a life and death issue – to encourage someone to risk the penalties of which we are so well aware.'

Abbot Richmond considered the Cistercian with a pensive air. 'I agree with Brother Gregory,' he pronounced at last. 'Until we can find a motive for the coincidence of two not clearly accountable deaths we can make no assumptions. Tell me, Peter, how do you account for the deliberate blocking up of the air vents in the apple store?'

'A prank, my lord. The novices are clearly guilty but are too frightened to admit it. When the shock of what happened as a result of their misbehaviour has faded no doubt one or two will creep into confession to make a clean breast of the whole thing.' He gave a tight smile. 'We cannot force them to speak out. They have their loyalties. No doubt the names of the miscreants are well known to the rest of them. It is only a question of time before a confession is made.'

Hildegard spoke up. The shock of a woman speaking sent a tremor round the chamber, except for the Cistercians who knew Hildegard. She asked Hertilpole: 'You claim it was a prank, but on what grounds, my lord? Where is the gain in jollity from such an activity? Who is mocked? That is the usual purpose of a prank.'

160

'They are boys, domina,' he stated, as if that was explanation enough and was about to turn away when she continued.

'More, if you permit.'

The men shifted in their seats.

She continued anyway. 'No-one to my knowledge says they saw any of the novices near the store. Someone must surely have seen the little fellows; they do nothing without making a commotion about it, even when they see themselves as being most discreet. Further, the fact that the garments used to block the vents are assumed to have been taken from the aumbry in the boys' dortoir, supports the suspicion that the boys were involved. I grant you that. But I am not so sure those little gowns came from the dortoir . . .' She broke off.

The line of garments hanging to dry when she went to hang up her own in the laundry drying room was something she had given little thought to until now. It had gnawed at her because she knew she had seen those garments somewhere recently, but it was only now that she understood how significant it might be that they had been hanging up in the drying room.

Aware that it was not the time to draw attention to the fact, she recovered and said, 'No-one saw the boys doing anything they shouldn't. They are kept busy at their lessons in the cloister. The novice master would know if any of his flock were missing. I wonder if you've questioned him.'

She recalled Torold's night-time escapade.

Glancing from the prior to the bursar she saw

that, fortunately, they did not suspect that the novice master was less than meticulous in his head-counting.

'I feel we must not accuse those children until we have more than prejudice to go on. Some evidence,' she finished, 'is needed before we can rush to judgement.'

'I thank you for your contribution, domina.'

The abbot turned at once to a different topic in the way some men do when they feel they have given enough time to a woman's comments and want to get on to the more important concerns of the men. Hildegard was pleased to find he was of that school. She did not trust him or any of his inner circle and wanted him to forget as quickly as possible what she had just hinted, before she had time to work out its implications. A glance at Gregory made her eager to find out what he would think to her theory. Sharp as ever, he had noticed her slip.

But the laundry? Was it relevant? Apart from the workers in there, scrubbing and drying and smoothing, who else frequented the place? People such as herself, to save the servants the trouble of having to gather up their soiled garments and afterwards return them. Who else would bother to go into that steamy, noisy place?

She pictured Darius in his *cuir bouilli*, his boiled leather hunting gear, with the shirt he had been ranting about. He could easily have picked a few little surplices off the drying racks and bundled them under his cloak. A further question would concern the likely reason for

162

him wanting to get rid of Brother Aelwyn. Her running thoughts baulked there.

Another thought entered her head almost immediately. It was a question, wasn't it, but did he ever wear anything with gold thread in it? It was difficult to imagine him strutting around attired like a courtier. His father might. But then he had a young wife to impress. Could Darius also want to . . .?

She broke off her ruminations when she realized Gregory was already bowing them out of the abbot's presence.

'So what trail are you following now, Hildegard?' Gregory looked sternly down at her. 'I could see you felt you had said enough in front of those three.'

'Was it obvious?'

'Only to we who know you.'

'I hope I didn't give them the possibility for further attempts to cover up the truth.' She pulled a face. 'No evidence for that last remark, Gregory. Nor do I have any theories about it. But it's surely possible that anybody could have snatched those little garments off the drying racks in the laundry and used them to stuff into the air vents.'

'It's interesting to hear you use the word cover-up,' interrupted Egbert. 'I was thinking along the same lines myself. But why? What's their motive?' They fell silent as Hertilpole and Allerton came out on to the path behind them and, black robes billowing, began to catch them up.

They drew level but did not pause longer than for the prior to say, 'We are as eager as you fellows to find out the truth. However, we cannot allow the spread of rumours that will unsettle everyone. I trust you will bear that in mind.'

'Perhaps if you have any further ideas you will bring them to us so that we can thoroughly discuss them?' Hertilpole's dark features were arranged in what must have been intended as a smile.

'We most certainly will,' agreed Gregory pleasantly. 'We must all work together for the peace and grace that comes from furthering God's will.'

'Amen to that.'

The two of them strode on.

'Fellows, he called us all,' Egbert grinned. 'They do not regard women here. It's difficult to remember that Whitby was once a double foundation with an abbess in charge in the days before the Conquest. I wonder what Hertilpole and Allerton would have made of that?'

'Don't be offended, Hildegard.'

'I'm hardened to insults, Gregory.'

'You shouldn't have to be.' He took her arm.

'They make little difference to me when they fall from the lips of those I do not respect.'

He chuckled.

*The cloisters. A little later.*

Many people were hurrying about, to and from the church, in and out of the various chambers, intent on business.

Egbert said to the others, in a quiet voice, 'At

164

least Hildegard has secured an invitation to see the holy relic today instead of having to hang around until Epiphany. That might mean we can make up our minds whether we want to continue in the auction or whether we can call it a day and head back to Meaux.'

'And in the process, leave the mystery of these two deaths unsolved and unpunished?' Gregory gave him a sidelong glance. 'Do I have your argument safe in my understanding?'

'You do, except for my conclusion.'

'Which is?'

'That even if we judge our bid to be rejected, we stay – whatever encouragement to leave the abbot carefully sets in our path.'

'That's what we would expect you to conclude. Abbot Richmond has clearly not got our measure.' Hildegard turned to Brother Luke. 'You agree, Luke?'

'Most fervently. If you had decided to leave I would have found an excuse to stay. Not only for Sabine,' he added, blushing. 'I mean for those two fellows who died so ignominiously, unshriven at a guess. They deserve our compassion.'

'And if finding out who murdered them is compassion, they shall have it,' announced Gregory. He reached out to clasp Luke's right hand, and the oath was sealed by the rest of them in like manner.

'Now, for this episode of the laundry, Hildegard, tell us more.'

She did so, again pointing out that the novices in her opinion were blameless. The little surplices that had been taken away must have been damp

165

like the ones remaining and as well as that they were hanging up high on the drying rack, well out of reach of such little fellows. True, they might have managed to find something to stand on, unfastened the cord that raised and lowered the rack, but they would have had to do it without being noticed. Unlikely in such a busy place. Someone tall enough to reach up to take them down had been in the laundry and it was obvious now they must have fully intended to block up the vents in the store shed.

As for the mystery of the gold thread, it might be that it had been left on some other occasion and had nothing to do with anything that followed.

'These apples,' Gregory interjected. 'The spaces left in the rows showed that they were probably taken in an orderly manner from the end of the nearest row as you would expect, yet six were taken from another rack as if chosen on purpose—'

'A different kind,' Luke observed. 'Demonstrating a preference.'

'Yes, and they were placed within reach as if Aelwyn, maybe feeling faint through lack of air, had decided to lie down for a moment.'

'Could the murderer have placed them so neatly next to him?'

'For what reason?'

'To suggest that he died from natural causes, from an undiagnosed inner complaint, a sudden apoplexy maybe, and, chore complete, thought to rest before starting the climb back up to the precinct? It would make it look natural—'

'As we are being encouraged to believe.'

'Yes, this is certainly the suggestion being

rumoured among the fraternity,' Egbert agreed. 'Someone spread the idea that Aelwyn was not as hale and hearty as they all assumed.'

'Have you asked the infirmarer what he thinks to that?'

'He said he had never heard anything to that effect before.'

'What you're saying,' Luke butted in with some impatience, 'is that we can discount accident from all this. So let's get it straight: he was murdered. Whoever did it cleverly blocked off the vents with garments from the laundry that no-one would immediately miss, then he waited for Aelwyn to go into the store, locked him in, then waited for him to suffocate.' He furrowed his brow. 'How long would it take to die from asphyxiation? He would have had time to place beside him the apples he had chosen.'

'So what about the gold thread? Where did that come from? Aelwyn wasn't wearing anything of that nature. But it was there, close to the space from where someone had taken the apples.'

'Who wears gold thread round here?' Hildegard asked.

'Definitely not Brother Aelwyn.'

'Or any of the monks.'

'Guests?' Gregory suggested.

'Let's find the garment. Has anyone searched his cell?'

'I will.' It was Luke, looking thoughtful for some reason.

As they began to separate to their different purposes, Hildegard had one last word. 'I've only seen gold thread once while we've been here.

167

For all their reputation for high living, the monks don't give much thought to the grandeur of their apparel.'

'Those black robes are the work of the Devil en masse,' Egbert mocked. 'It's like being in purgatory already.'

'But listen, I have seen something. Surely you've noticed the cope worn by the prior at mass?'

'Are you suggesting he went down to the apple store in it?' Gregory asked in a scathing tone.

'No, all I'm saying is that he's the only one I've noticed wearing a garment with gold thread in its weave. Maybe the abbot does too, for all I know. I've never seen him when he's not been sitting in front of his fire, but maybe a thread from the prior's garment caught on something and was transferred—'

The looks of disbelief mirrored Hildegard's own feelings about the theory. 'Oh, well, I can't think of any other reason for a thread of gold being there,' she finished.

'Let's get a closer look at it,' Egbert suggested. 'If we can get near enough we might find a pulled thread.' He tucked his hands inside his sleeves. 'I'll volunteer for this one. Anything's worth a try no matter how unlikely it seems.'

They were all unconvinced, but with little else to go on, as Egbert said as they strolled back across the abbot's enclosure, it was worth a try. While he was at it, he suggested before they parted, he'd also go and talk to the kitcheners to see what they could come up with – after he'd cozened them into a good mood over a jug of ale.

# Twelve

The invitation to visit the shrine of St Hild came a little later. At the time Hildegard was on her way to the stables, drawn there by the sound of raised voices.

The boy who delivered the message was gasping as he ran up. 'Come when you will, domina, now or after the next Office?'

'After the next one.'

'I'll tell him so.' He ran off.

She continued towards the stables and the sound of shouting, having already decided to see how their horses were being cared for and, more importantly, what might be said about Sir Ranulph's black stallion and Edred, when the unusual sound of a woman's voice rising to a desperate level attracted her attention.

When she entered the cobbled area behind the storehouses, Edred's wife was standing in the middle of the yard, pleading with a couple of men who were throwing a few meagre belongings down into the yard from the loft above the stalls where she was living with her children. They were apologising all the while, the children were wailing, and a man shouting orders and telling them to get on with it was only interrupted when the bursar appeared from under the arch opposite leading from the monks' precinct.

It was obvious that someone had over-stepped themselves and was now having the widow thrown out of her home.

Expecting him to put things right, Hildegard was astonished when he gave the widow a supercilious stare as she dropped to her knees with hands clasped. 'Stop this howling, woman. You're disturbing the prayers of the brotherhood. We can hear you all over the abbey.'

'But my lord,' she sobbed, bursting into a flood of tears, 'how can you throw us out? I have three small children. What are we to do? Where can we go? Please, my lord, help us!'

'How dare you! Are we to give you free lodgings? What if everyone came to us on their knees, blubbing and demanding special consideration? What then? Are we to give free houses to everyone who asks?'

'But, my lord, my husband gave you good and faithful service—'

'What? When he swindled us and stole our gold from our very coffers? You dare say he gave good service?'

'My husband was an honest man. He would swindle no-one. He honoured the Church and was faithful to its doctrine all his days!'

'Lie upon lie! Hold your tongue!'

'But what am I to do now? To be thrown out on to the streets! Are we to wander like vagrants now he is dead? Please help me!'

'Look to your problems yourself and don't bother me with them.'

'But it's because of you that we're in such dire straits!'

170

'How dare you speak to me like this? Get up, woman. And then get out! Take your belongings with you.'

The toddler began to howl again and the two older children stood as silent as mutes, shocked to see their mother in such distress and to witness the inexplicable anger, as it must have seemed, of someone they had been taught to revere.

Hildegard took a step forward but was forestalled when the widow clutched the bursar round the knees and cried, 'But, my lord, how cold your heart is! Please give us time! I implore you!'

The bursar pushed her away, kicking out until he broke her grasp round his legs. 'How dare you touch me! Get away!' he shouted. 'You say you need time. I ask what for? Why do you need time? What have you to wait for, woman?'

'But he's not even in the ground!' Her sobs were heart-rending.

The bursar was unmoved. 'He's dead. Do you think he's going to resurrect himself? For sure, God won't do it. The man was a thief and a liar. The abbey will be wealthier without him.'

Bursar Hertilpole half-turned with such a snigger of disgust it made Hildegard catch her breath. Even then he had not finished. Glaring back, he rasped, 'Now get out! I give you until sunset to remove yourself and all your chattels.'

Without another word he stormed from the yard.

Hildegard ran after him then stopped and returned more slowly to the woman. She could not even remember her name. What was it? Anna – that was it.

'My dear Anna.' Hildegard bent down so that they were on a level and took one of the widow's hands between her own. 'I heard all that.'

'He is throwing us out, domina!' The woman began to sob again. 'I have three children, one of them no more than a baby. Are they to sleep rough in the street? We have no-one. All our friends – such as they are' – she cast a baleful glance up to where the two men were standing in the open aperture of the loft – 'are here in the abbey. We have lived here ever since we married. Edred gave his life to making things easy between the town and these . . .' She wiped the back of one hand over her tear-stained face. 'These contemptible men. They were happy enough to go along with him when they were getting paid for their trouble, but now we need them they stand gawping. Where's their friendship now?'

Unnoticed, the yard doorways had filled with stable hands and house servants drawn by the sound of the quarrel. One or two shifted uneasily and stared at the ground.

'Listen, I'm not from here and know of no-one whom I might approach on your behalf . . .' Clearly it was no good asking for leniency from the bursar. 'But you will not be thrown on to the streets so long as I am here. Trust me. If it comes to it I will pay for your lodgings until we can find somewhere more permanent.'

'Pay?'

'Of course. My priory has the means. We can

spare enough to help you now you're in need. What else is our wealth for?'

A shadow fell over them both where they knelt. When Hildegard glanced up she saw that it was Hertilpole again. He loomed over them, his dark face tight with repressed rage. 'I see you have misunderstood the situation, domina. If you will allow me to speak in confidence – away from the servants' – he cast a black glance at Anna – 'then I will acquaint you with the facts of the matter. Come!' He held out an arm to invite her to rise.

Hildegard squeezed Anna's hand. 'Wait for me. I will not abandon you.'

She rose to her feet.

He stretched out an arm to invite Hildegard to precede him. Then she was ushered underneath the arch into the abbey precinct.

He led the way to a shadowed corner of the north cloister at present empty. When he turned to face her his glance was bleak.

'Your compassion does you credit, domina. But then, we revere our nuns for that very quality. They are the bleeding hearts of our ministry. They guide us in the ways of the weak and humble and we are the better for listening to them.'

Hildegard was on her guard. She could almost read his thoughts as they hammered in straight lines towards the words he next uttered.

'You see,' he continued as if to a small, rather stupid child, 'it is like this. I mean it as no criticism, but I would not expect you to understand the subtlety of these people. That woman and her misguided husband have been living off the abbey's resources for years. They have enjoyed a comfortable bolt hole on our property at our expense for far too long. Their needs have been met. They have never complained. At first we were pleased to have found a man who could speak on behalf of us with the rough-hewn fellows in the town. Let me tell you, they are always pushing for some exaction, first one thing, then another, always some grievance which they bring to our door as if we are responsible for their wretched lives.' He gave one of the thin smiles that never reached his eyes. 'The fact of the matter is we need to get her out because her husband had outstayed his welcome, and this is as good an opportunity as any. Besides, with a new man coming in—'

'So you've already found a substitute for Edred?' She made no attempt to disguise her disbelief.

'Not yet, but soon. Of course we shall. You must try to understand the practicalities of our needs. This is a large and busy monastic establishment. We are the most important land-holders in the region. We have many visitors. We need a man who will work on our behalf. In return he will need somewhere to live from where he can fulfil his duties. It is obvious the woman cannot stay. She cannot stay! And that's final. There is no room for hangers-on!'

'And her children?'

'Exactly. It simply will not do! I'm sure you can see that.'

'I feel you've been precipitate, my lord. She is grieving for her man. He is scarcely cold. He is not yet buried. And you uproot her and her children so hastily? I would have expected more concern for her welfare and her understandable grief at such a time. If we nuns are tolerated for the compassion we bring to the monastic orders, then we should at least be heeded. This is a clear case of injustice.'

Hertilpole drew back as if bitten. 'This sounds like a criticism.'

'Take it as you wish.'

'I must remind you, domina, you are a guest here.'

'As I am aware, my lord.'

He leaned forward to say softly into her face, 'Your privilege can always be revoked, my lady. I don't care what Order you belong to. You are here in our domain now. Do not forget it!'

With this warning and without another word, he swept away. She watched him stride down the entire length of the vault towards the church before she turned.

Anna was standing among her scant belongings with her children clustering round her when Hildegard returned to the yard. A few onlookers had come forward. They were in two camps – those who had the courage to risk their own jobs and support a woman in distress, and those too frightened to do so. 'What did he say to you, domina?' Anna looked apprehensive.

'He uttered only a warning to keep my nose out of his business. Nothing to worry us. Now, what do we need to do next?'

175

'I have a friend or two here, after all, bless them,' Anna replied. 'I cannot reveal the names as they are given me in confidence, but I'm told there's a small lodging available at present through Master Dickson. He will charge rent but not much as the place is no more than a single chamber. It's near the footbridge and will be enough for me and my little brood until we can think more clearly about our future.'

'Can you pay the rent?'

'I will find a way.'

One of the bystanders stepped forward. 'They've taken everything of value from her, even the contents of her purse, saying Edred stole whatever she had and it now belongs back in the abbey.' He spat to one side. 'We've had a whip round and have come up with enough for the first week's rent.'

'Then let me meet this Master Dickson and settle the rest long enough for her to find her feet. Will that help, mistress?'

Anna gripped Hildegard by both hands. Tears sprang to her eyes. 'I am more than grateful, dear, blessed lady.' She dropped to her knees and a sob shook her before she regained control. 'I shall pray for you, domina, for your kindness. You have no need to concern yourself with us. We are only servants.'

'No need for thanks, mistress.' She helped her to her feet. 'I am honoured to be able to contribute at all. I fear the problem goes far deeper than your own personal grief.' She thought it better to say nothing more.

Anna was beginning to regain a vestige of hope

and it gave her the confidence to address the group that had gathered round.

'My husband was an honest man. You all know he was. I will not have his name dragged into the mud because of what these monks say! Take warning, you silent ones with your disapproving faces! The next man to be vilified might be yourself! Then look to your friends if you still have any!' She scooped up her baby from where it clung to the hem of her skirts, hoisted the toddler on to one hip and called for the third child to follow. 'We'll go down to meet Master Dickson straight away.'

'I'd like to come with you but I have something to do here before I can come.'

'Then if I may, I'll wait for you. I shall be honoured if you will come down with us.'

The fellows who had been throwing her belongings out of the upper floor had descended into the yard and one of them, in a shame-faced way, interrupted to say, 'We'll carry her things down there now before Dickson rents it on to somebody else. We best be quick about it. There's enough here,' he jingled some coins in his palm, 'to secure it.'

*A few moments later. The church.*

An acolyte met Hildegard at the west end to conduct her behind the timber screen that cut off the laity from the rest of the nave. When they went through she gasped at the unexpected splendour that met her gaze. Behind the screen, hidden from the eyes of the *poraille*, the spectacular

177

edifice of the nave was awe-inspiring in anyone's eyes. Massive columns painted in strong colours of dark red and black ranged from one end to the other. Halfway down, a further partition screened the choir from view but the soaring columns were visible over the top where they held up the carved wooden vault like great oak trees supporting the massive canopy of a wood.

High windows let in a rainbow of vibrant colours, every pane telling a story from the books of the Bible, type and anti-type, as she remembered from her time in York at the glass-painter's house. Everything with its opposite, its mirror image. All of life. The dark side and the light.

Finding it difficult to avert her gaze or forget the troubling thought that she was being beguiled by the abbey's grandeur, she stumbled after the acolyte who led at a brisk clip through the choir to the east end with its enormous painted window where the high altar stood. But he did not stop longer than to bend his knee and make the sign of the cross before conducting her swiftly behind it to the farthest end of the building where, in the space behind the altar, there was a small, plain shrine.

It was nothing much more than a simple ledge covered by a linen cloth. On it was a bursa worked in Opus Anglicanum and inside, she assumed, lay the reliquary, and inside that, the precious lock of hair. She knelt in reverence to honour St Hild.

Eventually the rustling of a trailing garment on the polished tiles made her lift her head to witness the arrival of the abbot. His feet shod in embroidered kid-skin boots made almost no sound as he approached. It was the soft garments, silk brocade over a long linen under shift, trailing behind him that announced his presence.

Without speaking he knelt beside her to offer up a prayer then rose to his feet, inviting Hildegard to do the same.

'Here it is,' he breathed. 'Our most precious relic.' Several rings glinted on his slender fingers as he indicated the little altar.

'It must be a great sorrow to you, the Chapter and the entire fraternity of monks and novices to be forced to put a price on so singular and precious an object,' she murmured.

The abbot's pale-blue gaze acquired a suggestion of unassuageable sorrow. 'Our duty is first to the Lord of mankind and then to our brethren. We are committed to poverty and yet we must feed ourselves or become a burden on the community of Whitby like the friars with their continual begging for alms. We delight in divesting ourselves of anything that might obstruct us in our duty of praise, humility and obligation. St Hild will always remain in our hearts and prayers.'

That over, Hildegard waited to see what he might do next.

After a pause for another short prayer to the saint as intercessor, he reached out to open the embroidered bursa to reveal the reliquary, a small container of lavish design fashioned out of dark gold and studded with stones. He lifted it up and held it so that the light from the great east window struck it, causing it to sparkle with a million jewelled lights. Holding it in the palm of one hand he offered it to Hildegard and suggested she open it.

Cautiously she lifted the lid and looked inside.

A clipping of russet-brown hair tied at one end with a string lay on a purple silk cushion.

'May I?' She wanted to touch the hair to see if it was real. At a nod from the abbot she reverently ran a finger along the curving tress. It felt coarse. There was a suggestion of some resin-like substance to the touch. That first impression may have been disappointing because she had unwittingly expected more.

After a suitable hesitation when she silently questioned whether it might be human hair, she asked, 'And may I be told how it came into your possession, my lord abbot?'

'We have always owned it. In the dark days of the Northmen's invasions it was hidden in a secret place by one of the monks fleeing the flames when the abbey was burned to the ground. From there its journey is unknown until on the day the foundation stone of the new abbey church was laid it appeared as in a miracle and has remained secretly in the shrine to St Hild ever since.'

'I and my prioress at Swyne were in ignorance of its existence until your courier arrived with a missive to announce the fact. We are most grateful to be included in your invitation to possess such a rare and precious relic, should you eventually deem us worthy.'

'The fact that you are here, domina, is proof

enough that we consider you worthy owners of it. St Hild will guide us to its resting place of her choice.'

'And how can we ascertain her views on the matter?' She made a small, regretful smile. Hildegard herself would not give tuppence for a switch of horse hair, no matter how solemnly presented. Her prioress, however, for reasons of her own, might still be willing to pay whatever it cost. She had to take the next few steps with care.

Replacing the lid, she handed it back to the abbot with due reverence.

'May I know the procedure we must follow?' she asked meekly when he rejected her invitation to speculate on the manner of Abbess Hild's guidance.

'You were chosen as the first to view it. After you suggest what you are prepared to offer as adequate exchange, the lord bursar will invite the other applicants to view it, one by one, and they will be expected to do likewise.'

'And your final choice between these offers will not be made until the feast of Epiphany?'

'I'm sure we can hasten things along should your offer be acceptable. We will not expect you to remain away from your cloister longer than necessary. I know you will wish to return to Swyne as soon as possible.'

Hildegard inferred from this that he wanted rid of the Cistercians, unsettling his monks with their questions into matters that did not concern them. If she offered what he deemed a good price they could all be off back to Meaux at once, Epiphany or not. She wondered how he would square this with the other applicants who were left hanging around. Unwittingly he supplied the answer.

'Our discretion in this matter will be absolute. Our formal announcement about its new custodian will not be made until the Saint's feast day on the seventeenth of November next.'

'But that's almost a year hence.'

He bowed his head. 'As you say.'

Did it mean she might barter successfully if she had the nerve to offer what in other circumstances would be a derisory figure? What could she get away with? Had she really understood what the abbot was hinting, that the price of the relic was what he would pay to get rid of them – thereby leaving two murders unsolved and the abbey able to sink back into its private bed of corruption?

She thought it best to kneel and say some inaudible prayer to St Hild, the protector of women and nuns in particular. If there had been Cistercians around in her day, she felt sure the abbess would have been an enthusiastic supporter just as she was for her own Benedictines.

*The guest refectory.*

Preparations for the main meal of the day were bringing servants in and out of the kitchens with loaded platters and shouts of 'Mind your back!' And 'Make way, there!'

The two musicians, a lute player and a piper, the ones who had entertained the guests before, were running through a few tunes in the space between the trestles. None of the guests had made an appearance yet. Hildegard sat down to wait for Gregory and the others and considered all that had happened.

She was still somewhat dumbfounded by the possible implications when Luke came to tell her that the others were waiting for her in the gatehouse to hear what she thought of the relic.

'You've seen it?' he asked.

When she nodded he said, 'Tell me about it when we meet the others.'

Rumours about the eviction of Edred's widow had already flown round the monks' warming room and now she told him she intended to go down to meet this Master Dickson who was playing an invisible part in the matter.

She dragged on her cloak. 'It looks as if it's snowing again.'

He shook a few flakes off his shoulders. 'It's more like floating frost. The very air seems frozen. I'm glad the climate in Holderness is milder—'

'Except when the east wind drives straight off the sea!'

Smiling and blowing on his fingers, he accepted a quick offer of mulled wine. When they were ready and well wrapped up they set off.

*Outside the gatehouse.*

'So how much are they asking?' Egbert came straight to the point as soon as they stepped on to the foregate out of hearing of the porter and his man.

'This may be my mistake,' she began, 'but I got the impression that he will accept whatever it takes to get rid of us. I'm told I have to discuss such prosaic matters with Hertilpole.'

'He'll drive a hard bargain. They have a dire need of more gold to add to their coffers. He'll have to make up the loss of a year's rents unless they can find the gold Edred is alleged to have stolen.'

'It's not as straightforward as that . . . I believe horse hair costs little, even here.'

'What?' Gregory raised his eyebrows.

'I may be wrong but it felt . . . odd. Coarse. Sticky. I don't know what sort of hair those Anglians had but it cannot have been so very different from our own. Each strand felt thicker than human hair. It must have been treated with a kind of resin. Was it to preserve it . . . or was it a hair dressing? It was too much like horse hair in my view.' She paused and bit her lip. 'Who would know?'

She told them about the secrecy the Whitby monks insisted on until they announced the transfer of the relic on St Hild's feast day in November the following year.

Gregory's lips puckered. 'Would they be capable of pulling such a trick – to produce several so-called relics?'

Egbert considered the matter and both men exchanged glances, then began to roar with laughter.

'They truly think we're sot-wits!' Gregory exclaimed.

'And,' Egbert pointed out, 'anyone who gave gold to obtain something that was a fake would never admit it. They'd be mocked from here to kingdom come! Is it likely we're faced by such cunning?'

Luke was shocked. 'I say, brothers, these are monks, you know, not pardoners!'

'Whatever the case, we can't leave yet. Not until we've solved the mystery of the two murders.' Gregory was firm.

'I agree.' Luke was equally firm despite the sudden collapse of his certainty in the existence of natural goodness.

'Let's offer a low sum and see what happens,' Hildegard suggested. 'Even if they accept out of eagerness to get rid of us, they cannot renege. Then we can think up a reason to stay on. We'll have time to unknot the mystery, here at the heart of Whitby Abbey.'

That settled, they decided to accompany Hildegard and Edred's wife to the rented house by the bridge and, with a small child apiece sitting on their shoulders and the third skipping ahead, the monks accompanied Hildegard and Anna down the cliff side into the town.

Once they were safely installed they helped Anna find a cooking pot, laid a fire for her, and seeing that all was as well as could be expected, eventually left her so they could settle things with her new landlord.

# Thirteen

*Harbour House, Dickson's headquarters.*

Master Dickson was the fellow Luke had already
met in passing and who had so outraged his sense
of monastic privilege. It seemed the fellow was
a close colleague of the Master Selby who owned
the house where Sabine was lodging.

A big, bluff, red-faced man in early middle age,
Dickson's pock-marked face was not pleasant
to look at. He made up for any shortcomings in
personal beauty by attiring himself in a rich
collection of velvets and expensive furs –
ermine, pine marten, imported silver fox from
the Russias – and most of it, Hildegard noted,
forbidden him under the Sumptuary Laws. But
then, who was going to bother to report him in
this remote place where the cold made such
protection necessary? Come to that, who would
have the temerity?

Not a thread of gold among any of it, she
observed. It had become her habit now to check
everybody's garments, no matter how far removed
they were from any connection with Aelwyn's
death.

It turned out that Selby, despite his show,
was only one whore master among several and
this Master Dickson was the main man, owning
several 'houses' up and down the coast in other

ports where he employed similar fellows and one or two women. Not that the information was conveyed to them in such stark terms. It was only obvious how far his fiefdom stretched because he could not resist a little boasting about his power, with no attempt to conceal the source of his affluence.

'I like women,' he confided as he sat down with them in a large bright chamber overlooking the harbour and poured what happened to be an exceptionally good Rhenish into expensive-looking blown-glass goblets. 'I'm happy to help Master Edred's wife and children. He was a good friend to many of my clients.' He did not elaborate. 'The lady's too old to work for me, of course, not the right type either, but if she can pay her rent she's welcome to that little house at yon end. She'll be comfortable there and can no doubt keep an eye on what's going on by the bridge for me. I may even be able to find some work for her as I've recently taken over another business to support the fishermen.'

By comparison with Dickson, Hildegard judged her three companions impoverished in their threadbare habits and thin cloaks. Dickson had noted this too and made some comment about the half-starved and frozen brotherhood and that such poverty was shaming, a sure sign that monastics in general lacked common sense. 'But then,' he added with a kindly smile, 'not all of them could aspire to become abbots and live in idle luxury, could they?'

He also gave a thorough appraisal of Hildegard when he thought she wasn't looking but what conclusion he drew from it she could not guess. She gave him a careful scrutiny in return: not a thread of gold could be seen among any of his showy garments, no matter how close she stared.

'I like my women to look rested,' he resumed, pleased to have an audience. 'I like them to be well fed, beautifully gowned, with a smile of enjoyment at the pleasures bestowed on them. Every girl I employ walks and talks like a lady. They can mix with the highest in the realm. I'm proud of them. They're willing to make something of their lives. You fellows may say it's vanity and venery and should be punished, but I say it's natural pride in themselves and the pleasures God bestows. They do not need to go on the streets to beg. With a little prudence they can raise themselves from the gutter where Fate – or God or Lady Fortune – has thrust them and they can lift themselves up and live in comfort to the end of their days. Do you know, some of my girls own property themselves by the time they stop working for me. Ask the bursar up there, Peter Hertilpole.' He nodded in the general direction of the abbey. 'He rents from me. He even rents a house from one of my girls near St Mary's in York where his visiting brothers can stay.' He gave a placid smile. 'She accepted payment in a gift of wine the other day, so little need has she for rents now. In return she sent him a pair of red garters!' He pushed up his sleeves. 'Now, I hope I've set your minds at rest on the sad matter of Edred's widow? She'll be safe with me.'

Gregory's expression was inscrutable.

Dickson had a clerk brought in with a receipt for the payment Hildegard made on Anna's behalf.

'Have no worries. She's in my care now. As I said, I'll find a little job for her if she's willing.'

Hildegard placed the receipt inside her scrip alongside the phial and its contents and as she did so she remarked with an air of innocence, 'It's a mystery why anyone would want poor Edred out of the way. He was popular among many, in the abbey as well as in the town, so I understand – and that's no mean feat, the way things are.'

'It's my opinion,' stated Master Dickson, with a hard stare, 'that he stepped on the wrong toes.' When his eyes met hers his pupils were like the entrance to a long and empty corridor.

Outside, the street was busy and normal-looking. 'Glad am I to get out of there!' announced Luke. He shook himself.

'I propose we now ask ourselves the obvious question about Edred.' Gregory seemed impatient to move on.

'Which is . . .?' Egbert asked, detaining him.

'Why did he go up to the fish pond in the snow last night?'

'Was he on his way to the farm? Anna didn't mention it. If she had known I'm sure she would have told me. But maybe Edred had some last-minute business up there? Or with the brewery adjoining it?'

'All right, Hildi, let's go up there and find out.'

*The headland. A little later.*

When they had ridden up the lane from further down the coast the day they arrived they had passed a collection of buildings lying outside the perimeter of the precinct. Made gauzy under a shroud of rain then, now they were submerged under drifts of snow. It was clear, close up, how extensive they were. A foreman met them in the yard.

Yes, he knew Edred well. It was a sad affair. And no, the fellow had no reason to come up there that night. No-one would have expected it. They had battened down their shutters against the storm, confident that no-one would come visiting.

He admitted that Edred came up most days on abbey business to do with the town. They supplied ale to the taverns down there as well as to Master Dickson. Edred also came up after the day's work was done to meet one of the monks and they would pace along the track from the precinct to the far end of the pond and back, talking, always talking.

Edred was like that. A great man for opinions.

Of course, on the night in question, there was no Brother Aelwyn, his usual companion, because of his terrible accident, and it was believable that Edred might have done away with himself as was being rumoured, in his desperation of grief at losing an ally in these disturbed and turbulent times.

On that night, the one in question, he himself had seen no-one but they were at liberty to ask

190

among his labourers and house servants if they wished.

The answer was the same. The blizzard had kept everyone inside. There were a few quips about not wanting to get their balls frozen off, which made Hildegard smile to herself and, as they were talking, a kennel lad came in and stood listening with an open mouth.

Before they left he blurted, 'I saw summat up there near the pond last night.'

'You? . . . What could you see from your corner, sleepy-head?' one of the brewsters asked.

'I had to get up for a piss,' the lad replied. 'Duke was restless so I took him outside with me and we went for a little walk.'

'Took him with you on account of being afeared of ghosts, more like,' somebody jeered, ruffling his hair.

'I am. I admit it. Right scared and so would you be if you'd seen one. I told you I've seen St Hild and she told me not to listen to you lot.'

'Tell us about this other thing you saw,' Hildegard asked. 'Was it another ghost?'

'I thought so at first. Duke was growling and that. His hairs were standing up like spikes on a hedgehog. Then I made summat out through the snow that was still piling down. It was a dark figure floating along a bit like a ghost but like a man as well with another dark figure following it and then they locked and turned into one . . . I think that must have been when the following figure caught up with the one in front.'

'Could you tell what they were doing?'

191

'They were standing.'

'Not fighting?'

'Not doing nothing. Talking, like.'

'Did you hear what they were saying?'

'I wasn't that close and any road the wind snatched away every sound save for its own whining.'

'You're the one whining, Miggy. You'll be howling next. Don't listen, domina, he's always seeing summat.'

'Maybe they are not always ghosts,' she suggested. Smiling at the boy, she slipped a coin into his palm. 'If you remember anything else, do you know your way to the guest house?'

'I do.'

'Then come and tell me about it.' She bent down and, anxious for his safety, whispered, 'but don't tell anyone else until you've spoken to me, right?'

He nodded, proud to have a secret.

They left then and began to walk back towards the precinct.

'He must have seen Edred meet someone he knew well, to stand and talk in that weather.'

Egbert glanced about. 'That doesn't narrow it down much. He knew so many people.'

'Was it an assignation or an accidental meeting?' Hildegard wondered.

'I think we might have found out if it had been someone from up here, don't you? They couldn't guarantee that they hadn't been recognized and would have admitted it rather than be accused to their face. And no doubt they would have had an excuse ready.'

Gregory pulled his hood up. 'Let's get off this blasted headland.'

'We might go back by way of the pond,' Hildegard suggested.

The ice had melted and the long sheet of water lay like glass, undimpled, reflecting a grisaille sky. Only when they made their way to the farthest end and looked back did the abbey itself lie suspended, as it were, on the mirrored surface.

'Thick reeds all around the perimeter,' remarked Gregory. 'One or two places where the nets must be set. And here we are. This is where he went into the water.'

A scuffle of footprints in the slush obliterated any earlier prints. 'These are recent. Someone has been up here since we were here ourselves.'

'Looking for something that would interest us?' Egbert crouched down to peer more closely at the prints. 'Leather boots. The sort anyone would wear.' He straightened. 'We draw a blank every way we cast our gaze.'

'As Hertilpole suggested when he was talking about the novices, we may have to wait for someone to break.'

'He'll have a long time to wait for one of those novices to say he blocked the apple store,' Hildegard commented.

'Do you think that little ghost-ridden lad will come up with anything more?'

Hildegard strolled further off. Calling back over her shoulder she said, 'From the farm, or close to it, he could see someone standing just about here. The two figures. If I move this way' – she did so – 'or this way' – she moved again – 'he would not be able to see me. The rise of the ground hides the buildings from me, and I from anyone standing over there.' She bent down. 'And here it is. Look.'

In the short winter grass was a shallow puddle of ice and in the mud underneath the surface where the ice had broken were two different-sized prints.

She sighed. 'It cannot help us, can it?'

'At least these are man-made prints so at least the lad wasn't seeing ghosts again.'

'Better than nothing,' agreed Egbert.

Luke had been silent most of the time. Hildegard was beginning to feel anxious about him. His spirits seemed unusually low. Until recently he could always have been counted on to raise their own spirits with his unquenchable optimism, but now . . . She took his arm. 'What do you think, Luke?'

His melancholy smile pierced her heart. 'What do I think? I think we live in a well of evil. That we should have to pace this beautiful cliff top in the search for a murderer when we should rather be singing a paean to such magnificent natural beauty will forever remain the greatest mystery and sadness to me. Why should we have been set to spend the brief, precious moments of our lives in so gruesome a manner? Why must we dwell amidst evil?'

'Oh, Luke, we are human creatures; this is what it means. We live in a moral dimension. Animals do not have the privilege of our ability to make choices between good and evil. They do what they must. We do what we can. And today we can choose to bring justice to two men or walk away and let their killers go free.'

'Am I free to walk away?' His expression was desolate.

'Come on, Luke. Never give in to the canker in the soul. *Hinc illae lacrimae!* You would want us to find out who gave you a fatal blow, wouldn't you?'

'I would regard it as a blessing, Gregory – if, dead, I had the power to regard anything – but it's such a perfect winter day, the air so cleansing and pure, the sky like window glass, we should be able to raise our eyes to worship whatever power brings us here. But we can't! Some evil-hearted villain has chosen to crawl the earth in hatred, leaving a black trail of death behind him. Why?'

'That's a question for Abbot Richmond. He's the theologian here.' Gregory patted him on the shoulder.

The young monk looked thoughtful. 'I shall go and beg instruction from him then. Let's see what his teaching might be.'

Hildegard had walked further on. The path branched when it reached the abbey enclosure. When they first arrived they had taken the left fork, finding their way along the north side of the building until they came out on to the fore-gate. Another path, a trod of some kind, paved now and then, led straight down from the out buildings away from the abbey and continued on down the cliff. She guessed it might come out near the parish church of St Mary.

'I'm going to have a look further on,' she called back. 'I'll catch up with you in a while.'

The track undulated over the headland and, as she expected, joined the path to the parish church where the memorial for Brother Aelwyn had been held. Having already climbed up and down the cliff path enough times to know it would lead past Sabine's cottage, then down to the corner of Church Street and from there into the town, she concluded that anyone could have come up from that direction with no need to enter the enclave. The likelihood of anyone seeing them was remote too, especially on such a night when everybody was safely indoors sheltering from the blizzard.

If Edred had set off to meet Hildegard on the foregate, he must have decided to go up to the pond first. It would not have been far out of his way. But why? Who would he want to meet with such urgency?

Returning to catch up with the others, she found that they had not moved on but were still staring into the waters of the pond. Gregory was lying on the bank among the rushes with one sleeve rolled while he groped about under the surface.

Egbert appeared to be giving him instructions. 'Try more to your right,' he was saying. 'Now a bit further out.'

Hildegard asked him what they were doing.

'Do you see how the wind blows constantly from the sea over the headland? It pushes the water into this little creek here, no more than an indentation pressed into the side of the bank.

You can't see the way the wind works today as the airs are light but that night it was howling along and the snow built up in drifts on this side. If anything had fallen – say something had been torn from a garment for instance – it might have been pushed along the bank into the reeds further over here.'

She glanced round. The snow lay in scabbed drifts over the ground. It was kicked about as if somebody had been looking for something – such as a weapon – and whoever had been up here must have been out before Prime. She berated herself for not thinking to do that first. She wondered if they had found anything.

She glanced at Egbert. 'They beat us to it, didn't they?'

Gregory grunted at this and withdrew his arm. 'I'll try further along.'

Rubbing his forearm to get some warmth back into it he knelt down and made as if to plunge it back into the ice water, but Luke elbowed him out of the way. 'Let me have a go. No point in catching cold.' He followed Gregory's example, reaching down at intervals and working his way methodically through the reeds along the bank.

Hildegard watched him lifting his hand out of the water then bending down to dredge again through the tangled roots.

Egbert took up her last remark while they watched. 'Only a fool would drop a weapon at the scene of a crime.' He observed Luke's efforts without any expectations. 'At least he'll have clean arms!'

He was just declaring, 'It was a good theory, Greg,' when Luke interrupted him with a yelp.

He jerked back on to his knees. 'Look at this! I don't know what it is but it's something.'

He held it up. It was water-logged and, when he pressed a finger over it, it gleamed bright green like a piece of fabric. 'It's a feather,' he announced. He turned it over in his palm. 'It's definitely not a gull's feather, nor is it from a hawk although it's large enough.'

'It looks like a cock feather. Must be from the farm.' Egbert tried to sound enthusiastic but it was clear he was disappointed if this was the sum of their search.

'Just a moment.' Gregory took it from between Luke's fingers and held it up. 'You know where this comes from? It's not from a cockerel at all. Remember those parrots we saw in Outremer, Egbert?'

Suspiciously the monk took it and wiped off some of the mud. 'You know, brother, you may be right. But what in the Devil's name is a parrot feather doing up here?'

Hildegard returned to the abbey with the others but left them while she went to speak to the bursar.

He was busy, she was informed, but she had already written down their offer for the relic on a square of parchment and now she left it with the sub-prior. It was a derisory figure. Let them make of it what they will. They would never accept it, not unless they were mad to have them leave at once. And that in itself might prove something.

The others were waiting in the cloister. The feather had had clean water run over it and was dry now. The colour was a dazzling viridian. They agreed that it must come from a parrot. Luke stroked it to make it lie flat. He claimed to have seen a parrot at York fair where it seemed to curse the onlookers in a language no-one understood. Egbert and Gregory had seen many, flying wild in the trees on their travels.

'And you, Hildegard, do you take our word?'

'When I was at Handale of all places, there was some outrage involving a priest at Whitby in which he was poisoned. His family were well known and came from a manor further south called Thweng. Their emblem happens to be three green parrots – or popinjays, as he called them.'

'A Crusader family?'

'Possibly.'

'Any other connection with Whitby?'

'Only, as I say, through the priest, a younger son. He was the last male of his line which brought problems to the female members over their property rights. I cannot see any connection now. I'm sure it must have been resolved. He did happen to mention the live parrot they had when he was a boy, but I would imagine it's long dead by this time.'

'Another dead end too,' observed Egbert. 'Unless any of us happen to spot a parrot on somebody's shoulder.'

# Fourteen

Even as the foursome began to make their way back towards the enclave they could hear the evening's revels from below the cliff. Faint in the distance it sounded as if a band of pipes and tabors was wending its way up the hill towards them.

'This must be by special invitation of the guests,' Hildegard remarked, her heart sinking at the thought of having to face yet another night disturbed by the Twelve Days revelry.

No wonder Dickson had made that comment about how he preferred women to look rested. He must have taken one look at her and decided that what she needed was a good night's sleep.

If he had dared to say anything to her about preferring his women to look rested she would have retorted that she preferred men to keep their opinions to themselves – especially when engaged in the running of brothels.

Gregory noticed her dismay and must have guessed the reason. 'You could always beg a comfortable corner in the infirmary if it gets too much.'

'Maybe they won't stay late. It's early now. They may be going on somewhere else.'

By the time they reached the foregate the band were already at the top of the cliff. They had attracted a large crowd of followers from the town who were toiling up the path in their wake. A few children ran alongside, banging their own small drums and tootling shrilly on little wooden flutes.

It was soon revealed that the musicians were the harbingers of a group of mummers who came toiling up the cliff side behind them. They were masked mostly, and wearing weird garments suggesting devils, angels, and a version of court dress that mocked any pretensions King Richard's courtiers may have had to elegance. Enormous shoes, the poulaines of the Bohemian court, with exaggerated points attached by chains to their knees, made walking a problem. They struggled up the path with hoots of laughter and much falling about. There were also men dressed as women with long string wigs, trailing skirts, fake bosoms and over-painted faces, and others of no particular gender like the angel with trailing wings of grubby white goose-feathers who was either a beautiful knave or a large-eyed maiden, and one followed after with a waist-length fake beard, either a fat ale-wife or a corpulent, ale-quaffing husband, and the leader of the band in a turban covered with silver stars wore a wooden scimitar stuffed in his belt and something like walnut stain on his face. In and out of this mob were jugglers, concentrating on their tricks, a conjuror in cap and bells producing eggs from every orifice to the raucous delight of his followers, and the stilt walker from the previous evening, the stilts carried by the little man who himself was a one-man band with cymbals attached to his knees, bells and rattles jangling from his headdress, his elbows, and anywhere else they could be attached without impeding his climb up the path.

The stilt walker kept flicking back strands of hair from the flaxen wig with a graceful hand while urging the crowd to follow. 'Every step brings you closer to Heaven, my darlings. Onwards!'

A dragon-headed figure wielded a bag on a stick to entice those out of range to part with a few coins. 'Silver or gold!' he kept bellowing through his mask. 'We are not choosy! So long as they're coins with our dear king's head on them we shall be delighted to thank you in our prayers tonight. Come on, you misers! Put your hands in your pouches!'

The drums rolled with a flourish every time a coin was dropped into the bag.

'Still they come!' murmured Gregory as the crowd swelled. A boyish look of delight was on his face. 'They must be fellows from the Mysteries in York, surely? Look at that bishop! Dressed almost as lavishly as the real thing!'

It was a child being carried on a small palanquin made up of boards and covered in rough cloth. He was blessing the crowd with a benign expression as his carriers jolted him along.

Somebody began to shout, 'Make way for the King!'

The crowd of folk still toiling upwards parted to allow a group of white-winged children to scramble into view. Behind them a tall, emaciated fellow with curly blond locks spurting from underneath a huge wooden crown was attired fully in gold. To cheers he came striding up the hill using his sceptre to club stragglers out of his way.

'Is that a pretty girl under all that stuff on his face or an equally pretty boy?' Egbert queried.

The king was smiling and blessing his jostling followers and in a surge of noise and the whirling legs of acrobats he was conducted on to the foregate to a blast from a sackbut.

As Hildegard suddenly noticed, visitors at the guest house, obviously forewarned, had appeared in the doorway. There was Sir Ranulph, smiling as genially as ever, with one arm round an excited Amabel; Darius gazing ironically down on the rabble; Sister Aveline, positioned close to Amabel, with her hand on her arm; the three corrodians within sight of each other, and the Glastonbury fellow in the furs who had been whisked away that first night when the hunting party returned with only slightly less noise than the mummers were making now. Body servants and others crowded in a chattering mob behind them.

The king strode into the centre of the space carved out for him and took up a position. He raised his sceptre to begin a speech.

Before he said more than half a dozen words the brick bats started to fly. Clods of earth, small stones, something that looked like a dead gull, fish heads, apparently brought along for this very purpose, hailed down on him and the mummers. The winged children fled shrieking and giggling in a little flock. A couple of guards wearing fake armour began to sing a Te Deum.

The king himself scurried behind them and tried, with mock inefficiency, to hide. Then the whole lot surged towards the porter's lodge to push their way inside the enclave.

Remaining on the foregate, Hildegard heard the minstrels strike up as soon as they entered the garth while more and more onlookers pushed inside to set foot on forbidden ground. It was a hurling, raucous confusion of colour and clamour, the noise ricocheting from the high stone walls and doubling its effect.

Gregory caught Hildegard's eye. 'You saw it too? Let's not lose sight of him! Come! Follow me!'

Luke pulled at Hildegard's sleeve. 'What's he saying?'

'Hurry! Keep up!' She knew what Gregory had seen.

He had already merged into the crowd with Egbert close on his heels by the time Hildegard, dragging Luke behind her, managed to force a way inside.

'Tell me what he said!' he repeated. 'What is it?'

Half-turning she mouthed, 'The popinjay!'

Luke nodded, not entirely understanding, but followed her without further delay.


With everyone pressed into the small area of cloister garth and several brawny Northumberland pipers appearing from somewhere to join the minstrels, it was a scene of carnival within.

The music invited everyone to dance. People linked arms with anybody who happened to be standing next to them and, kicking up their heels, women swirled their skirts, men stamped and shouted, the jugglers performed their tricks and anyone who could sing raised their voices to the old tunes and sang their hearts out.

Only one group did not join in. Apart from the Cistercians, the monks of the abbey, hoods thrown back, faces smiling much as Darius had been smiling, with a bemused condescension, were ranged around three sides of the cloister in silence.

'This way,' muttered Gregory in Hildegard's ear.

He forced a path behind the crowd who were now preparing to dance a salterello as the music changed. They came out on the opposite side of the garth where the king was still brushing himself down after his costume had been despoiled by the missiles hurled at him. The dragon-headed character strode into the middle and shouted through his mask for the musicians to hold quiet.

One by one the instruments fell silent as a troop of actors launched themselves into a play in which the dragon itself was a chief character. A surgeon in realistically blood-stained garments drew out an enormous knife and made a few feints with it.

One luckless fellow was roughly plucked from the crowd while the rest of the players joined in with gusto. After a chase they tied their victim down while the crowd cheered.

The stilt walker presided over the surgeon's antics from on high and in a loud horror-stricken voice described the operation with relish. 'And now he puts both hands inside the gaping wound and draws forth his organs . . .' Fake entrails, or real ones from some butchered beasts of the field, were drawn as from the victim's belly as the crowd groaned in mock horror and sniggers of derision.

'There, see him?' muttered Gregory.

'Or her,' Egbert replied, following his glance.

Hildegard peered over to where Gregory had indicated.

In the milling crowd someone wearing a white smock with a pair of red horns on their head was yelling as lustily as everyone else.

On his shoulder: a live bird.

'A popinjay!' breathed Hildegard.

At that moment, astonishingly, the man stepped forward into the play's action and began to berate the surgeon. In response he got a bucket of convincing-looking blood thrown over him. The green parrot sheltered inside his capuchon to the delight of the crowd.

In response the man encouraged the bird to jump on to his wrist and pose like a hawk until he sent it flying round the garth. Everyone watched open-mouthed to see if it would make a bid for freedom, but to loud hoots and cheers it swooped down on to the man's wrist again and squawked something only those standing by could hear. The fellow held the bird aloft and took a bow. The parrot mirrored him.

Hildegard noticed the fellow's eyes as he lowered his head and how they darted from side to side over his audience. 'Gregory, is that our man?'

Egbert flexed his fists.

Luke was frowning. 'What are we going to do?'

'Wait,' suggested Gregory. 'An opportunity will come to observe him at closer quarters.'

The abbey brewster, one of the men up at the buildings on the perimeter of the enclave they had met earlier, had commanded a team of muscular lads who had manhandled a few barrels on to the garth and the crowd began to jostle for free drinks. Hildegard wondered how the monks were going to clear the place when the time came for everyone to leave, or whether they would have to retreat to their dortoir in the face of such mayhem, leaving the security of the abbey in God's hands.

Unobserved, however, the garth and the town folk in it were being surreptitiously controlled because all around, where people might have thought to wander off to find some unattended gold chalice or crucifix, the abbey servants, many of whom she now recognized, stood with folded arms at the exits and entrances to the private areas of the precinct.

After a word from one of the sub-priors the musicians were soon playing music suitable for a farandole at which, gradually, as the sound and the rhythm penetrated their hearing, the players began to link arms to form a snake that started to wind its way around the garth.

When everyone saw what was happening they joined in and soon the living creature with a thousand legs was jigging in and out of the cloisters and eventually snaking back at the same cheerful pace through the gatehouse and on to the path to town.

It took time, and no-one was bothered about that, but with the sound of the drums and pipes fading down the side of the cliff the entire rowdy mob gradually returned from whence it had emerged.

The tolling of the bell put the final seal on things, drowning out the last whisper.

The Benedictines, their abbey safe again, were already filing into church but Gregory, pushing his companions on ahead of him, suggested they join the last of the followers. 'We'll see where this green parrot goes. Its keeper might be a townsman, or one of the mummers as seems more likely. We'll find him and talk to him after he's had a few stoups of ale.'

'*In vino veritas*,' muttered Luke.

Already dark now, the flares lighting the path helped them keep their footing on the steep track. A few figures in outlandish glitter could be seen heading past the parish church. With the red horns in their sights the Cistercians tagged on behind.

*The town. Moments later.*

A febrile atmosphere had the streets and alleys in its grip by the time they reached the bottom. Every door was open. Groups still arm-in-arm reeled slowly from one house to the next. The loudest sounds of revelry came from Church Street where the crowd was thickest, and when they reached the corner they saw that it was impassable, thick with onlookers and the crowd following the procession meeting another one forcing its way up from the direction of the quay.

The two groups clashed somewhere lower down near the moot hall. Flames leaped upwards. An explosion was heard. Cheering onlookers reassured those too far away to see what was happening that everything was going well.

'It looks as if the mummers are putting on their show again,' Gregory reported from the height that enabled him to see over the heads in front. 'The other procession seems to be in charge of the tar barrels.'

Luke was searching the faces of the crowd with a strained expression and when Hildegard noticed the girls hanging out of upstairs windows and shouting down into the throng below she understood why. Sabine would surely be in the Selby house. Not out here on the main thoroughfare.

'There he is!' exclaimed Egbert, catching a glimpse of the red-horned devil with the parrot through a gap in the crowds. They pushed forward, leaning into the wall of bodies until it gently opened, received them, then closed behind them. In this way they managed to press forward until they were close enough to the horned figure for Hildegard to make cooing noises to the bird. Its owner turned.

'*Salve, ma donna*!'

'*Salvete*,' replied Hildegard including the popinjay in her greeting.

A young, beard-less, nut-brown face with taut, wind-honed skin and dancing eyes was visible when he pushed aside the mask. Without speaking he encouraged the bird to step off his shoulder on to his hand, then he offered it to Hildegard. The well-trained creature knew how to behave. It stepped fearlessly on to Hildegard's wrist and began to speak and bob its head.

'Is it Latin?' she asked its owner in astonishment.

'A good Christian popinjay,' he boasted. 'Take him. He likes you.'

'He is so sleek and fine,' she murmured, running one finger down the parrot's chest. Its feathers lay as smooth and soft as silk over its bony chest.

'Take. He is yours.' He made as if to move off.

'I have no way of keeping him,' she explained.

'In your house. Your husband like? You make pretty hat with feathers?' He ran one of his own fingers down the sleek side of the bird and gave Hildegard a penetrating stare.

Was he a Fleming, a Lombard? He seemed to have mistaken her habit for a player's garb. She touched it at the neck and as she pulled forth her little wooden cross a look of astonishment flooded his face. Then he roared with laughter. 'You keep him. Teach him prayers. He speak good Latin. Go to popinjay heaven. Maybe he become Pope?'

He took her by the other hand and squeezed it as if to convey some kind of meaning. The crowd pressed them close together and the bird stepped on to her shoulder. The merry eyes of its owner hovered close to her face and he bent his head. 'Aren't you a mummer, after all?'

She shook her head. Pulling a face he took the popinjay and, speaking gibberish to it, replaced it on his own shoulder. '*Vale, ma donna.*' With a quick bob of his head he slipped away into the crowd.

Gregory swooped down. 'What was that about?'

'He tried to give me the popinjay. It speaks Latin. I feel I've missed something.'

'There he goes.' Gregory, still taking advantage of his height, gestured down the street. 'He seems to be trying to give it to someone else now. A friar by the look of him, although he could be a fish merchant in holy day garb.' The crowd milled about them and Gregory asked, 'What was the bird saying?'

'I couldn't tell.'

'All I can say is he didn't look as if he was likely to hit somebody over the head and push them into a fish pond.' Egbert still had his eyes on him. 'There he goes, predictably into an ale house.'

'You can slide into a drinking den without being noticed, Egbert. Why don't you go and listen to that mysterious bird to find out what it's saying?'

Egbert adopted a parrot's voice and said something about his master pushing a nice fellow into a lake. 'Huzzah! Huzzah!' he squawked, causing heads to turn. 'I always get the rough end of the stick,' he pretended to moan. 'Ale drinking . . .' He shivered.

'We'll wait for you in the street . . . Ready to carry you home,' Gregory called after him as Egbert followed the horned head piece down the street to one of the houses with broom over the lintel where it had disappeared inside.

\* \* \*

211

Hildegard felt disillusioned. 'I feel we're on the wrong track. He's a foreigner. He can't have anything to do with Aelwyn or Edred, can he?'

'So how did a feather from his popinjay get into the fish pond close to where Edred's body was found?'

'*If* it was from that and not another bird. I feel we've missed a turn somewhere.'

'The truth is we've never seen a turn to miss because we've never even been on any track.'

Leaning against a corner of a house, they stood a little apart from the milling crowds lining the street to watch the first of the barrels being dragged up the slope. Once at the top they would be set alight and allowed to roll down so that youths could risk setting themselves on fire as they leaped over them.

'You can't escape the fact,' he said, 'that there's been precious little to go on.'

Turning her back on the activity in the street, Hildegard suggested they went over what had happened so far. 'First Brother Aelwyn.' Remembering Dickson's comment, she asked, 'Whose toes did he step on?'

'Some animosity from the town?'

'They seemed to like him if the comments at his memorial service were anything to go by.'

'From the brotherhood then?'

'That's more likely. His flagrant disregard for celibacy must have angered some of the purists. Or,' she said, 'maybe he became too involved with the followers of Wycliffe?'

'A reason for doing away with him? Surely it's not enough except for the most arrant purist willing to risk hellfire for his absolutism? And anyway, the law deals with heretics. I can see no reason for anyone to take matters into their own hands over it.'

'The Duke of Gloucester and his friend Richard Arundel have recently made it a hanging matter to shelter heretics.'

'That's true. But Gloucester's a long way off. Up here they have a disdain for Westminster law if it doesn't suit them, especially if it comes from him. Surely it must be something more local?'

'Or more personal?'

'In such a tight-knit community – I mean the abbey as well as the town – it's unlikely that anyone is going to drop any hints to us. We're outsiders.' He frowned. 'I can't help feeling the abbey high-ups are aware of the fact and hope to play on it. That's probably the main reason the matter was handed to us.'

'You don't trust them, do you?'

'No I don't. And that's personal!' He gave one of his tantalizing smiles. 'They regard us as fools and you know how that rankles!'

'That aside, Gregory, let's look at the facts again, so far as we know them: Aelwyn's movements were common knowledge. Everybody knew he used to go up to the apple store most days. They wouldn't have troubled to steal the means to block up the air vents if they hadn't. But they would have to time it so that he was the last one to go up that day.'

'So it seems to mean that someone managed to lure him there at a specific time. I'm thinking of a tryst with Sabine, for instance, now we know of their relationship.'

'Surely she wouldn't harm Aelwyn? According to Luke she was distraught the morning she heard he'd died.'

He made no reply.

Instead he reminded her of how the path up to the abbey passed Sabine's house lower down. 'It would be easy for her to walk up from her house to the top of the cliff, but instead of entering the abbey she could have taken the path towards the orchard without even going inside the enclave.'

'With the intention of meeting Aelwyn? . . . Hmm.' After a pause she said, 'To meet him, yes, I can accept that . . . but to lure him into the store so as to kill him?'

'We know so little about these people. That's our problem. We're groping in the dark trying to understand their loves and hatreds. And what about Edred's death? Do we suspect that the person who murdered him had also earlier murdered Aelwyn?'

'I think we're assuming so.'

'But again, we have to ask, why? What's the link?' He paused. 'Such a theory would surely exempt Sabine. Can you see her pushing a man into a lake?'

'As for a link between Aelwyn and Edred?'

'Talk. To swap opinions? Edred's body was found close to the farm buildings. With Aelwyn dead, though, his usual purpose was thwarted, so what took him up there that night?'

'Maybe he had a message for someone there?'

'Despite the blizzard?'

'Yes. And he walked up, bypassing the abbey enclave where he was to meet me, and instead met the man with the popinjay?'

'But why? How would he know him? And what do you think he was going to tell you if he'd managed to turn up?'

'Brother Dunstan was vague. He thought only that it might help us understand a little more about the undercurrents sweeping the abbey.'

Remembering the friar in the tavern on the day of their clash with the abbey mercenaries, Hildegard mentioned again a link between supporters of Wycliffe, the desire to be able to speak out freely, and for Edred as with many, a desire to question the official doctrines like those associated with the Eucharist and to have the Bible in translation so that all could freely read it.

'The desire for bonded men to attain their freedom is a strong pressure on many to join the rebels, whatever the religious arguments. Plenty of folk live in the woods to escape the bondage of a master. They're open about fighting the scourge of slavery. They vow never to give in, to fight on to the end, whatever the penalty.'

'And both Aelwyn and Edred appear to hold similar views. It's not too much to call them allies. It seems to be fairly common knowledge around the abbey precincts that Aelwyn was a sympathizer, tacitly at least. He must have been something of a rebel as a novice, transgressing the Rule when he was a youth. Then, for some reason being allowed back into the fold . . . Was it at a price, do you think?'

'What do you mean? . . . As a spy?'

'It would be useful to have a grateful brother reporting back to the abbot anything that might harm abbey interests. And Edred might have been a useful source of information for him, given his connections in the town with men like Dickson.'

'And thus they stepped on someone's toes?'

'By the way, where is Luke?'

Gregory glanced about. 'He was here a few moments ago.'

Hildegard stood on tiptoe and stared down the street. It was too crowded to make anyone out.

They exchanged glances.

'At least let's go and rescue Egbert from the claws of the demon drink.'

'And then approach the sanctuary of Master Selby to rescue Luke?'

# Fifteen

By the time they pushed their way inside the ale house they found the centre of attention to be the popinjay and Egbert himself. He was offering it a little dish of ale while it stood on his wrist. It pecked at the ale with every sign of enjoyment and when it finished it jumped on to Egbert's head and began to clean its feathers to the delight of the onlookers.

Egbert said something to it in Latin and the bird replied, although whether it was simply a response to familiar-sounding words or to their meaning it was difficult to assess.

The owner of this exhibitionist bird stood by with a stoup of ale in his own hands, smiling round at everyone with his bright, noticing glance. Although he gave no sign, Hildegard felt that he was aware the minute she and Gregory stepped over the threshold.

Very slowly he began to entice the popinjay back into his keeping.

Egbert, losing his partner, sank back among the group of drinkers and in a moment appeared beside them. 'Harmless enough,' he murmured. 'Come outside.'

When they were a few paces away he said, 'He says he's a priest from a vill near Bruges. He follows the trail of the trouvères, picking up enough scraps to stay alive, getting rich at times like this and living poor the rest of the time.'

'A priest?' queried Gregory.

'Ex-priest. Thrown out on his ear for fornicating . . . or so he claims.'

'That doesn't surprise me.' Hildegard recalled the way he stood so unexpectedly close when he was trying to offer her the bird. 'Didn't he find anybody to take that popinjay then?'

'I think it was something else he was offering.' He grinned. 'Not what you're thinking. It seems the bird is a sign understood by those in the know. A play on the word pope? Pope – popinjay? When I reached the ale house he was in a corner talking to a friar—'

217

'Was it the Friar John who was so useful at Meaux last Lukemas?'

'That's where I've seen him!' Egbert exclaimed. 'I thought he looked familiar. He's grown a little forked beard since then. Just like the one the king is said to have adopted.'

Gregory and Hildegard exchanged glances.

'What?' Egbert looked puzzled.

'We were trying to find a link in all this and came up with the idea that it might be something to do with the king's likely support for the men in russet.' He lowered his voice as a well-armed fellow, whose mail-shirt looked like the real thing among all the motley, paced beside them down the street with exaggerated unconcern.

Gregory had need for caution. He was referring to Wycliffe's disciples who travelled the country wearing rough russet gowns and reading openly in English from the parts of the Bible already translated – and risking persecution from the barons who ran the King's Council for doing so.

To be seen as a Wycliffite was a dangerous activity now that the new regime of King Richard's enemies was running the country. That the queen, Anne the Good, was a supporter of the theologian's ideas, as were all her Bohemian court, strengthened the view that King Richard himself was a supporter of more freedom in religious matters, as his mother, the Princess Joan, had been too.

Egbert, however, seemed unconvinced. 'I would imagine there are enough disagreements here without dragging in the king and his enemies. What about the animosity between the fishing folk and the abbey? That's contentious enough.'

The armed man, apparently having heard enough, walked on.

'You think Aelwyn and Edred trod on too many toes over that?' Gregory asked, watching the fellow stride off down the street.

'It's as good a reason as any. Get shot of the troublemakers. Without a spokesman like Aelwyn the fishermen are more easily managed. Rid yourself of a go-between like Edred, and replace him with a sot-wit who'll do your bidding: your job's complete.' He cupped one hand. 'You've got them in your palm.'

'That's a grave charge against the abbey hierarchy. We were thinking more along the lines that the abbey were using Aelwyn to keep an eye on their own enemies. Whatever the case, how do you explain the feather in the water and our friend from Bruges?'

Nobody had any ideas.

'Have you seen Luke, anyone?' Hildegard asked when it was obvious they were getting nowhere. 'He was with us one minute then gone the next.'

'We're trying to second-guess him and are meandering our way down to Selby's house,' Gregory explained.

Egbert nodded. 'Lead on.'

The alleyway, known as Grope Lane and by other more ribald epithets as well, was as busy

219

as the high street with crowds rolling shoulder to shoulder from one house to the next.

Doors were wide open to the houses where the girls were stationed and their strong-arm protectors lounged genially outside, swapping banter with the clients they knew. When they reached the house at the far end where Master Selby lived, its windows were ablaze with lights. A minstrel could be heard wailing some love ballad in the hall.

They noticed Luke at once. He was standing on the opposite side of the alley, gazing up at one of the first-floor windows.

'How young and innocent can a man be?' Egbert asked. 'What does he think he can achieve?'

The door-man recognized them from when they had been here before looking for Master Dickson. 'You after that young fellow of yours?' He pointed.

At that moment the window opened. The perfect oval face of a madonna appeared. It was Sabine. She shouted, 'Are you still there, monk? Go away!'

Luke had the grace to look abashed. Even so he shouted back, 'I must speak to you, Sabine. Come down.'

'You can't afford for me to come down. Do you have silver? . . . No, I thought not!'

'I beg you. Look, I'm on my knees.' With that he knelt, all the while looking up at her.

'Don't you understand? I'm working!' The shutter slammed.

Luke got up and went across the alley to the

door of the house. Before the door-man could stop him he went inside.

The man laughed. 'How quick do you reckon he'll be?' And before anyone could reply he exclaimed, 'That didn't last long! Here he is now!'

Luke came tumbling out of the house in the grip of two thick-set men who dumped him out in the street, dusted off their hands, and returned inside.

A shutter opened a crack and Sabine stared down. 'And don't come back!' She sounded irate but something appeared in her hand and she threw it out to land at Luke's feet. He stepped forward to conceal it under the hem of his cloak. Further shouting ensued and then the shutter slammed again.

The door-man, distracted by the arrival of potential custom, did not see Luke quickly bend to pick up the item.

'Let's go. Talk later.' With that, scarcely waiting for the others, he made for the end of the lane where the old path led up to the abbey. They followed.

Away from the seething crowd, Luke said urgently, 'I knew there was a reason for that thread of gold. I just hope and pray I'm wrong. Wait until we get to the top then I'll show you.'

They set off briskly up the steep incline. It was extraordinarily quiet once the town was left behind. Drifts of snow hung precariously from the cliff face and frost glinted on the paving trods forcing Gregory, who was leading the way, to issue a warning about where to set their feet.

Concentrating on not slipping and breaking a limb, they trudged after him as he picked his way upwards into the darkness. Starlight was inadequate to light the way. They began to slow down, out of breath at the steep climb, confused by the winding of the path into deep shadow and out again, until suddenly a shout was heard from out of the blackness in front. It sounded as if Gregory had fallen. Next came the unexpected clash of steel. It was followed by Gregory's unmistakable warning to get back.

'Does he mean us?' Egbert pushed past Hildegard towards the sound.

Just then a couple of figures heavily swathed in cloaks and hoods swarmed out of the darkness below them. They kept coming on without a pause as if to mow them down.

Egbert swiveled, sword somehow in hand. Hildegard gaped. She had not known he had thought to arm himself. The lead figure reached out and tried to push her off the path so he could get to Egbert. Without thinking she lashed out, catching him by chance in the face.

She felt her fingernails snag down the length of his cheek to his jaw bone. He snarled something and lunged towards her. She side-stepped but he twisted quickly to catch hold of her wrist until he could grasp her round the neck. His face, up close to her own, visible as his hood slipped back, was fixed in a snarl of rage.

'Don't waste your time, nun. Out of my way!'

It was clear he had some more definite goal

in mind. Ahead, Gregory must have drawn a sword. Her attacker plunged up the path to the place where his confederate had been lying in ambush. In the confusion it was impossible to tell how many had followed them up from the town. Blows and shouts and the shudder of steel on armour plate came confusingly from different directions out of the darkness.

A pale shape loomed beside her to materialize as Luke. He gripped Hildegard by the arm. 'Leave them. They've got steel. Run for it!'

'No, Luke. I have a knife.' She drew out a long blade visible in the pale starlight. 'Gregory is up ahead. It sounds as if he's surrounded. Let's go to him.'

They could hear Egbert taunting his attackers and two lumbering shapes appeared above them, indistinct in the shadows. There was a flurry of movement, difficult to make out, then one of them pitched over the edge of the path to roll with a curse down the snow-covered cliff until he was halted in a dark clump of thorns.

On the path the fight continued, first Egbert emerging from out of the darkness then his assailant followed before he too went to join his companion down the cliff side. Egbert shouted to the full extent of his lungs and, further up, out of the blackness of the night, Gregory's answering shout was heard. He sounded hard-pressed.

Without hesitation Egbert flung himself towards the sound of battle with Hildegard at his heels.

Four figures in concealing cloaks were crouched

ahead, two above and two below with Gregory trapped between them. If he had been of a mind to escape, the cliff, sheer at this point, was not an option. He had no choice but to fight his way out.

Silhouetted against the night sky they saw him rise to his full height, lift his sword in both hands, then wait until one of his assailants made a move. The man sprang for Gregory's throat but the monk brought the haft hard down on to the bassinet of his attacker who groaned at the impact and slid off the path into the shadows. A second man approached.

Having the advantage of the higher slope, he launched himself on to the place where he must have seen a glint of Gregory's sword and the two of them locked and, still fighting, began to roll down the path, sliding almost to Egbert's feet. He bent and grabbed the man by the sword arm but he wrestled free. As Gregory regained his footing, Egbert stuck the point of his sword under the attacker's guard and twisted until he broke the sword loose from his grasp. A knife quickly appeared, dragged from the fellow's belt, and he slashed out to ward off Egbert's attempt to force him over the edge of the cliff.

Gregory, felled by another attacker's full weight as he lunged out of the shadows, rolled out of range of his whirling blade and from his position on the ground was able to smash the edge of his sword hard across the greaves the other man wore. It did no harm but it made him stumble and gave Gregory the chance to scramble to his feet and beat him back, thrust by thrust, until he too made his way down the cliff to join his companions. Any other assailants had reckoned up the odds and melted into the night.

'How many were there?' Out of breath, Egbert peered through the darkness.

'They're gone. But what did they want?' Gregory too was breathing hard.

'Cutpurses,' Egbert replied with asperity.

'Well armed for cutpurses,' Hildegard observed. She licked blood from the back of her hand.

All three stared intently down the side of the cliff to catch sight of any movement but, whether wounded or not, their opponents must have been making off in a definite silence towards the street.

'I recognized that fellow who came bumping up behind us.'

'How could you, Hildi? It's too dark to see your hand in front of your face.'

'His hood came off and he was close enough for every line to be visible. He was one of the abbey's hired men.'

'You mean you'd recognize him again?'

'Definitely. Especially as I gave him a good clawing down the side of his face.'

A muffled shout came to them. It was from somewhere off to the left where Luke had last been seen.

They all peered to where a dark shape was groveling about in a snow drift some way off the path.

'Is he wounded?' Egbert stepped to the edge to get a closer look. 'Want a hand?'

'No, I'm coming up now.'

In a moment he was standing beside them. He was shivering and his chattering teeth were audible. He began to brush the snow off himself. Hardly able to speak, he muttered, 'I know what they wanted. I threw it into the snow so they couldn't get their hands on it.' He patted something in his sleeve. 'Let's get back up to the abbey in case they come after us with reinforcements.'

The urgency in his voice sent them on at a brisk pace to the top without wasting time.

The refectory was in pitch darkness and they only found a candle and tinder after groping around in various niches. Bending their heads in the pool of light they inspected the object Luke now withdrew from his sleeve.

'Why, it's like the bursa the holy relic of St Hild is kept in!' Hildegard exclaimed.

It was an object of great beauty. The workmanship was the finest Opus Anglicanum. It had once been a precious and expensive piece of work made to the highest standards of the Guild of Broiderers. There could be no doubt that it had once belonged to an abbey or similar place. The only obvious faults to mar it were a slight discolouration of the red dye where it had evidently been left in strong sunlight for too long, and several loose strands of embroidered gold thread.

Opening it they found nothing much inside apart from some dried leaves and flower-heads and, mysteriously, a tooth.

'I'm glad none of us got killed for this.' Egbert looked on it with some disdain.

Hildegard took out the phial containing the gold thread and laid it in between the close threads of gold. It would have matched if any of them had been missing. She turned it over. Everything seemed intact, although it was roughened in places by too much handling. 'So this is what Sabine threw down to you. I wonder how she got hold of something like this?'

'She told me about it,' Luke explained. 'It was the one that covered the relic until the Abbot decided it did not do St Hild justice.'

'I expect Hertilpole also judged that the reliquary would look more impressive with a new one.'

Luke nodded in agreement. 'This one was acquired by Aelwyn but I know not how, some favour to the sacristan perhaps. The point is he gave it as a gift to Sabine. She was using it to contain a few keepsakes as you see: a flower Aelwyn had given her and the first milk tooth shed by Torold. And then you found that single give-away thread, Hildegard. I just thought, if I can persuade her to let me have it for a while so that we can see if the threads match, it would maybe help find the murderer.' He looked confused. 'I did not want to suspect her. And now I see there is no torn thread. We have no reason to believe she was in the apple store after all.' He looked as if he might shed tears of relief.

Hildegard gave the little bursa a careful appraisal, saying, 'You thought the thread we found might match?'

The bursa was passed from hand to hand until it reached Luke again.

'So how did you think a thread from it might have appeared in the apple store?'

'I asked her point-blank if she'd been up there. The reason is obvious, isn't it? No-one is above suspicion. This is something I noticed she always held close. When I asked if I might see it again she said it had disappeared the night her cottage was set on fire by Dickson's men.'

Gregory gave a sceptical shrug. 'Convenient.'

While the men talked Hildegard felt something snag on her fingernail. When she looked the smallest thread was torn and clinging to it.

'So one of them stole this thing,' Egbert was saying, 'and then they stole some novices' garments from the laundry, blocked the vents, chose some apples, barred the door to prevent Aelwyn from getting out, and then walked away?'

'And the bag finishes back with Sabine?' Gregory could not have looked more sceptical. 'If she had not thrown it down to you with every sign of being willing to do so, I would not believe her story. I would imagine it was she who had prevented Aelwyn's escape from the store and therefore done away with him. But as it is . . . she would have been taking a risk letting you get your hands on this.' He shrugged and looked thoughtful.

Hildegard held her tongue. It was a small thing she had discovered but its meaning might be momentous. She needed a better light before destroying Luke's dreams again.

'Why would anybody be carrying it when they went to the store?' Egbert was asking.

'To put apples in?' Hildegard turned to Luke. 'So how does she say she got it back?'

228

'I know not. You saw how it was. She would not speak to me. I was as surprised as anyone when she decided to throw it down. Have you thought she might be shielding someone, perhaps because she's afraid of retribution? You know how things are here.' He looked worried.

'If they only knew, they need have no fears,' remarked Egbert. 'We're as far from discovering who they are as we are from discovering what the moon is made of.'

To Hildegard it seemed like a deliberate gesture by Sabine to throw them off the scent. If it had been stolen on the night of the fire by one of Dickson's strong-arm louts, why should they believe he had returned it? A pang of conscience? That seemed unlikely. A thief and a mercenary would be more likely to sell it on to somebody for a profit.

Maybe Sabine, never having lost it in the first place, had thrown it down to Luke in an attempt to show she was innocent? Or maybe she really was frightened of retribution and Luke's worried face was justified?

She touched him on the arm. 'If I'm sure of anything, Luke, it's that Sabine can look after herself.'

It didn't mean she thought she was innocent.

Sister Aveline poked her head out of her adjoining chamber when she heard Hildegard in the corridor some time later after the men had left. 'A message for you. A young lad came looking for you but he said to tell you he would return.'

'Was it Torold?'

'Don't expect me to know the names of these wretches. It's not one of my obligations.'

Her door closed.

After debating the matter with herself for a while, Hildegard eventually pulled on her cloak once more to go outside. She found the contrast startling.

While they'd been discussing the bursa indoors, outside there had been a fresh fall of snow. The foregate lay in ghostly silence. Her boots crisped into it and left a trail of prints as she entered the cloister garth through the night gate. The monks were all abed by now and nothing disturbed the stillness of the night.

With a forgotten childish delight she made the first prints into the perfectly even snow on the garth and headed to the door that would lead through various passageways and courts into the infirmary. It must surely have been Torold who had come looking for her. She would quickly speak to him then go back to bed.

The door from the garth clicked shut behind her. Something about the delay in the sound was unexpected. She half-turned her head. There was nothing there.

The slype lay ahead. It was a narrow passage running between the separate buildings in the abbey. The cresset at the entrance had gone out. She set off into the darkness with a hand on the wall on each side to guide her.

Ahead lay the infirmary. It was visible at the end of the slype as a shadow hulked against the sky. Its sloping roof lay under a fresh blanket of snow.

Within, tended by Brother Dunstan and his assistants, would be the sick and old, tossing sleeplessly in private pain. With luck, Torold would still be busy if Brother Dunstan had made good his promise to keep the lad close in the early days of his grief.

With hands groping into the darkness, she stepped between the narrow walls and had almost reached the end when a definite sound behind her made her halt. This time she knew she had heard something. The uncanny silence that followed made the hairs on the back of her neck rise.

'Who's there?' she called.

There was no answer.

'I know there's someone there. Why don't you speak?' Anger made her voice sound overly loud and the echo bounced between the stone walls. There was still no response.

She held her breath and listened. A sound came with the stealth of a cautious footstep. Slowly a shape was beginning to emerge out of the darkness. Ghost-like, it was making its way towards her – not in silence now but with the steady tread of iron-shod boots as it came near.

She waited, scarcely breathing. It wasn't a monk then. It was more like . . . Was it a mercenary, one of the armed men used to frighten the fishermen?

Because it was so dark, with no window slit to allow in any light, she could not tell how close they were when they stopped. Enraged, she shouted, 'If you're not going to speak to me then back off!'

Turning, about to run out into the open, she felt something grasp her cloak, and drag her to a stop. She hit out to free herself but whoever it was holding on to it had a strong grasp and would not let go.

'Get off! Who are you?'

She had a sensation of body-heat as the unknown figure loomed over her. A wreak of ale was almost reassuringly human. It was not a wraith from the land of the dead. A silent struggle ensued as he grasped hold of her and tried to wrestle her to the ground. She grasped at leather, at gauntlets, at part of a hauberk, difficult to identify as they eluded her grasp.

A strip of linen was tied over the lower part of his face in the style of a mercenary and, still silent, he began trying to bundle her towards the end of the slype. She saw the glimmer of starlight and the blue waste of snow on the paving stones in the next yard.

Tumbling out into the open, she was almost glad to have been forced outside until she saw that the yard was enclosed by walls. It was a trap.

In a glimmer of light the figure gripped her round the neck.

With an angry dash, she ripped off the linen strip to reveal a face. It made her stiffen with dread.

Claw marks made a bloody track down one cheek as far as his jaw. Instantly it told her he was out for revenge.

He might have been thought handsome in a ruthless, aggressive, hard-mannered way except that his eyes were set too close together. Now they sparked with hatred.

One hand gripped her chin and turned her face up to what little light there was.

'I knew it was you on the cliff side earlier with those cloister creepers,' he ground out. 'Why waste your time with them?' He was breathing heavily. The sour stench of ale was stronger as he looked down into her face. 'What you need, nun, is a real man, not a monk.' His lips twisted in derision. 'What about it? I can do more for you than those two brothers-in-arms. Are they sodomites like all their kind?' He dragged her against his hard, muscular body. 'I can tell you, I'm not.'

She tried to draw back. 'Why did you attack us?' Her voice wavered as her thoughts speeded up. Where was her knife? Surreptitiously she felt for it in her sleeve but he was alert to her slightest movement.

'Is this what you're looking for, my lady?' With a sneer he brought up his left hand. In it the long blade of her own knife flashed close to her eyes.

'Are you going to blind me?' Her voice was under control now.

He registered the change. 'Not so, my lovely. I want you to witness every holy moment of our union. This'll be the first time I've had a nun.'

Without any other preliminary he was already reaching under his mail shirt to fumble at the buckle of his belt.

It was her only chance. Dashing a hand against the knife he was grasping she rammed one knee hard into his groin. In the moment before his head snapped forward and knowing that she must not waver, she wrenched her knife from out of his briefly weakened grasp and drove the hilt up under his chin, ramming his head back with all her strength. He gagged, recovered and jerked forward again, trapping her against the wall.

She gripped his hair in her free hand, pulling his head backwards, and as he broke free and plunged towards her she used his own momentum to yank him forward so she could side-step and smash him face-first into the stonework.

He sank to his knees.

Not waiting to watch him struggle to his feet, she ran as fast as she could to the far side of the little yard with the knife still miraculously in her grasp and only when she felt sufficiently far off did she dare swivel to face him again.

He was kneeling in a cursing heap at the foot of the wall and clutching his face, not going anywhere.

With a gasp of relief she pulled open the wall door and stepped into the adjoining passage.

Something soft and living was on the other side.

She screamed.

*In the forbidden precinct.*

A hooded monk in black took hold of her.

It was Hertilpole.

Apart from a sharp intake of breath he made no other sound at her sudden eruption from the yard but merely gripped her by both shoulders and thrust her against the wall.

'Let me go!' she gasped, astonished at his roughness.

Illuminated by the flickering flames from a wall sconce nearby, his face creaked into a smile before his lips twisted at a sudden thought. He asked, 'Have you come to see me? Is that it?'

She gaped at him.

'I've been expecting you,' he continued. 'But at night? No, I didn't expect this!'

'No, I . . .' Why would he imagine she would visit him?

He lowered his head so he could speak more intimately. 'Have you come to add something to that insulting offer for the relic? I'm very willing to discuss matters at greater length. I did not entirely expect you in the middle of the night, but if that is your choice and desire, I accept, most readily, my dear.'

Smiling with his terrible, humourless smile, he gripped her by both arms and began to push her rapidly along the corridor ahead of him until suddenly he thrust her backwards and there was nothing behind her and she was falling and realized it was a door that had opened into a candle-lit chamber and she was falling backwards, unable to help herself until she landed on a heap of something soft amid the unexpected scent of old vellum and parchment. She realized with astonishment that they were in the muniments room and she was lying on a pile of documents. She had hit them with sufficient force to knock the breath from her body.

Hertilpole was on top of her at once. He stifled her as he found her mouth and pressed lips like cold marble over it. He was pressing hungrily to urge a response.

For one vile moment the memory of her returning mercenary husband when he had lured her into the crypt of St Bartholomew's surged before her. The remembered horror of imminent rape by a man she had believed to be long dead gave her the strength to resist this new and shocking attack by a monastic now. This time there was no Rivera to save her as there had been then.

Calling on the power of an angelic host for strength, she fought to free her mouth from his lascivious searching and punched him about the face and head to his obvious astonishment.

'Be still!' he hissed. 'Make no noise!'

In the glowing light of a dozen candles she saw his eyes narrow with contempt at her resistance. At first he pretended it was due to excitement until he began to realize it was repugnance, a personal affront, a challenge to his authority and sense of entitlement. That a mere woman should resist him enraged him.

Sprawled under him she could scarcely move off the mound of documents, the writs, the affidavits, the leases and cartularies, the lists of tolls and fines and ancient obligations recorded in the archives, and when he gripped her face between wiry fingers so that he could force open her mouth she gagged as he inserted his tongue between her lips.

Revolting as it felt, she had no choice but to clamp her teeth together and bite as hard as she could. He roared with pain and flinched back. She saw him raise a fist in fury.

The brief pause gave her time to wriggle from under him. His fist pounded into the pile of vellum, missing her by inches. Crawling over the mound of documents, she hurled herself on her knees towards the open door but he followed with a shout of rage, dragging her back by her skirts and with a handful of fabric in his grasp began to haul her back into the chamber. He was surprisingly strong.

During the intense struggle that followed he knocked against the candelabra with its rich complement of beeswax candles and as it swayed hot wax fell on the documents underneath. The candelabra fell, setting alight the dry pages they were lying on. There was a flash and a sheet of flame engulfed the chamber. It gave Hildegard time to scramble from his grasp and drag herself into the corridor.

The narrow vaulted passage yawned in both directions. First she tried one way, plunging into the darkness, her gasping panic taking over but then, after a backward glance noticing a line of light under a far door, she fled towards it as recklessly as a moth to a flame.

# Sixteen

Divided by wooden partitions were rows of beds on both sides of the chamber, visible in the half-light between the arches. Brother Dunstan was at the far end talking to a lay brother. Both started back in alarm as Hildegard burst inside.

'Fire!' she croaked. 'In the muniments room. Brother Hertilpole . . .!'

The chamber swam away from her until she managed to hold on to consciousness long enough to repeat the alarm. Then she sank to the floor.

As if from a great distance she heard Brother Dunstan order a couple of his assistants to get to the muniments room at once.

She felt him take her by the arm as everything swam back. 'Be seated, domina.' His kindly old face showed concern. 'What has happened?'

'Attacked . . .' she muttered, then broke off. She would not be believed if she accused the lord bursar, Peter Hertilpole, of trying to rape her. 'One of the abbey guard – did not see who – but the fire!' she repeated.

'Worry not, domina. Those assistants of mine will see to it. Did a candle topple over?'

'Much worse – the candelabra . . .'

He looked thoughtful. 'You mean in the muniments room? I wonder what took you there? Only the lord bursar and his clerk enter therein.' He patted her arm. 'No matter. You can explain later in your own good time. Let me get you something to assuage your shock.'

He padded down the chamber to the far end where a small brazier, enough for the cures and hot water needed by the patients, was burning brightly on its tripod.

When he returned he handed her a steaming liquid, which he persuaded her to sip. He surveyed her with a thoughtful look. 'I see your habit is somewhat torn.' Leaning closer he asked, 'Is this to do with Edred?'

'I don't know . . .' Was it? In the chaos of her thoughts she could not say for certain. Everything had happened so quickly and unexpectedly. The hired guard appearing out of nowhere, then falling into Hertilpole's clutches as she sought safety. 'I don't know,' she repeated.

Brother Dunstan's concern darkened. 'If it is to do with Edred then I am responsible.' He put his head on one side. 'I had no idea I was putting either of you in danger. No inkling that it might go much deeper than . . .' Detecting her alarm he put out a hand to reassure her. 'You're safe here, domina. I'll make sure of that.'

'Is Torold about?' she managed to ask. 'I believe he tried to find me at the guest house with a message.'

Dunstan got up, went to a partition near the door and poked his head round. In a moment Torold appeared looking puzzled. 'No, domina. I didn't come. Should I have?'

'It's only that someone of your description wanted to speak to me. I know now who it might have been.' It would be the kennel lad, Miggy. *I must go up there*, she thought in some fear. What did he want to tell her? Was it urgent? What if he had put himself in danger by appearing at the guest house? She had to see him.

She rose unsteadily to her feet. 'I must go.' The thought of the long, lonely walk up to the isolated farmhouse was terrifying, but she had to do it.

239

Dunstan protested. 'Take a moment to rest, domina. What is it to make you leave here in the middle of the night? Rest awhile. There's a spare bed reserved for guests—'

'It's someone . . .' Remembering the way one of the patients had been sitting up in bed listening to everything that was said last time she was here, she allowed the rest of her explanation to trail away. 'Trust me, brother. It is necessary. Another life may be at stake.'

A racket in the passage leading to the muniments room made Dunstan hurry out to see what was going on.

Torold walked with her towards the main door opening on to the garth. 'It's dark out there, domina. Shall I come with you?'

'Better not, Torold, although I thank you for your offer. You'll be safer inside with Brother Dunstan. He may need help when they bring Bursar Hertilpole in.'

'Him? I wouldn't help him if he was the last man on earth and I know I'm damned for saying it but I don't care!'

Gently she pushed him back inside. 'Go, stay out of trouble.'


The cold was as sharp as a knife. It took her breath away and she knew now why the mercenary had wound a scarf round his face. He must have followed them up the cliff path in the freezing wind after the failed ambush.

Pulling her own hood tight and tucking it into the neck of her cloak, she gave a thought to Gregory and Egbert. If she knew where they were she would ask them to come with her but she would never be able to get inside the dortoir to find them without causing a scene and having to make up some excuse for her bizarre encroachment into the monks' private sleeping quarters.

She set off, taking long strides that might at a glance fool anyone watching with malevolent intent into believing she was a figure to be reckoned with.

*The headland.*

It was the effect of night with its looming shadows as she passed beside the high north wall of the abbey church, the sudden screech of a disturbed sea bird, the sense she tried to ignore of someone following her, that made her quicken her pace up the headland. Icy fingers seemed to crawl up her spine.

The night was moonless. Ahead lay, she knew, but could not see, the distant humped shape of the outer buildings with the monks' graveyard beyond it, stretching away to the brow of the cliff. There was a long fall from the heights. And then the sea. And the haunting sound of the regular ebb and flow of the surf on the rocks.

Lower down the headland, cupped in shadow, lay the sinuous shape of the fish pond where Edred's body had been found under its carapace of snow.

By now the constant scourge of the wind had swept most of the snow away, leaving only drifts

241

lying like living creatures in the night. One of them seemed to move towards her but she could not say what was real and what was imagination and the doubt kept her away from the mounds as she began to run.

*There really is something behind me*, she thought, a few moments later, increasing her pace. Something. A ghost? Or someone?

She thought she heard panting and when she stopped there was a skittering of stones as the thing stopped too. A hurried, alarmed glance back down between the snow mounds showed no movement. Inhuman stillness prevailed.

The silhouette of the abbey loomed behind her, massive against the night sky. Behind that was the town, a few far lights on the other side of the estuary. Nothing.

A breath, delicate as air, like someone trying to make no noise, then a clammy sense of the blackness folding in on itself, taking form and coming towards her – a hand, touching hers.

Almost fainting, she jerked away, but before the scream rose in her throat came a whisper.

'Domina . . . Walk on as if you haven't seen him. I have a sharp stone in my hand.'

Another whisper, incredulous. Her own reply. 'Is that you, Torold?'

'Forgive me for disobeying. I saw him leave after you.'

'So let's walk on. Come.' Strangely reassured by Torold's sharp stone and, when she came to think about it, her own knife, she stepped boldly on up the track.

A light shone in one of the windows of the

farmhouse. In a few moments they were in the yard; nobody had followed them in and Hildegard was knocking softly on the shutter.

It opened a crack.

She breathed again. 'Where will I find Miggy?'

'Here, I'll get him.'

A scuffle and a few whispers followed, then the pale oval of the kennel lad's face appeared in the space between the slats. 'What?'

'It's Hildegard. Did you come down earlier to tell me something?'

'Yes. Wait there if you will.' The slats clapped shut.

Hildegard glanced down at Torold. 'Did you really see someone follow me?'

'Yes. Some fellow in a cloak. He came out as far as the fork in the path, took a few paces along it, then seemed to melt away.' He glanced hurriedly over his shoulder. 'I can feel it. He's still out there.'

'You must have overtaken him?'

'I floated like a wraith and he would not see me. I've had long practice.'

The farmhouse door creaked slightly as it was opened. A hand beckoned. When they entered they had to fumble round a few obstacles in the dark until they found themselves in a lobby and a large hound was inspecting them, sniffing, licking, pushing its big, brute body against them with Miggy whispering for the animal to hold its noise.

A voice from the depths of the house called, 'Shut 'im up, Mig. Take him outside.'

'I am.' And in a different tone he hissed at

243

Hildegard, 'Listen, who's this? I didn't reckon on having an audience.'

'I'm Torold.'

'I know that. You're that abbey lad born in sin with the monk father—'

'Say one more word and you'll get this.' A movement in the darkness suggested a bunched fist.

'I've never had a dad, let alone a monk dad. Not got a mam now neither. So what? Are you going to push my face in for that?'

'Come now, boys—'

'I didn't mean it.' Torold sounded shame-faced. 'I've had enough of them, saying stuff.'

'No offence taken. I get the same thing. I want to tell her about what else I saw that night they done in Master Edred.'

'Quickly,' she invited.

'I couldn't work it out at the time. It was so frail, like a dream, almost as if it hadn't happened. I couldn't tell you with all that lot jeering about ghosts. He threw something into the pond. One of them did. I suppose it was one. I heard the splash. It might have been a bird or a fish but it was more of a splash than either of them might make. I was trying to work out how many of them were there at the time and didn't take enough notice till after when I began to think.'

'You said two—'

'Yes, but after. I saw it as two walking away in step, looking like one, bunched up, like. And because there had been two. But it wasn't two. It was one, by himself.'

'And you heard one splash?'

'Yes.'

It must have been the sound of Edred falling into the water. But she was puzzled. He said the man had thrown something.

'What makes you say he threw something? Did you see what it was?'

'No, it was too dark. I saw his arm go over. And it was a howling wind as well but you know how the wind suddenly drops for a bit and you can hear other things, sharp, like? It was like that. Howling, then in the silence this short, hard splash. And then the wind again. And the snow rattling and drowning everything else out.'

It must have been the weapon they had used against Edred. If it was a stone and even if they looked for it, it would be no help. She felt Miggy regarding her attentively through the meagre light.

'That's really useful to know,' she assured him.

'You're being like a nun should be, kind, not wanting to hurt my feelings. I can tell you don't think much of it.'

'It's not that. It's just that it's difficult to tell one stone from another.'

'And if it wasn't a stone but something else?'

'Then it would be different, depending on what it was.'

He turned to the hound. 'Come, Duke, come.' He went to the door. 'You as well.' He included both of them.

Groping around in the darkness again they found their way outside. Miggy closed the door without a sound so as not to wake anybody and

245

led the way to the kennel yard. With as much familiarity as if he could see in the dark he went to one of the cages and, ignoring the hounds inside, fumbled about under some straw until he found what he wanted.

When he lifted it out he held it so Hildegard could see it.

She stared in astonishment.

'A dagger?'

'Summat like.'

She reached out for it.

It was a heavy, workmanlike iron weapon, not one of the fancy, tooled ones that men often wore in order to display their wealth. This was heavy iron, plain and businesslike.

She ran her fingers along the haft. 'There seems to be something embossed on the end of the cross hilt.'

'I couldn't make it out. You'll be better looking at it in daylight.'

'May I take it?'

'Aye, so long as you remember finders keepers. I had to get wet to fish that out.'

Alarmed, she asked, 'Did anybody see you?'

'I'm not daft. I took a fishing net and pretended to be dredging for fish.'

'I'm sorry I doubted the usefulness of your story, Miggy.'

'That's all right. I wouldn't have believed me myself unless I'd been there.'

They made their way back towards the farmhouse.

Torold hung on Hildegard's arm. 'That fellow's still out there. I can feel him watching.'

Miggy whispered, 'Who is it?'

'We don't know.'

'He followed me and Torold saw him and bravely came after to warn me.'

Miggy chuckled. 'Whoever he is, he must be up to no good to be out here at this time of night. It'll be Matins soon and if he's a monk and outside his cloister, he'll be in for it. Let's have a bit of fun.'

Before either she or Torold could guess what he was planning Miggy whistled to the hound, who came loping away from whatever he had found and waited for his master's orders. It was a lymer, valued for its skill in hunting in silence. Now Miggy whispered, 'Go find, Duke, go find!'

With a silent bound Duke disappeared into the night.

A moment later a yell resounded from some yards away. A man's voice, shouting and cursing, could be heard as he tried to free himself from the jaws of the hound. Miggy doubled up. 'What shall I tell him? To bring him in or let him go?'

'Let him go for now.' Hildegard peered into the night. It was best not to show their hand without something to link the night wanderer with the murderer if it turned out that there was a link.

The boy whistled again and Duke reappeared with a strip of cloth in his teeth. Someone crashing down the path below where they were standing told them that the follower was making good his escape.

'Now all we have to do is find out who has a ripped cloak!' Miggy chortled. 'I hope I'll see his face when it's matched up!'

Proud of the skill of his charge, he wanted to show more. 'I'll let him chase him as far as he can run. Give him some exercise. Go, Duke. Seek!'

Torold had been silent while this was going on. Now he said, 'If the devil who murdered my poor father is the same one who murdered Master Edred, he might even be this creeping fellow, skulking in the night looking to murder the domina. I think it's well done to give him a fright. Maybe we should follow to find out who it is.'

The pursuer, Duke the hound, was silent, and the pursued, whoever he was, tried to be silent, but they could hear his boots slipping on the trods and sending small stones scattering down the hillside. He must have been wearing black. Except when he ran across the white heaps of snow he was invisible. Then he became a mere wraith as insubstantial as a shadow.

Hildegard was convinced it was her assailant in the slype, although he did not seem to be wearing steel on his boots. Nor was there any sound of his chain mail as he ran.

*It can't be anyone else*, she was thinking as they all three followed briskly from a sufficient distance to hear where he was going. *It can't be Hertilpole, can it?* How severe was the fire in the muniments room? It had flared up and she had caught a glimpse of the bursar's hood on fire, and then she had fled in fear. It might be best to apprehend him after all.

A moment later Duke appeared in front of

them. He ran to Miggy. By now they were at the abbey church wall. The lymer began questing back and forth, sniffing out the man's scent and now and then sitting on his haunches in disappointment in front of a side door in the north transept. He began to scratch at it.

'He's gone inside. It must have been one of the monks out of his cloister. Does that mean one of them is a murderer?' Miggy asked in wonder.

Torold pulled his hood up. 'You can't go inside, domina. I'll go.' Before she could stop him he had slipped through the door, leaving Duke, after trying to push his muzzle in, to prowl back to his master when the door closed in his face.

'We'll wait. What a good thing you have such a well-trained hound,' Hildegard remarked. 'It's a strange thing, but I used to own a lymer called Duchess. She got me out of many a dangerous situation. I miss her. But she died long ago from old age.'

'Maybe you should get another one, domina. There's nowt like them. I can go anywhere with Duke beside me. It's what Brother Aelwyn should have had, though I can't say that now in front of Torold. And Master Edred, come to that, a lymer might have saved him, though he was too much for dashing about to take time over a hound.'

'I'm told he used to fly a hawk up by the fish pond,' she mentioned, wondering how long Torold would be and what he would find.

'That's right, but they looked after it for him in the mews. He only came out when he felt like it. He should've taken her with him that night. Let her take out that murdering devil's eyes!'

'What did he fly?'

'A peregrine, but he'd fly all sorts. Anything he could carry on his wrist.'

'Have you ever seen him with a popinjay?'

'One of them parrot birds? I can't say I have. There's a mummer in the town with one. They say it speaks Latin better than the abbot!'

'Is he a mummer? I thought he was a Flanders priest?'

'No, he's a mummer with the lord Percy's troupe. He just pretends to be a priest.'

'Have you seen him up here?'

'I might have.' He paused, then told her, 'Them mummers come up here yesterday to see how high the cliff is and were planning to climb down it. Put on a show, like. With wings and that. But they couldn't agree on how to do it. Or where the audience would stand. Then there was something about gulls' eggs and letting the little fellow down in a basket, but he didn't like that idea and there was a lot of talk about it not being worth their while after all.'

'Which mummers were they?'

'The usual lot. That lad on the stilts for one—'

'Lad?'

'Aye, the one with the flaxen wig that knocks around with them minstrels and the rest of 'em, the lord Percy's lot.'

'Are they up at the earl's stronghold usually?'

'Somewhere like. On the move from one end of the county to t'other. Not bad if you like that

sort of thing. I prefer my little nest and Dukey.'
He fondled the lymer's ears and bent down to
kiss him.

The side door opened and Torold slid out
without a sound. 'The brothers are filing in for
Matins. I couldn't see anybody with torn clothes.
There was only the sacristan and his assistant
going round lighting candles when I first went
in. I went up to them and said, has somebody
just come inside? And they said yes but we
don't know who because he had his hood up it
being so cold tonight, but he's gone now. Which
way did he go? I asked and the sacristan accused
me of being a gossip and why did I want to
know? So I told him a bit of a lie and said he
dropped something and I thought to give it back
to him. And he said, he went out through the
south side but I daren't follow because that's
the monks' privy chambers over there and I'm
forbidden to set foot.' He scowled. 'Sorry about
the lie, domina.'

'That's to the good, Torold. You've both helped
me more than you can know. I think now it's
time for you both to go back.'

'Will you come back to the infirmary with me?'

'Yes, why not.' No doubt he would want her to
excuse his absence to Brother Dunstan.

'I'll be off, myself. Not much chance of catching
a glimpse of St Hild's ghost floating down the
nave with that lot chanting!' Chuckling, Miggy
plunged off up the incline with Duke at his side
without another word.

'That hound is nearly as big as he is.' Torold
seemed to look longingly after them both and

Hildegard asked, 'Would you like a hound of some sort?'

'I'm more a herb man myself. Brother Dunstan wants to train me up – whether I'm a child of sin or not,' he added.

# Seventeen

A scene of confusion met them as soon as they stepped back inside the infirmary. Through it all the old fellows in their beds slept on.

Not so Brother Dunstan and his assistants. There was no sleeping for them. Two of the tougher lay brothers were helping Hertilpole pace across the floor. He was groaning and shaking his head from side to side as if to rid himself of a swarm of bees.

It was unclear what they were hoping to do but the bursar resisted them, pulling away and tearing at his habit then clutching their arms as if they could protect him from something, all the while groaning and crying and bellowing, *mea culpa, mea culpa.* Dunstan himself was trying to persuade him to drink from a medicine cup. There was a strong smell of chamomile. Several others were rapidly making up a bed and another was mixing something over the brazier.

Hertilpole was forced on to the bed where his charred habit was stripped down to his waist amid violent protests. He was expertly turned on to his stomach and the extent of his burns became visible. It was not as bad as Hildegard had expected. His tonsure had been burned to reveal a red scorch mark up the back of his neck, but the thickness of the fabric seemed to have protected him from the worst of the flames.

An assistant approached carrying a bowl of liquid honey. While the strapping young men held him still, the assistant dipped a strip of cloth into the honey then transferred it to the back of Hertilpole's neck and held it there like a poultice. His struggles began to subside. Now it could be heard that he was muttering something again over and over. It sounded like a prayer of contrition.

Dunstan noticed Hildegard and Torold standing agape by the doors. He came over.

'His burn is not serious. It took us a while to persuade him to leave the chamber. He would not come out. Once the fire was doused by my boys he seemed to feel he should stay there. The burn will cause some discomfort but from what he is saying, that is the least of his concerns.'

His expression was ambiguous when he reached forward and touched the tear on Hildegard's sleeve. 'Easily fixed, domina. I'll get somebody to do it for you. Now, why not stay the rest of the night in our guest chamber? That's what it's there for. It's now Matins. You can get several hours' sleep before Lauds. Tomorrow will be a day of revelations. We must brace ourselves.'

He beckoned one of the lay brothers. 'Provide the domina with what she needs in the guest chamber and a drink of something warming, if you will. Young master Torold will assist me. Come, lad. Let me show you how we treat burns.'

Revelations? Hildegard could not sleep. The last thing she wanted was for her humiliation at the hands of Hertilpole to be whispered about the abbey. It would be a matter of controversy and she knew she herself would not escape criticism. The questions were all too easily imagined: *What was she doing in the bursar's privy chamber at midnight? . . . How she must have led him on . . . playing the temptress Eve . . . What did she expect? . . . She must have been asking for it.*

What about Hertilpole himself? What was his defence to be? She doubted whether he would admit responsibility for his own heinous actions when he recovered from his punishment by fire.

Later the turmoil resolved itself into one stark fear: that Abbot de Courcy – Hubert – would perhaps hear the rumours before she could return to Meaux. What would he think of her then? Would he believe that his trust in her redemption was a mistake after all? Might he even go so far as to carry out his threat to excommunicate her?

The latter seemed like nothing compared to her shame that he might feel she had betrayed him again. She cringed with the injustice of such a possible outcome. Meanwhile she was helpless, caught in the middle of events not of her own choosing, trapped until a resolution could be found.

Tossing and turning, she could bear it no longer. She got up, pulled on her boots, laced them, then went soft-footed to the door. Slipping out into the vaulted chamber beyond, she could see by the light of a candle at the far end Dunstan's peacefully sleeping face.

He was sitting bolt upright in a chair as if he had meant to keep watch over his patients but now, overcome by sleep, he only moved his head a little at the sound of the great doors being opened. The frosty air swept in as she stepped outside. Snow was thick on the ground.

In her own chamber she opened her saddle bag and checked that the locked pouch had been undisturbed. Then, at last, she fell asleep.

'You look exhausted, Hildegard. Bad night?'

'For sure Master Dickson would not approve of me!'

'Come now. Has something happened?'

'Gregory, you could prise secrets from a stone.'

'Then let's get out of the garth and allow the smug participants at the Office of Lauds have the place to themselves while I prise more from you.' As they set off, he murmured, 'Not that I mean you're a stone. But I know how well you can keep a secret. Remember, you're among friends. We're your designated guards as much as your warders. Hubert was insistent we keep you safe.'

Blushing at the thought that she had been discussed between them she accompanied him as far as their corner in the cloister then asked, 'May I crave your help?'

'You know you can.'

'Will you accompany me through the slype that leads to the back of the infirmary?'

Without asking questions, he led the way. Egbert and Luke joined them.

All four walked slowly between the walls of the narrow passageway and waited for her to explain.

In daylight it did not look sinister in any way. When they reached the small yard further on, she held up her hand. 'Wait. Where are the abbey guards quartered?'

'Over by the stable yard.'

'So why would one of them be here?'

'They should not be. They would have no business here, unless one of them was summoned.'

'One of them was here in the night. It was one of those who lay in ambush for us on the cliffs.'

'Did he see you?'

'Yes.'

'Did he explain himself?'

She bit her lip.

'Come! What did he say?'

'What, indeed? A nun alone, near midnight, a man who kills for pay? What do you think he said?'

Gregory took her arm. 'And?'

'I gave him a bashing to remember, thanks to your instruction in unarmed combat.'

Gregory squeezed her arm. 'Good. But say on . . . I can tell there's more.'

'I escaped him – but ran, quite literally, into Hertilpole through that door over there.' She pointed. When Gregory started towards it to fling it open she restrained him. 'No, I'll tell you what happened next. He dragged me into the muniments room and there managed to set fire to himself!' At their smiles she said, 'He's in the infirmary, recovering. I need to know what he's going to say about the matter. Luke, I have nothing to confess that others may not hear. But if Hubert should get hold of a rumour that I was—'

'There's already a rumour – it almost takes my breath away, so scandalous is it.'

'Already?' Her glance flew from one to the other.

'Rest easy. Your name was not mentioned. Only Hertilpole's. He'll be the one to do penance unless he has a good story everyone can bring themselves to believe.'

'Tell me what they're saying, will you?'

'The gold! The treasure he accused Edred of stealing . . . it's been found!'

'What?' She was puzzled by his elation and cautiously relieved.

'It was found, Hildegard, in the muniments room in a chest hidden carelessly behind a chair. What it means is that Edred did not steal it! It means that Hertilpole – the bursar – must have known all along where it was hidden. That it was not stolen at all!'

'It was a fit-up! I knew it!' Egbert punched one fist into his palm.

'What I don't understand is how it came to light.' Gregory looked puzzled.

'I'll explain. Some lay brothers found it when they were putting out the fire. They had to move everything about to stop the fire spreading – and there it was!'

'So it was revealed because of Hertilpole's lust!' Hildegard exclaimed. 'When he dragged me into that place and . . . tried to . . . and I pushed him off, he knocked over the candelabra and set himself on fire—'

Gregory was laughing with astonishment. 'He did what?'

Egbert slapped him on the back. 'God works in mysterious ways, brother. We have always known it.'

Luke interrupted. 'I heard something else. That he believes an avenging angel with a flaming sword swooped down from heaven to punish him for some sin he committed. My informant could not tell me what the sin was, so I assume we were intended to believe it was covetousness.'

'It's over. Worry not, Hildegard. Brother Luke is keeping notes. He'll inform Hubert of the truth if he should be misinformed by anybody else.' Hildegard closed her eyes and gave a long sigh of relief. Hubert's opinion was worth more than anything that might befall her. It was all in all to her. 'But now let me show you what I retrieved from the adventures of the night.' Making sure they were not observed, she opened her scrip once more and took out the dagger, telling them how young Miggy had retrieved it from the pond.

In daylight it was even more rough-hewn than she had imagined. It weighed heavily in her hand and the haft was worked roughly like an apprentice piece. She rubbed the embossed end and peered at it for the first time.

Handing it to Gregory, she mentioned how it had come into her possession.

Egbert put out his hand. He moved it experimentally, commenting as he handed it to Luke that it was an ill piece of work and unfit as a dagger for anyone – although its use as a club was not in doubt.

'Look at the blade.' He ran a finger along it. 'Too blunt to cut butter. I don't believe this is meant to be used as a dagger at all.'

'What's this little emblem?' Luke asked. 'It looks familiar.'

'It should do.' Hildegard watched them all in turn.

Gregory took hold of it again for a closer look. 'It's the seal for Whitby Abbey! Look, Egbert.'

The dagger – or seal – or whatever it was – was passed from hand to hand. Hildegard mentioned Miggy's version of what had happened that night and it was superfluous to add the obvious conclusion.

'Someone here in the abbey – but not just someone, not a mere monk, but an obedientiary with access to the abbot's seal . . .?'

'Unless, of course, it was stolen.' Gregory as always looked for alternatives to any theory.

While the others were pondering the implications she reached inside her scrip once again. 'And then this, a gift from Miggy's lymer, Duke.' Again she outlined what had happened and how it had come into her keeping.

'That kennel lad is wasted. He should be helping the sheriff track down felons in York.' Egbert rubbed the scrap of cloth between finger and thumb. 'It's what the monks wear here. Hard-wearing stuff for the climate.'

'So now we search for a torn habit or cloak. Or, more easily, a needle in a hay-cock.' Gregory took a closer look. 'From what you've been telling us, Hildi, I would want to have a look at Hertilpole's cloak and ask him why he was meeting a mercenary in the dead of night. But since he was in the infirmary while the hound was doing its duty he seems to have the perfect alibi.' He frowned. 'We shall be like lymers ourselves and hunt on in silence. Come, brothers, we're in to Prime soon. Eyes sharpened.' He glanced at Hildegard. 'No wonder you look tired. What a night! Why not get some rest and meet us when we're set free again with news of our findings?'

She replaced the piece of cloth and the dagger that was really a seal in her scrip. They lay alongside the phial containing the gold thread from an unidentified source. 'One at least must lead us to the murderer of Edred. From there to Brother Aelwyn?'

'And from there to a motive for such evil,' concluded Gregory.

# Eighteen

Hildegard had no intention of going back to bed, not when everything was coming together: the seal used as a weapon, the torn fabric from the garment of a prowler in the night, and the gold thread found at the scene of the first murder. Not to mention the remark Miggy had made about the man with the popinjay. What was the truth? Was he a player or an ex-priest? What had he to do with events at the abbey?

As soon as she left the others to go into Prime she made her way down the cliff path beside the parish church into the town. It would have been quicker to walk down the monks' trod to the bottom of Grope Lane, but the memory of last night's ambush was still too raw to make her want to risk that way. Although it was daylight the path would be isolated, best avoided.

The sun was still low on the horizon and just beginning to seep from behind the frosty haze over the estuary. It made everything close by stand out sharply against the snow.

Below the cliff the thatched-roof dwellings could be seen, small and perfect, like a drawing on glass. From that direction came the faint shouts of traders opening their premises for another day's trade, the sound of carts carrying produce from the fields thundering over the cobblestones, the barking of dogs, the random cries of children – a normal day.

Even as she slithered down the slope the sky was turning to a shade of blue above the headland that might have reminded Luke of Sabine's eyes.

What was the woman's role in all this? Had she tired of Aelwyn? Did she want him out of the way? Was she as grief-stricken as Luke believed?

There was only one way to find out.

As Hildegard reached the street she noticed signs of last night's revelry. The Twelve Days, or more accurately, the Twelve Nights, were almost over. Soon it would be Epiphany and, as it had been decreed in the courts of heaven, it was also King Richard's birthday.

His grief must outstrip anything most people would ever experience. Elder brother: dead; father: dead; beloved mother: dead; the Smithfield rebels hanged without trial. And then in the last twelve months his surrogate father, Burley: cruelly executed without a legal trial; thirteen of his closest allies bloodily executed likewise. And he, the king, the once beautiful boy, still only in his twenty-second year.

How would he withstand the horror in such isolation? Would he go mad and rave impotently in his palace, or sink into a melancholy as some predicted? Or would he set out on a murderous trail of his own?

It was the custom of kings to seek revenge against their enemies. The bloodiest revengers acquired an astonishing respect from the Chroniclers. Barbarity did not fit with this most pacific and cultured of monarchs. It did not seem in his nature to root out his enemies with any kind of ruthlessness. While admiring him, Hildegard also feared for him. He must be living in constant fear of a knife in the back. How could he survive the treachery of the court as long as his uncle Woodstock, the Duke of Gloucester, lived?

Troubled by the large scale of the ills and

dangers of the world, she reached Master Selby's house and knocked loudly on the door.

A ground-floor window inched open and a fellow in a nightshirt poked his head out. 'Oh, it's you again. Where are your friends this morning? Sleeping off the abbot's wine?'

'Probably. You know what men are like. Drunkards and willy-wavers all. May I speak to Sabine?'

'She'll be asleep after last night.'

A window above their heads flew open. 'No, I'm not. That damned rooster woke me. Who is it?'

'Hildegard of Meaux.'

'Send her up.'

'Bloody nun,' grumbled the door-man. He vanished from the window and in a moment appeared in the doorway wrapped in a blanket. 'Go on up, then.' He stumbled sleepily back into his chamber and allowed Hildegard to find her own way. Sabine was peering through a crack in the door on the first landing when she reached the top.

'What's happened? Is it to do with that Brother Luke? I hope he hasn't sent you to plead his cause. What does he think *I'm* going to do?'

'May I come in?'

In answer Sabine stepped back but as soon as Hildegard entered, she said, 'I'm not listening. He can go and—'

'It's not on behalf of him I'm here. It's to do with Aelwyn.'

Sabine froze. 'What?' Her face turned to stone.

'He seems to have treated you well. A kind

man, I would think. He fulfilled his obligations over Torold. You have a son you can be proud of.'

She gripped Hildegard by the arm. 'Is Torold all right? Has something happened to him? Is that why you've come? Is he hurt? Tell me what's happened—'

'Stay calm. It's not him. Nothing has befallen him. He's quite safe.'

Sabine threw herself down on the rumpled bed and dragged a blanket over her nightgown. 'Go on then, what?'

She picked up a length of nettle, ripped off the leaves and began to split the stem as if it was all that mattered.

'May I sit?'

'Do what you like.' The blazing blue eyes that had so broken Luke's heart were like chips of ice now she knew her son was safe.

Hildegard returned her glance. 'I understand that it was an embroidered bursa you threw down to Brother Luke last night?'

'So?'

'He's puzzled. Why would you do that?'

'Has he talked to you?'

'Yes, he has.'

She focused on linking the nettle stems into twine as if there was nothing more interesting. 'I suppose he would tell you everything. Thick as thieves, aren't you, your lot?' She lifted her head.

'And your lot?'

Sabine gave a hollow laugh. 'Who are my lot? The fellows that come tramping up the stairs every night for what they can get? Or Selby and Dickson for what they can make out of me?'

'And are they your lot?'

'What do you think?'

'I think you're able to find a better lot than any of them . . . if you want to.'

Sabine rubbed a hand over the eyes that seemed to cause most of her problems and Hildegard felt a twinge of sorrow for her. Maybe she was not as hard and manipulative as she had first seemed. Although, she reminded herself, this act now could also be part of her manipulative nature. Maybe she could not help herself.

She gave no answer now but continued to stare stonily at Hildegard in open challenge.

'I'm fond of Luke,' Hildegard admitted. 'He's very young. He was given to the abbey before he really knew what life was about. He has no knowledge of women, no defence against us. You've turned his life upside down. But he wants to do the best for you, whatever that might be.'

'The first thing is he can stop pretending he can help. It puts their backs up, Selby that is, and his wife. They think I'm passing information to him.'

'About what?'

'Them.'

'Why should that bother them?'

'They have too many secrets.' She gave a scathing laugh and picked up the twine again. 'Open secrets, most of them. The fools. As if the whole town doesn't know what's what. It's just that nobody can do anything about it . . . unless they want to finish up dead, like Aelwyn and Edred. You want to warn Luke if you like him so much.'

265

'Is it this cartel of Dickson's?' she asked.

The blue eyes flashed over her. 'How do you know . . .?'

'You said it was an open secret. It's so open Dickson himself was boasting about it to us, although I imagine his purpose was to impress on us how powerful he is locally and to warn us off in case we had a mind to interfere.'

'He would do that. Even monastics can be put out of the way, as you've seen. It wouldn't bother him. He has no fear of hellfire.'

'So Dickson is behind all this?'

'He had a nice deal going with the abbey through Aelwyn . . .'

'So what went wrong?'

'He and Edred got sick of the way the fishermen are being treated. They'd been talking to that Lollard fellow.' She hesitated and then decided to take a risk. 'And you know about the others?'

'The others?'

'The opposition that was beginning to form – since the Lent executions in Westminster?'

'I was appalled by that, as were we all. It was brutal. An obvious way of isolating the King. What about these others?'

Sabine changed tack as if she regretted touching on something too dangerous to mention. 'I was talking to that disgraced priest, the one with the popinjay . . .' She waited as if for a sign of some sort.

'I understand he's no priest but one of Lord Percy's mummers.'

Sabine breathed a sigh of relief. 'I didn't tell

you that. So you'll know what they feel about the executions?'

'I imagine they're angered enough to consider revenge.'

Sabine lowered her voice. 'Aelwyn too. That's why . . .' She bit her lip and if the tears that suddenly made her eyes seem larger still were fake, she was worthy to join the mummers herself as she whispered, 'Someone had to get rid of him. I don't know who's behind it. He had enemies in the abbey because of – well, because of me. The canker in the rose, someone called him. But to me . . . he was the rose itself . . .'

Making a shot in the dark Hildegard remarked, 'But the red rose continues to threaten the white?'

Eyes never leaving Hildegard's, Sabine nodded. 'He knew that. Lancaster's men are everywhere. Using violence to force their will.'

'It's the same in York . . . The Duke of Lancaster subsidizes the abbey there, St Mary's, a Benedictine foundation like Whitby. The monks here have friendly dealings with them.' She suddenly remembered what Dickson had told them about a house of his in York, managed by one of his girls. He was perfectly placed to pass on information. And the other way about. 'A few years ago,' she explained hurriedly, to account for her sudden hesitation, 'Lancaster's place-men tried to fix the election of the York mayor. They failed, I'm pleased to say. For once the townsfolk were too strong and would not be intimidated nor bought off. But the Lancasters have spies even down in our abbey at Meaux. We need to tread with extreme caution if we have dealings

267

with anyone in their world.' Even for me, now, she reminded herself, am I going too far? She was only guessing where Sabine's allegiance lay. There was no proof of anything.

So far she had not answered Hildegard's first question and it might be thought clever, the way she had avoided answering it.

She tried again.

'There is one thing you might tell me, Sabine. Why did you throw down that bursa for Luke to pick up?'

Smoothly she came back, 'Because I know that whatever I do he will look after it for me and treat it as a holy relic, so besotted is he, and should I ever get out of here I shall know where to find it. In it are the few possessions dear to me. One day . . .' She shrugged and gave a faint, rueful, melancholy smile. 'Let me not put my hopes in dreams.'

'So it has nothing to do with Aelwyn's death?' Sabine looked puzzled.

'How could it have?'

'Why did you throw it down?'

'Because he asked me too. He wanted a token, I suppose. I thought it would make him go away and not cause more trouble.'

'You lost it the night when Dickson's men set your cottage alight.'

'That's right.'

'It was the night Aelwyn died.'

'I know that. Two losses in one night. I hadn't thought I would feel it so deeply – I believed I wanted a man, not a monk, but he was . . . he held my heart in some strange and good way

268

that was rare and . . . I treated him with such contempt . . . taking it for granted that he would always be at my beck and call . . . and he bore it with such grace . . .'

Hildegard began to believe that her tears were genuine as they coursed down her cheeks. 'We often don't realize that love exists until we've lost it.'

'Is that what it was? Love?' Sabine flashed a glance through her tears that might have been recognition that Hildegard was more than the Cistercian habit she wore. Rubbing at her cheeks she asked, 'Have I been of any help, domina . . . any help in finding the murderer of my son's father?'

'Help in eliminating a suspect, maybe.'

And yet, Sabine had still not admitted how the bursa had been returned, nor when, exactly, it had been taken. She asked, 'It must have been a shock to find your cottage on fire in the middle of the night?'

'It was late, towards morning when most revelers had already gone to their beds.'

By then the gold thread from some other piece of embroidery must have already been accidentally left in the apple store.

'I'm surprised the thief didn't sell the bursa on and make the profit he expected.'

Sabine laughed in scorn. 'Can you believe the sot-wit? Of course he couldn't sell it! Everybody who saw it knew it was mine. I put out that it was cursed – and it reappeared, intact, by sunset!'

Before Hildegard left, the door-man sprang

after her. 'I hope you're not persuading her to join you?' Sniggering, he followed her to the door. 'She's worth her weight in gold.'

'In that case I hope she sees some of it.'

He stared at her. His glance went to her small cross then back to her face. 'All right then. I'll mention it.' Looking thoughtful he unlocked the door for her and let her out into the fresh air of the street.

The monks were filing out of the church when she returned. Some made for the warming room, others for a bite to eat in the misericord. Thinking how lax they were in their daily life she waited for the white robes of the Cistercians to appear and went to them as soon as she saw them.

Egbert greeted her first. 'To our chagrin the brotherhood are most correctly attired. Not clean, perhaps, but their garments not torn to ribbons by a lymer's savage teeth either.'

'But we have not given up,' Gregory added. 'Luke is to search the dortoir in case there's a torn cloak lying about and I'm to stroll over to the abbot's lodging to have a look round there, leaving Egbert to scrutinize the cells of the obedientiaries as soon as the next Office begins.'

Gregory fixed her with a hard look. 'Did you catch up on your sleep, Hildegard?'

She shook her head.

'I thought not.'

She explained, concluding, 'I admit I doubted her, Luke. And now . . .?' She looked undecided.

Luke was still smiling over the curse Sabine

had pretended to put on the bursa. 'As clever as she is beautiful,' he remarked.

She hoped for his sake he was beginning to sublimate his carnal love into something more spiritual.

Agreeing to meet again after they had fulfilled their intentions, they separated.

Hildegard thought it a good time to look in on the infirmary to find out how matters stood there. Hertilpole's explanation for his accident – or punishment by an avenging angel – was something she was eager to hear first-hand. It would confirm her innocence and assuage any fears that Hubert would hear rumours to her detriment.

Torold met her at the doors. 'I'm collecting herbs for Brother Dunstan,' he told her the minute she appeared. 'He's over there, pouring sleeping drafts into him as fast as he can. He's demented,' he added.

'Who? Brother Dunstan?'

He grinned. 'No, the lord Bursar. He has committed sin after sin to hear him rave. I feel virtuous by comparison.'

'I hope you always do!' Smiling she went on in.

Hertilpole was still stripped to the waist and the honey-soaked bandages were in place but Dunstan's two stalwart assistants were having a hard time persuading him to lie still.

Every so often he would raise his head and try to scramble to his knees, hands clasped before him, eyes rolling up to the vault above his head

271

as if to a throng of angels in heaven. '*Mea culpa,*' he kept repeating in feverish tones. 'Forgive me, oh Lord. I was beguiled. *Peccavi me.* I was tempted and failed. *Mea culpa, mea maxima culpa.*'

Dunstan was looking exasperated. When he noticed Hildegard hesitating near one of the pillars, unsure whether to approach or whether it would make matters worse, he came over to her. 'He's kept this up since you were here last,' he told her. 'Listening to him leaves no doubt he's got a lot to answer for.'

'Theft and attempted rape at least,' she replied, looking with distaste at the writhing, raging monk, 'but what about murder?'

'Strangely, no mention of that. Theft, yes. Theft of his own rents. He hoped to incriminate Master Edred and thereby cast blame upon his defence of the fishing community, claiming that he was handing money over to them. A sad and mean little plot. The justice of their case stands by its own merits.'

'I came to see if there had been any new developments.'

'Nothing of use to you. Only further confirmation that we are led badly in these dark days. Our Lollard critics can continue happily in the knowledge that they are acquiring by the day yet more evidence that the Orders should be dissolved.'

'Do you see that as likely?'

'In the long run? It is not an option. It could never be initiated. The Pope's men are everywhere here. They would straight away get word back to Rome. Opposition to the Pope would have his armies breathing down our necks in no time. The taxes he raises from us are too valuable to lose. If the King opposes him and tries to take power back into his own hands he'll find he'll be sidelined. His royal power will be seen for what it is, something bestowed on him by the authority of the Pope, who'll encourage vociferous support here. Fools will flock to what they see as the stronger side.'

'King Richard will not like to feel he is not sovereign in his own realm,' Hildegard observed. 'To owe fealty to a foreign power whether in the spiritual realm or this one will not fit with his idea of Englishness.'

'Sadly, there are plenty who will not see it as treason to transfer their allegiance to Rome for the purpose of personal gain.'

'Dark days, brother, as you say. Let them soon be ended.'

A monk entered through the far door, the one that led into the passage to the muniments room. It was Hertilpole's clerk. He was without his writing desk. Catching sight of Dunstan he came over. After a perfunctory obeisance to Hildegard he demanded of Dunstan what was being done to bring Hertilpole back to reason.

'I've done all a man can do and what he now needs is time and absolution.'

The clerk scowled. 'Then give him time. Give him absolution if you can.'

'It's not for me to involve myself with the sickness of his soul, magister. That's for his confessor and his priest.'

273

The clerk moved his shoulders about as if they were stiff, gave one last, cold look at Hildegard as if at a trespasser, then turned and departed with the words, 'Inform me of any other fantasies he dreams up.'

Dunstan said nothing but his glance as he watched him leave said it all.

Hildegard decided to take her leave as well. 'If there's nothing I can do to help at present, brother, please do not hesitate to approach me later if anything comes to mind.'

'Let him stew, domina. It will do his soul good to experience the extent of its limitations. I thank you for your concern. His ravings make it clear what he attempted. He does not deserve your compassion.'

Chilled by the truth of Brother Dunstan's words, she could do little to change things. Even the clerk's manner saddened her in that brief meeting just now. His was not an unusual view of women. *We are tolerated at best*, she thought. *Such men would prefer it if we did not exist at all.*

In the past, during Anglian rule, before the Normans ravaged the country and destroyed its more benevolent customs, women were treated with greater justice. Norman arrogance had brought limitations on all women who wanted to take a full part in public life.

Rare ones still made their mark, like those who in the fullness of their characters flouted man-made laws and went their own way, and managed life to their own satisfaction. All praise to mystics like Julian of Norwich, she told herself, even Margery Kempe, and especially the nun who made the hermit Richard Rolle famous for his prolific writings, the anchoress Margaret Kirkby, along with many others who modestly set about establishing their independence in a way that usually only the royal and the rich could enjoy.

She wondered what Wycliffe would have said and done if he had not died so suddenly? There were no women among the preachers in russet. Was that because women did not want to set themselves up to speak in public? Or did he believe along with generations of theologians that women were the source of evil, whose only purpose was to tempt men to venery in order that they could preen themselves when they occasionally resisted temptation?

At least within her Order women, though living separately, played an unfettered part in contributing to their own finances, successful in the wool industry and in many other ways useful to their financial wellbeing on the same level as men. *Labora et ora.* That's what the Benedictines said, although here, now, there seemed to be more *ora,* prayer, than work, the former often easier than the latter.

Deep in thought, she merely lifted her head in a dazed sort of way when someone nearly knocked her over as he swept on to the foregate. It was Darius again. He never seemed to look where he was going and he was always in a hurry. Now he tossed his cloak over one shoulder and muttered what might have been meant as an apology.

'You did rather walk into me as if I were a ghost,' he complained.

'Did I?' She glanced at him. He had a bruise on one side of his jaw. No doubt it was that rendering him as bad tempered as ever. 'Is that painful?' she asked.

Self-consciously his fingers went to his face. 'Tolerable.'

She had been about to offer some salve but decided against it. From somewhere Dunstan's words floated into her mind: *Let him stew.* Maybe that was the kindest thing to do sometimes, to allow people to suffer their problems in order to understand them.

She was about to walk on towards the guest house when he said, 'Do you want to know how I got it?'

Biting back the honest answer, she waited for him to tell her.

'It was last night. Some wild man was travelling down the cliff path at a rare clip and I happened to be in his way and for no other reason than that he took against me and landed me a blow on my jaw!'

'What did you do?'

'Gave him as good as he got until he stumbled off.' He chuckled. 'It's a rare thing when you can't walk about at night, ain't it?' He fell into step beside her. 'And how about you, domina? We thought you'd gone back to Meaux as we haven't seen you around much. That Glastonbury merchant is cock-a-hoop at winning the holy relic for the monks of Glastonbury. That'll mean lower rents for him and other advantages as well, no doubt, but—'

'Just a moment. Did you say he'd been offered the relic?'

'We assume so. Why else would he be looking so pleased with himself and making preparations for the long journey back to Somerset?'

Her brow wrinkled. 'Nobody has informed us about the abbot's decision. We understood it would be made at the Feast of Epiphany.'

'Well, certainly Sister Aveline isn't building her hopes up. She's convinced her little priory will be closed if they can't offer the pilgrims anything so she's decided to ask permission to return north with us as my step-mother's companion.'

'How unexpected,' she observed.

'She's moved quickly. I'll give her that. We'll be having prayers dawn till dusk. I wonder how that'll go down with Father! At least it gives me an excuse for going my own way. The old fellow doesn't understand he could make more money from sheep than he can from his peasants working the land. What if there's another bad harvest, I say to him. Sheep can live off grass and we can trust that to keep on growing. But he thinks he knows best. In fact, domina, I would relish the chance to talk to your brother Cistercians again about how they run their flocks so successfully . . .' He smiled with no sign of guile and she understood why he had suddenly become so affable.

'I'll let them know. They may be interested in talking to you too. Do you have much land?'

'A fair bit,' he admitted with a modest smile. 'To hell with peasants. There's more wool on a sheep – and you can eat them. Neither applies to an average labouring villain! Yes,' he affirmed with satisfaction. 'My mind's made up. This is what I'm going to do as soon as I get away from here. It's settled.'

They were at the door of the guest house now and before they went inside she asked, 'This fellow who waylaid you – would you recognize him again?'

He shook his head. 'Too dark. There was something – I can't quite put my finger on it. A smell? A scent of some sort? Not unpleasant.' He shook his head. 'No, I wouldn't know him if he was standing plumb in front of me.'

They separated when they entered the hall, Darius to call for a flagon to be sent up and Hildegard to go over to Aveline who happened to be descending the stairs.

'Is it true that the holy relic has been offered to the emissary from Glastonbury?' she asked after a brief greeting.

Aveline looked smug. 'I told you we hadn't a chance.'

'But has it been announced? No-one has mentioned it to us.'

'I expect they'll make an announcement later. I only know what I've heard.'

'And Darius got this from . . . .?'

'Amabel – lady Amabel. She told me in confidence, but as you seem to know already I suppose it's permitted to mention it between ourselves.'

\* \* \*

278

So they had travelled all this way and suffered the villainies that followed for nothing? Everything had gone wrong from start to finish. The sooner they left Whitby the better. First, however, Abbot Richmond's decision must be verified. Only then would they be free to leave. He would have to solve the crimes that had been committed within his purlieus himself.

Dissatisfied at leaving the murders unresolved, she rammed a few clothes back into her travel bag and flung it on to the bed so she could leave at a moment's notice.

There was little else to do.

Once she had told the others she had failed to obtain the relic they would no doubt be ready to leave as soon as the horses were saddled. *If we ride like furies we can even be back at Meaux for Epiphany*, she decided. Back to that paradise where Abbot Hubert de Courcy presides.

Despite this tantalizing image, her feelings were not unmixed. What would Hubert think if she returned empty-handed? More to the point, what would her prioress say? Neither of them would be pleased. It couldn't be helped, however; the entire situation from first to last had been out of her control.

But what about the far more serious matter of two young men, dead? Again it was out of her control. Someone here was a murderer, but now it was up to the monks themselves to find out who it was and deal with him.

Dissatisfied with her failure she went out with a token irritated slam of the door.

*The abbot's lodging.*

The abbot's servant greeted her with the same surly expression as before. This time there was no Gregory to sweep him aside and she had to insist before he would let her in.

Richmond kept her waiting as before for what seemed an unduly long time. She wondered what important task engaged his attention and what he thought to the ravings of his bursar, which by now he must have heard about, remote though he was from the gossip in the misericord.

Idly taking a closer look at the diamond-shaped panes of window glass – green tinged, she noted, Rhenish, perhaps imported along with the pipes of wine – she heard a sudden loud crash as the main doors in the hall were flung back against the walls.

Heated voices were heard and the door to the abbot's private chamber was wrenched open. The prior could be heard demanding to know what was afoot. Several servants made stuttering answers that did nothing to quell the outrage he obviously felt at having the peace disrupted. Abbot Richmond's querulous tones could be heard above the rest and eventually the explosion simmered down to a rumbling mutter.

By now Hildegard was across the chamber but then she hovered, undecided about whether to reveal her presence in the midst of a private argument or not. In the confusion, she appeared to have been forgotten.

She heard the abbot questioning Allerton again

and then there was a slam followed by silence as if everyone had hurried from the building.

Carefully Hildegard nicked open the door into the passage. It was empty.

Clearly she was not going to be able to discover who had won the relic now. She went to the entrance to let herself out, in time to see a group of black-robed monastics flapping across the yard towards the gatehouse. *Now what*, she wondered.

Bracing herself for what was to come, she followed, unnoticed, in their footsteps.

# Nineteen

The big iron-studded oak doors, which prevented anyone gaining access through the gatehouse, were shut and barred from the inside. This was unexpected given that it was still well before noon and they were usually left open during the day so that business could be conducted with the outside world.

Underneath the archway a group of Richmond's high-ups were standing in a cluster talking worriedly and with some arm-waving. The abbot was being ushered inside the porter's lodge with Prior Allerton. A number of monks had gathered and, guessing that it might be something to do with Hertilpole, Hildegard wandered close enough to overhear what was being said. It made no sense.

'Get the captain to see to them!' she heard from one.

'Clear 'em out like chaff from the threshing sheds,' said another.

'We can only pray,' advised a third and immediately fell to his knees.

'My master will advise the utmost retribution,' observed a fourth who Hildegard recognized as Hertilpole's clerk. 'How dare they approach us with their illegal demands? They're nothing but an ignorant rabble of ne'er-do-wells. Trouble-causers. Half of them on the run from their masters. The sheriff will have to be informed.' A rumble of agreement followed this remark. Encouraged, the clerk went on, 'He must be summoned from York at the earliest opportunity with properly armed militia. We'll see who runs this town!'

One of the monks, in a tone of great daring, interrupted. 'But I'm told they were invited here by a messenger sent from our lord bursar with the idea that we might discuss their complaint about the nets.'

The clerk turned in fury on the hapless monk. 'So you listen to rumours, brother? Shame on you! Surely your confessor will need to hear this! I pray he's near enough to witness your tomfoolery.'

'Yes, I am,' said a voice. 'But if it is true what Brother Martin says then it is no tomfoolery, is it, magister?' He spoke in such a tone as to suggest that the clerk should get back to his quill and leave thinking to his betters.

The insult was not lost on the clerk. He was a tall man with the beginnings of a paunch, and although usually stooped over, clutching his portable writing desk, he now rose to his full height and through clenched teeth suggested that his respected brother might address his remarks to lord Hertilpole himself.

Undeterred, Brother Martin's confessor agreed that that would be the best course. 'As soon as our lord bursar is himself again.'

The clerk jerked away and pretended he had more important things to be getting on with than listening to ill-directed sarcasm. He grabbed a passing boy by the scruff of the neck and sent him to fetch the guards at once, the better to earn their pay, from their quarters near the stables. The boy ran off.

From outside on the foregate the battering at the doors continued. Shouting at various levels of intensity accompanied this pounding and eventually resolved itself into a loud and persistent chant of *'Ut! Ut! Ut!'*

Each guttural was accompanied by the beat of clubs on the shaking doors.

'Worry not, brothers, they cannot get inside! We are quite secure!' The speaker, whatever his name, moved back to a safer distance.

Brother Martin risked himself again. 'That is hardly the point, brother. These men have been invited up here to discuss their grievances. It was a clear invitation. The least we can do is to keep the bargain that was made with them.'

'Do you want to volunteer to go out to talk to them?' came another voice. A rustle of consternation ran round the group at the word 'volunteer' and everybody stepped back.

'They have knives, like as not. In this mood I wouldn't guarantee anybody's safety.' It was the porter. 'Best stay safe inside, brothers, until they quieten down and go home.'

One of the younger monks went to the flap that opened out to identify anyone on the other side and shouted through it, 'Go back to your homes!'

His suggestion was met by jeers and catcalls. The chanting resumed along with a more determined beating of the clubs on the iron-bound doors.

Gregory and Egbert sauntered up. 'We could hear this even inside the infirmary,' they explained to Hildegard. 'What's happening?'

She told them what she knew.

'Pigeons coming home to roost.' Egbert looked as if he would add, 'I told you so,' if any of the Benedictines approached, but they were more concerned about their safety and the strength of their doors than about talking to guests.

The noise outside continued with increasing ferocity. The fishermen sounded desperate. The gist of their complaint came through, fragmented, furious and driven by a sense of raging injustice.

The huge fines imposed on them – for breaking what they saw as a rule invented for the abbey's own profit by the bursar – were forcing them into starvation. They had women and children to feed. Days and nights working on the treacherous sea for no reward could be tolerated no longer.

Were they not free men with rights like any

other? Even the other day their boats had been turned away from the beaches at Filey and they could not land their catch.

And yesterday the abbey had sent down armed men to clear their own beaches with the result that their nets had been destroyed. Without nets how were they to fish? And when they tried to sell to the inland towns the abbey took tolls on the catch even then.

All this was interspersed with the continuing war-like chant of *Ut! Ut! Ut!* in the deep and threatening Anglo-Saxon tones of men used to physical strain and strength. If they got inside there was no doubt that those cowering behind the doors would be in danger of bloody noses or worse.

A fracas erupted in the cloister and, from the direction of the infirmary, accompanied by a straggling crowd of Dunstan's assistants, the half-naked figure of the bursar appeared. His narrow, emaciated chest gleamed white and his face was contorted in an agony of regret.

'*Mea culpa!*' he kept bellowing as he forced his way into the middle of the group and fell to his knees, beating his bony chest and pulling at the tangled folds of his habit. 'I have brought this disgrace on you all!' he continued in a loud voice. 'It is my doing! I believed I could talk to these ruffians, that I could persuade them to retract their plea. It is my fault! I own it! I brought them up here! Now, I must send them away again. Open the doors and let me at them!'

He sprang to his feet and hurled himself at the great bar that held the doors shut and tried to lift it. At once the porter and half a dozen monks threw themselves against him to prevent the last protection being removed.

'Come now,' the porter said in the tone of one used to straightening out disorderly persons, 'leave it until tomorrow. It's near on the next Office. Tell them that. They'll understand.'

'I'll tell them, my lord.' It was the clerk. He elbowed everybody out of the way and opened the flap. 'Listen, you fellows! We are obliged now to attend the most holy Office of Sext.'

Jeers greeted this information.

The clerk persisted. 'It is our bounden duty. Go back to your homes and we'll discuss this matter fully in Chapter tomorrow morning. Someone will come down to speak to you and we'll sort out your grievances before sunset.'

There was a gradual silence from the other side while this olive branch was considered. Evidently it met with some scepticism but the power of the obligations the monks were under, to hold Offices eight times a day, was one the town respected. It's what monks were here for, after all. A murmuring discontent arose nevertheless, and the spokesman asked, 'How can we trust you?'

With extraordinary calmness the clerk replied through the flap, 'I assure you, we are holy men. Our word is our bond. If we say a thing we mean it. Now, go home.'

'If nobody comes down to us before sunset tomorrow, we shall return. We will not be fobbed off. We are mariners and owe no allegiance except to our king. We need to dry our nets on the beach and we do not need to have you idle folk stealing the cost of our catch every time we do so.' His voice faded and he must have turned to face his comrades because everybody standing under the gatehouse arch heard him ask more distantly, 'Agreed, lads?'

There was a reluctant cheer and some grumbling and the spokesman came back louder again. 'Till sunset tomorrow then. But no later.'

The monks glanced covertly at each other.

Hertilpole's clerk turned to them with a smirk of satisfaction. 'We'll make sure this abbey and all its gates are firmly barricaded by then. Come, my lord.' He held out a hand to invite Hertilpole to his feet. 'Let's go back into the garth.' To those standing nearest he said, 'Escort the lord bursar to the infirmary to allow him to rest.'

The group attached to Hertilpole drifted off.

The Cistercians watched them leave in silence.

Egbert was incensed. 'He didn't mean a word of that! Those fishermen must be as honest as the day to be so taken in. It can only get worse if Hertilpole and his lackey continue to treat them with such contempt. Is the abbey so short of cash they'll force men to violence to feed their families? What good will it do to drive them to starvation?'

'That clerk went too far,' Gregory agreed. 'I wonder on whose authority he was speaking? Nobody contradicted him even though they must have known he was lying when he made such a promise. I wonder what Abbot Richmond thought if he was listening?'

'Hertilpole was only sorry he caused an affray, not that he'd tried to dupe them into paying more tolls. It is unequivocally lacking in justice,' Luke agreed. 'Look, here comes the abbot now.'

Richmond was white-faced when he came out from the porter's lodge. He stood under the arch while he inspected his monks, then with a curt nod he led the way towards the church.

Brother Dunstan had prophesied that tomorrow would be a day of revelations. It looked likely to be somewhat more than that.

While the monks went off to fulfil their holy obligations, the clerk and one or two others clustering round him discussed the mariners' affray, as it was now being called.

The clerk was already unslinging his writing table. The strap was slung over one shoulder and, pulling it into place to set it level, he snapped open the lid and laid it ready with a piece of vellum, his ink, his quill sharpener, his quill itself and the wiper for it with one or two other things and demanded, 'Names?'

The young monk who had shouted at the fishermen to go home said at once, 'The Breks. All five of them.'

'Trouble-causers. Their cottages need burning. That would sort them out. Who else?'

A list of names followed. Some discussion ensued about whether a Master Driffied had been present this time or whether he'd learned his lesson, but when they could come to no agreement the clerk put his name down anyway.

As he wrote his tongue came out from between his lips and it reminded Hildegard of his master. She wished these fellows would keep their tongues inside their mouths. The sight repelled her.

From where she stood she could see that despite her revulsion the clerk had a fair hand. Fairer than his physical aspect, which, along with his lolling tongue, was a contortion of rage suitable for a chap-book sketch of the Seven Sins.

She had never taken a good look at him before. He was a man always in the shadows of his masters: the silent figure in the corner when she first visited the abbot, a brooding presence when she returned with the others, always present when the bursar was present. At the same time, in a way she could not explain, he was not present, he was an absence, an ambiguous nothing. Now, it seemed, he had come into his own.

She guessed he must be around thirty to thirty-five, tall but now crook-backed to bring him down to the level of the others. Lean, dark browed, with a thin, black line of hair along his upper lip and a clipped, pointed triangle of hair on his chin, he expressed no patience with what he evidently saw as stupidity by those helping him.

In terms of ambition he had probably gone as far as he could in the monastic hierarchy. If he was ambitious he must be living with constant disappointment. Whitby was far from the seat of power. Whether that made him bitter she could not tell.

He was certainly angry, disdainful to those under him and obsequious towards his master, a staunch aid in the furthering of Hertilpole's ambitions. If the latter's madness had changed his aims somewhat to include regret, she could not tell that either, but if he persisted in his ravings his clerk would surely feel betrayed when the purpose for which he had made himself hated in the town was cast as naught in the sweep of Hertilpole's penitential turn-about.

When his sharp-eyed glance fell on Hildegard now he asked, 'Did you wish to say something, domina?' The hint of a sneer in his voice irritated her.

'My gratitude for your valued attention, magister, but since you so kindly invite me to speak, I have to admit to some wonder that you can imagine the fishermen will give up on a matter that is clearly as important as life or death to them. Surely it would be better to come to terms with them?'

'I did ask if you had anything to say, agreed, but I did not expect to have to endure censure from a woman, especially a nun with scant knowledge of the world of men.'

'Forgive me, magister,' she replied in a tone that failed to match her sentiments. 'I believe our actions as monastics or seculars are best served by compassion and understanding. Diplomacy is the better part of valour, is it not? The fishermen, it seems to me, seek only fair dealings in order to carry out their trade. Where words prevail not, violence prevails absolutely.'

'I have no time to discuss this business with

you. There are practical considerations to take into account that you can know nothing about. We have until sunset tomorrow to fortify the abbey. I excuse you from our presence.' He gave an impatient bow and at once turned back to his coterie. 'You know what to do, brothers. Go! Do it!'

As they scattered to their tasks he spread chalk over the list of names he had inked in to dry them, shook it off in a fine cloud that settled on the sleeves of his gown, folded his writing implements away after wiping the end of the quill on a piece of cloth, and shut the lid. Slinging it under one arm he made off in the direction of the church.

Hildegard stood staring after him for longer than she realized. Then, aware of the consolation of friendship, she went to wait for the emergence of her fellow Cistercians from the Office of Sext.

She did not have long to wait. The midday Office was short. As well as that she had the impression from the brisk way everyone filed out that they were eager to get on with preparations for something extraordinary.

Egbert saw her and came over. 'So we're going to be under siege. That'll be something new! How long will it last? We could be here for months, Hildegard!' He chuckled. 'I, for one, will be delighted to break it by flinging the gates open, traitor though I should be dubbed! Can you believe they can ramp up their problems to this extent?'

'Maybe common sense will prevail and someone

will go down to talk to the fishermen and sort it out.'

'If they dare! I wouldn't give much for their chances the way those fellows sounded. What a pity Master Edred isn't here to talk them out of their difficulty.'

'I know of one man who might be able to do it. He already has their trust and could put the case for the fishermen with some authority.' She mentioned Friar John. 'I don't know whether he's still around. He may have moved on.'

'Who does he truly represent? Do you know?'

'I believe he's loyal to the king.'

'I wonder. He'll be ending up in a ditch one of these days.'

'This doesn't get us far, does it? What are we going to do? We've lost the relic as far as I know . . .' She mentioned what Aveline had told her.

When Gregory appeared they discussed the question of leaving again. But the murderer was still somewhere within the abbey and none of them wanted to leave the mystery of two deaths unsolved.

'The bodies of Aelwyn and Edred are lying side by side in one of the chapels,' Gregory told her. 'If things continue like this they will lie unburied for some time. It makes me wonder if Hertilpole is entirely aware in the labyrinth of his confusion that the abbey is about to be under siege – and for no other reason than his relentless pursuit of tolls.'

At that moment Torold appeared in the garth. He came straight over to the Cistercians. 'I was looking for you, domina. Brother Dunstan asks if you'll aid him in the infirmary.'

Puzzled, she followed Torold, and the others came along for support.

'It's the lord bursar,' Torold confided as they hurried along. 'Brother Dunstan thinks your presence may jolt him out of his madness.'

With some trepidation Hildegard entered the long echoing chamber with its low ribbed vault.

She was surprised at how quiet it was – no raving, no bellowing recriminations – and when she reached the far end where Dunstan kept this particular patient at a distance from the others Hertilpole was sitting up on his bed, his robes, though untidy, at least covering him with some dignity. He glared when she appeared.

Dunstan was apologetic. 'He won't hear of calling off his demand for payment from those desperate fellows. Money is money, he keeps on declaiming. *If they use our beaches, then they pay our tolls. If they fail to pay the tolls, then they suffer the consequences.* That sort of ranting.'

'But what can I do, Dunstan?'

'Maybe the sight of you will provoke shame. Once he can acknowledge that he has sinned in one respect, maybe it will bring him to acknowledge that he is behaving badly in another.'

She gave him a doubtful glance. This was not her measure of the man. She saw him as incorrigibly stiff-necked. His sense of his own importance seemed paramount. 'Tell me what I should do then.'

293

'Talk to him. See what that does.'

Emerging from between the pillars supporting the low roof vault, she made her way cautiously to the foot of Hertilpole's bed. He was staring fixedly at the tiles on the floor and did not look up as she approached.

'My lord?'

He stirred. As if being dragged from sleep, his eyes roamed about in an unfocussed daze until they eventually settled on the white-robed figure standing before him. He gave a startled grunt then gripped the edge of one sleeve as if to protect himself. He stared at her for a long time without bringing himself to speak until, from the depths of his vocal range, he ground out, 'You have come to torment me further?'

'I trust not, my lord. That is not my intention.'

'Are you adhering to your lies?'

'My . . .?'

'Don't play the innocent! Your lies, woman! The accusation you made against me! Are you still lying about me?'

He got off the bed and moved closer until he was standing over her. The smell of bad breath, sweat and his unwashed nether parts made her want to retch.

He leered down at her. 'What is your purpose in such lying accusations? Do you hope to destroy me?'

When she did not answer, not knowing where to begin, he poked his face into hers and asked, 'Did the Devil send you? Are you on a mission to bring me down to hell to copulate with Beelzebub himself? Do you want me to witness you writhing in his arms, your body aflame with lust and godless desire . . .?'

She broke in to stem the flow of his madness. 'I have told no lies about you, my lord. Indeed, I have spoken very little about you although there is much that could be said, as you well know.'

'And you will say it! You do say it! You will! You will! I know this! Your lies are shouted from the roof tops! You are the incarnation of evil, like all women! Daughters of Eve! Driving men to destruction in the pits of everlasting hellfire! Rightly were you thrown out of the Garden and rightly will you be thrown out of my abbey!'

'*Your* abbey?' she was stung to retort. 'I imagine Abbot Richmond and his chapter would have some claim on it and not wish to hand it over entirely into your keeping!'

'Aaaaagh!' He began to thump his chest. 'Take her away! Save me from this witch's vile false-speaking! Out, woman! Out! Back to your sink of iniquity! Back to your fiery pit!'

Hildegard turned to Dunstan, but he was already hurrying forward. 'My mistake, domina.' He turned to the bursar. 'Peter, this is a fever of your mind. She has said nothing. What do you imagine she has said?'

'She accuses me! She accuses me! Her lies will drag me down!' He put his head in his hands and began to sob.

'Of what? Say it.'

'Of sin! Of gross sin!' he blubbered. 'She caused me to touch her and a devil with wings of fire swooped down to burn me because I would not submit to her lust! Take her away! Take her from my sight!'

'Peter, calm down.'

Two burly assistants approached. One of them held a steaming beaker. 'Shall we give it him now, brother?'

'If you can, yes. Try to get him to sleep. When he wakes he may be sufficiently rested to be back in his right mind – enough to make reparation to the domina for his calumnies – and to instruct that clerk of his to make peace with the townsfolk. He's led us down the wrong track and I fear what will lie at the end of it if something isn't done to make us draw back from the brink. His madness is spreading everywhere!'

Hildegard had backed away and Dunstan came over to her to say, 'The abbot has retired to his lodging as if the matter will resolve itself. Meanwhile the mercenaries are taking up arms, eager to shed blood, and the monks are busy barricading themselves behind the walls. We shall be over-run, it will do no good, and my poor old fellows,' he gestured to the row of beds where the patients lay, 'hoping for a quiet end to their days are going to be under attack if not murdered in their own beds.'

'Why does the abbot not stop this now?'

'He is too holy to engage himself with the gross affairs of commerce.'

'But what about the prior? Surely he has the authority to do something?'

'You have seen, surely, what sort of leader he is? He is no more than Hertilpole's manikin, like one of those child's toys on sticks that can only dance to another's tune. He is in thrall by way of Hertilpole to Cuthred who, of course, will follow his master's orders to the letter and take joy in the bloodshed that will surely follow.'

'Cuthred?'

'Hertilpole's clerk and factotum. Without word from him the prior will do nothing.'

The Cistercians were waiting further off and came over when they saw Dunstan looking so distraught.

While Hertilpole started to rant again as the assistants tried to persuade him to drink their calming potion, Gregory and Egbert asked what they might do to help.

'Batten down the doors. Those fellows in the town may have right on their side but they've been drinking since Christmas Eve. They'll not be open to reason if they have to drag themselves all the way up the cliff side only to be insulted once more. They've been treated shamefully and when they realize how they've been cozened yet again there's no knowing what they'll do. I suggest that you, domina, bring your belongings into the guest chamber here. You will not be safe outside the walls.'

'We'll help her.' Gregory and Egbert said as one.

'I only have one saddle bag.'

'Nevertheless,' Gregory replied. 'We intend to come outside on to the foregate to see what's what and we'll help you bring your things back inside at the same time.'

# Twenty

The afternoon was already darkening under a scud of racing clouds from the east. Further snow looked likely, but so far it had held off. When they reached the guest house, after persuading the reluctant porter to open the night door for them, they discovered that the other guests were already forewarned and on the point of leaving.

'This is unexpected,' complained lady Amabel as soon as she saw Hildegard. 'We thought to celebrate here but it looks as if we'll be on the road during the Feast.' She pulled a reproachful face at her husband.

'Not so, sweeting. I have friends at a manor near Guisborough. If we start now we shall arrive not long after nightfall. It's safer to leave at once and, besides,' Sir Ranulph gave his son a covert glance, 'I have finished my business here.'

Darius raised his surly countenance from inspecting the straps on his bags. 'And what business might that be, my dear lord and father?'

'Ha! That's surprised you, hasn't it! You don't imagine I'm here for mere pleasure, do you?' He patted Amabel's hand to take the sting out of his words and indicated a velvet bag containing something not much bigger than a man's hand waiting to be taken out with his personal baggage to where the wagon would convey their possessions northwards. 'I consider

I have had a profitable few days here. When you find out why you'll congratulate me.'

He was looking so extremely smug that Hildegard paused to hear him say, 'I've always told you wealth resides most securely in land. I now have in my possession something a buyer is willing to exchange for a very large piece of land indeed. If you're still set on running sheep over it, so be it. I don't object to that. But it's land, Darius, land, and one day you'll learn there's nothing more valuable, not even sheep.'

Darius looked put out. Then the corners of his mouth began to lift. 'Why, you old schemer! Is it what I think it is?'

His glance fell on the velvet bag.

His father tapped the side of his nose and the two of them turned away with Sir Ranulph putting his arm round his son's shoulders like man to man.

Before he left he went over to Gregory and Egbert and extended one hand. 'A good joust, brothers, but Master Buckingham's need for payment, a bill I was willing to settle in full, swung the abbot in my favour. I hope you don't think it was underhand?'

'Well done,' murmured Gregory. 'It's good to know that after the imminent attack by the mariners the abbey will be rebuilt again by so prodigious a master builder.'

Sir Ranulph looked puzzled and when he worked it out he gave a bark of laughter. 'Quite so, friend. Quite so!' Still chuckling, he ushered his entourage towards the door with Sister

Aveline, giving Hildegard a final smile, tagging along behind.

'Did he mean what I thought he meant?' Egbert wrinkled his brow. 'But, Hildegard, I thought you told us that the Glastonbury merchant had obtained the relic?'

'That's what Aveline told me.'

At this moment the two body servants from Glastonbury were heaving a chest down the stairs, one at each end and when, puffing, they gained the ground floor, they dropped it down to have a short rest.

Behind them came the merchant himself in a blue hood, ready for the road. It was generally known that he had dined almost every day in the abbot's lodging. Now, before going out he offered a few opinions about the coming siege and wished the Cistercians well.

As he went to the doors he added, 'We've had a successful visit. Well worth our journey to this wild region. I'll have many stories to tell the monks when I return south. My commiserations to you fellows, however, and to you, domina. It is not without a qualm that I take home the very thing you yourselves hoped to obtain. However, we can but abide by the abbot's decision, can we not?'

With that he swept out followed by his two servants, his metal-bound chest, and he himself carrying a carefully wrapped object – no bigger than a man's hand.

The others looked at each other in astonishment. 'So who has the original and who the fake?' Hildegard's expression was close to hilarity as she looked from one to the other. 'I told you horse-hair didn't cost much!'

'They may not agree. It may have cost the buyers much indeed. I wonder what they paid!' The men themselves were close to hilarity too as they guessed what must have happened.

When they told Luke, who had tracked them down after a word with the infirmarer, he was incredulous. 'But do they not suspect?'

Gregory explained what the abbot had told Hildegard earlier, that the bidders in this sale had been sworn to secrecy.

'Each one will believe he has the genuine relic. Later in the year when they have a ceremony of dedication on St Hild's Day the truth may slowly filter out. But who will doubt that he himself does not possess a genuine lock of Abbess Hild's precious hair and that the others are fake?'

'Sir Ranulph has already got someone to give him land in exchange,' Hildegard told Luke. 'He'll deny any suggestion of its being a fake should he be questioned.'

'A case of *caveat emptor*, indeed,' concluded Gregory with a wry grimace.

The night passed in a state of uneasiness throughout the abbey. The guest house on the foregate sounded strangely hollow when the guests left and the kitchen staff disappeared with no work to do. The three corrodians had taken shelter in the dortoir with the monks. Hildegard, in the guest chamber inside the infirmary, was glad to be surrounded by some stalwart young men

301

to supplement her own ability to fight should there be violence.

The definite loss of the holy relic, if such a thing had ever existed, still disappointed her. With the help of pilgrims who came to pray before it, the nuns at Swyne would have been able to finance an extension of their own buildings to take in more sick and elderly with no homes of their own. The prioress had mooted the idea of an extension to the choir too, with the idea of taking in more pupils to prepare them for the Song School in Beverley. Now those hopes would come to nothing.

Before they could leave they had a mystery to clear up, but ahead there was the confrontation with the mariners to face. Although it was difficult to imagine that they would actually storm the abbey precincts, and even more difficult to believe they would attack helpless patients in their beds, it was an uncertain atmosphere that pervaded the place. As Vespers and Compline came and went, night extended its dark mantle over the world and the Great Silence fell.

Dunstan went round to make sure the doors were barricaded. 'Just in case,' he muttered when he came to offer a few words to Hildegard about Hertilpole's madness. 'He's sleeping now and we must pray that tomorrow his reason will be restored to a semblance of what it was.'

She wondered if the fishermen were waiting in the expectation that he would send someone to parlay with them after discussions in Chapter, and she wondered how long it would be on the morrow before they realized they were the victims of a hoax. The thought of their disappointment and rage was frightening. To the abbey it was a matter of showing who was boss. To the mariners it was a matter of life and death. With nothing else to lose it wouldn't matter to them what they did.

Now, on the surface, everything continued as usual. The bell tolled at midnight, bringing the silent monks down the night stairs and into the nave to worship at the great altar while Hildegard, somewhat uneasily, stood almost alone at the west end behind the screen.

A few servants showed up and at the last minute she noticed Torold slip inside with a couple of companions. One was the silent boy who had done as he was told on the day of her arrival. The other was Miggy.

They were up to something. When everybody began to leave, Hildegard went as far as the west door then lingered out of sight while the boys remained. Duke had evidently been told to guard the exit and was sitting erect and in silence when Hildegard patted his head in greeting.

As soon as the boys heard the main doors slam they started to behave in an extraordinary manner.

The silent boy was instructed to walk from the screen at one end of the nave towards the west doors where Hildegard was standing out of sight. The other two stationed themselves at a short distance on each side of him and watched carefully as he began to pace forward.

He was almost up to the doors when Hildegard stepped forward. Before she could speak there was a frenzied scream and the boy fell to the floor, his face pressed to the tiles and both arms outstretched as if grappling with an enemy.

Hildegard ran to him. 'Child! What is it?'

From both sides came gasps of shock and as Miggy ran up he was babbling about St Hild and ghosts and how you had to walk in a straight line down the nave and not deviate and she would appear to you in a white shift, but it was the domina, whose name was almost the same, who appeared but she was real.

He took a breath and clutched at her arm. 'You are real, aren't you?'

'You sot-wits!' she hissed. 'Look at this poor lad, frightened out of his senses. What are you doing making such fools of yourselves?'

Then she began to laugh. The atmosphere of impending doom seemed suddenly as ridiculous as these children playing at magic to summon a dead saint.

'Don't you know it's not true?' she demanded, ruffling their hair and holding the shivering silent lad against her to comfort him. 'It's just a tale people tell round the fire in winter. Heaven and Hell may exist for all we know, but it's as sure as anything that no-one has ever returned from either place to prove it. We only have the word of a few old men who want to keep us in awe of them, and story-tellers who share their outlandish fantasies merely in order to amuse us. Come back to the infirmary kitchen and have a tisane, then it's off to bed with you all. I'm ashamed sensible boys like you should believe such stories!'

As they calmed down and sheepishly followed her out through the side door with Duke's claws clicking over the tiles beside them, she asked, 'What would you have said if St Hild had appeared? Did you have some questions ready?'

Torold replied. 'We'd have asked her if she knew who killed my father.'

'That's the reason we cannot leave yet. Young Torold needs answers and nobody but us seems interested in finding any.' Hildegard and the other three Cistercians were walking up to the headland away from the abbey.

For a time their images were captured by the luminous dawn between Lauds and Prime, when even in winter the northern sea thickens the reflected light and mirrors it back to the land. Their faces were bathed in silver light like the features of saints drawn on grisaille glass.

They had decided to walk up the rise above the fish pond for no other reason than a desire to escape the gradually increasing hysteria inside the cloisters.

The brotherhood were behaving as if annihilation by the sword was inevitable. Some were desperately ready to be martyrs. A few silent ones were detached from it and moved about with thoughtful faces, but the rest flaunted their righteousness in loud condemnation of the mariners' defiance. It was as if Hertilpole's shattered mind had shed its fragments among them like the pieces of a broken mirror.

'There is yet time for the prior to assert

305

himself,' Luke said in a tone that suggested he had not much hope of that.

Egbert mocked the idea. 'Do you seriously see him going out on to the foregate to talk to them? He hasn't the nerve.'

'I would talk to them,' Gregory admitted. 'But it's no good promising them what the abbey will not deliver. I don't understand how the abbot can believe it will end in satisfaction for either party. Violence will achieve nothing. It begets only more violence. The fishermen cannot pay with what they do not have. Is the abbey going to ruin them? Where will that get them? The abbey needs them as much as they need the abbey.'

'It will go to law,' Hildegard suggested. 'They say the old abbot was always in and out of the courts.'

'Will this one choose that route? He's a sad example of what lack of leadership can do to a fraternity.' Egbert gazed moodily out to sea where the horizon was streaked with crimson as the sun began to shrug itself out of the water. Millions of red and gold lights began to blink across the surface. Everyone turned to watch.

Despite the daily yet always awe-inspiring beauty of the dawn, Hildegard's thoughts were still with Torold. He was right to ask who had killed his father, but she was beset by the creeping suspicion that the murderer might have slipped through their fingers.

The idea was too vague to share with the others yet. It made little sense. What if, she wondered, Aelwyn had known that the relic was a fake?

He had obtained the old, discarded bursa that had covered the reliquary and given it to his mistress. It was a pretty thing. He could have sold it on behalf of the abbey to bring in some needed revenue, and the fact that he had not done so made one want to ask how he had obtained it. Sabine had kept her keepsakes in it. Did she, too, know that the relic it had once housed was a fake? Would Aelwyn have told her – or not told her?

She gnawed over other possibilities. They seemed endless. They led nowhere. But what if, by some process she had not yet worked out, somebody thought Aelwyn was about to announce the truth? He appeared to have grown into an honourable man after his rampaging novitiate. His actions showed that. Maybe this subterfuge about to be practised regarding the holy relic now went against the grain? Again she asked herself, what if, getting wind of his intention, someone had decided to shut him up?

Then there were the guests to be accounted for.

It was in Sir Ranulph's interests to have a genuine relic, and the Glastonbury merchant would be of the same opinion. What if some loyal person among either entourage thought up that diabolical way of keeping the truth secret.

The same theory might be applied to Edred. He was considered by everyone but the bursar to be an honest man. For that very reason he might have decided it was time to reveal the truth.

Remembering the conversation in the hall between Sir Ranulph and Darius as they were leaving, it began to strike Hildegard as too overt, like a scene by a couple of mummers acting out a pretence at secrecy. It might have been intended to demonstrate their belief in the absolute genuineness of the relic – a ploy to cut off any suspicion that might arise about their involvement in keeping the truth out of it.

Darius seemed the type to have no compunction in getting rid of any man who stood in his way. There was that bruise he had been so keen to explain away, and he had been inside the laundry and must have seen the novices' little surplices hanging up to dry. Maybe they had given him the idea of stopping up the vents and thus preventing the truth coming out? The more she thought about it the more credible it seemed, even though it was all based on supposition without a shred of hard evidence.

Then there was the Glastonbury merchant. The loyalty of his servants was not in doubt but he had played such a small part over the last few days it was difficult to make much of him. Of course, he had dined regularly with the abbot and maybe a hint had been dropped, no-one the wiser. *Will no-one rid me of this troublesome knight?* Aelwyn, silenced, would safeguard the interests of both.

This brought her thoughts to the abbey men. What might be true of the guests might also be true of the abbey obedientiaries, the bursar in particular, either acting alone or on orders of Abbot Richmond?

It was almost inconceivable that a lord abbot,

a figure near the top in the hierarchy of the Order, should allow matters to drift so far out of his control that they were being forced to sell off their assets. It would be an affair of burning concern to him that the abbey should continue to pay its way. If a word of suspicion reached his ears that someone doubted the authenticity of the relic, wouldn't he want the truth smothered?

The manner of both deaths suggested a perpetrator without a weapon, or someone lacking the nerve to use one to draw a man's blood. And the battering of Edred with an iron weapon more usually used as a seal was something a desperate man might wield in the heat of the moment. The seal had not necessarily been stolen from the abbot's chamber where he conducted business affairs. It might be carried by anyone who needed to seal a document on behalf of abbey business – the prior, the bursar certainly, and others, chamberlain, sacristan, cellarist, bottler, almoner. The list was long. Every document that left the abbey would be moved by it and payment authenticated.

'It's going to be a fair day,' Luke said, breaking into her thoughts. 'Nothing to stop the prior sending someone down that cliff side with a message of conciliation.'

The sky above the headland was now flooded with crimson light.

'Red sky in the morning,' warned Egbert. 'Does that tell us something?'

With the feeling that they had witnessed an omen of things to come, they made their way back in gloomy silence towards the enclave.

* * *

When Hildegard entered the infirmary the old men in the beds lined against the walls were in a ferment of excitement. One had a piece of wood across his knees which he clearly intended to use as a club, another was flexing his fingers and saying with relish, 'Leave them to me, brothers. I'll show them what for.'

Brother Dunstan lifted his hands in mock despair when she asked him what was going on. 'They imagine they're young bulls of twenty. The years of living peacefully as cloistered monks have fallen away in the excitement of feeling young and unbound by any vows. They'll settle down once their blood cools and if there is an attack I doubt not that they'll sleep right through it.'

'Did you say I could get my sleeve repaired where it was torn?' she asked.

He directed her towards a door that led by a few winding steps up to a small tower room where the broiderers worked.

*The broiderers' chamber.*

When she entered she saw that it was festooned with fabric and the tools of their Mystery. A couple of laybrothers were sitting cross-legged, gossiping and stitching. When she made her request to them they readily agreed.

'No need to take the garment off, domina. We'll have that stitched up in a trice,' one of them told her.

He put aside the cloak he was working on.

It was ripped on one side. Hildegard stared at it. 'Whose garment is this?' she asked as he searched around for light-coloured thread to replace the black he already had in his bodkin.

'We have no idea. They just send them up willy-nilly and we stitch 'em.'

'Is it possible to find out?' she persisted.

'Doubtless. Go and see the chamberlain. Do you know where he is?'

'I can find him.'

Looking round while she waited until the seamster had finished with her sleeve, she noticed the stand containing different coloured threads. The men were obviously capable of stitching the complicated patterns required for a range of ecclesiastical vestments.

She saw gold and silver thread among the red, blue, green and yellow. A small piece of fabric stitched with a close pattern of daisies was lying half-finished on the side. The tips of the petals were picked out in red to represent the blood of Christ.

'I think I might have seen something like this somewhere in the town,' she told him. 'Is it likely to come from here?'

'Almost certainly.'

'It was being used as a little bag to keep things in.'

'Mayhap it was no longer fit for its original purpose, or it might have been an off-cut from a larger garment. We re-use where we can.'

When he finished mending her sleeve she thanked him and hurried out.

*The misericord.*

The chamberlain was cutting off strips of meat and stuffing them into his mouth where he stood. He was shocked and surprised to see a nun at the door. 'Are you permitted in this part of the enclave, domina?'

'I believe so. I was directed here. I have a question about a garment that is being repaired. It's a cloak belonging to one of the monks. I was told you would tell me to whom it belonged.'

'I really don't see what concern it is of yours.'

Inventing a lie with a speed that shamed her she said, 'But the seamster cannot remember who sent it up and they are in a hurry to return it. He thought you would know.'

'Ah, on an errand out of the compassion of your heart.' He put another sliver of meat into his mouth and, chewing, gave her question some thought. Eventually he said, 'Describe this cloak. I've sent several garments up there to be repaired.'

'Black. Not unlike many others. But the tear, quite distinctive.' She gave a small, false laugh. 'Almost as if some wild animal had torn it!'

His eyes darted before he replied. 'I might know the one you mean. I expect it was the cloak the bursar was wearing when he had a recent tumble down the night stairs. It's ready, is it?'

'Soon,' she smiled, all meekness. 'My gratitude, my lord.'

Bowing, she went out.

The bursar's cloak?

Did that mean he was out last night stalking about in the darkness of the headland? Following her? After that gruesome attempt to rape her when his swift punishment had nearly burned him alive?

But how could that be?

She was certain that after Brother Dunstan's assistants had rescued him and brought him back to the infirmary, mind-boggled and raving, he had been under the infirmarer's watchful eyes all night.

Now she wondered why the chamberlain was lying. He must know that Hertilpole was in the infirmary last night, everybody knew, so to name him could not implicate him in anything else. The little lie about falling down the night stairs was extra confirmation of his innocence.

That meant that Hertilpole had his alibi but someone else did not – the wearer of the bursar's cloak. If, in fact, it was the bursar's cloak.

# Twenty-One

The day was drawing to a stormy close as the red dawn had implied. The sky was like lead. A powerful wind was driving in from the sea turning it into an expanse of white foam. It was known as wreckers' weather.

Chapter had been and gone. The daily Offices had been sung at the appropriate times.

A messenger had been sent down to invite the mariners to partake of some ale up at the abbey

313

where matters could be discussed in a calm and courteous manner.

This was the story.

It was so astonishing it travelled round the abbey in a flash and created almost as much excitement as if no messenger had been sent and they were still crouching fearfully behind their barricades. It divided the fraternity into two camps, those who thought it a good and holy gesture and those who were appalled that they should cave in and have to listen to the whining of men they, in effect, owned.

'They should pay their fines and end the matter. If not, they deserve what's coming to them.'

Gregory wondered on whose authority the messenger had been sent and what promises he had been instructed to make in order to entice the fishermen to return.

Egbert told him he heard it was Prior Allerton who had extended the invitation. 'Attempting to break the strings that bind and follow his conscience?'

'And what is Hertilpole saying about that, assuming he's in a fit mind to say anything?'

'They say he is almost fully recovered, has faith in his prior, and is in complete agreement with everything he says.'

As if to confirm that he was back on the job the bursar himself, followed as usual by his clerk, came briskly out of the church and set off towards the gatehouse. They saw both men duck their heads to enter the porter's lodge and the door close behind them.

As everyone watched to see what would

314

happen next, Hildegard noticed with a shiver that inside each of the turrets at the corners of the roof was a figure. A glint of metal as the sun struck from between a gap in the thickening clouds suggested guards. She wondered if they were armed. When she pointed them out to the others they looked thoughtful.

Eventually Gregory said, 'Let's see if we can get out on to the foregate when the mariners and all the rest arrive, Egbert. For sure they won't come without support. I'd like to see what happens.'

'I'm with you, Greg. And you, Luke?'

'Indeed so.'

'Me too,' Hildegard added.

The regular chamade was already floating up towards them as the drums started up in the town the way they had struck up as darkness fell every evening. Usually the monks would be thinking of going into Vespers, but a surprisingly large number were still congregating in the cloisters with a disregard for the bell that began to toll. The abbey servants were much in evidence too.

Altogether the febrile atmosphere made Hildegard apprehensive. The threat from Hertilpole after his verbal attack earlier had shaken her. It made brutally clear how little regard some men had for women in general. The fact that such vitriol came from one monastic to another was against the spirit of the teaching and was shocking to witness. It made it difficult to believe that he had had a change of heart about the pleas of the mariners. It was clear that he had the same arrogant view of anyone, man or woman, who challenged his authority.

The sun found another gap between a crack in the clouds and began to pick out details in ominous streaks of crimson and gold, a carved gargoyle in the guttering, a vindictive face in the garth. Shadows caused by this brief effulgence deepened. The Cistercians went to stand outside the west doors on the little knoll that gave a view on to the foregate.

At present it was almost empty but the sound of the approaching townsfolk was increasing as they climbed the cliff.

*Which is worse*, Hildegard asked herself, *to be trapped inside an abbey where I know I have enemies, or to be outside among drunken seafarers bent on justifiable violence?*

The threat implied by the dark beating of the drums could not be ignored. A war drum added another layer of menace. The squeal of pipes was followed by a sackbut or two, and eventually the words of a marching song rose like an incoming tide as the procession approached.

It did not hurry.

It held to a measured tread.

It showed as surely as the spoken word that the seafarers would not be trifled with this time.

All the monks were in the garth now, ranged round about, dark, silent, and vigilant. The obedientiaries stood in a worried group near the gatehouse. Abbey servants were stationed at intervals along the walls. In the turrets the mercenaries stared down and a sound like the winding of crossbows could be heard.

'Hildegard, I fear there may not be the friendly outcome we've been led to hope for.' Gregory took her arm. 'Why don't you go into the infirmary and keep an eye on those patients of Brother Dunstan?'

'You mean because I'm a woman and weak and may get in the way?'

'I am not Bursar Hertilpole. I would never think less of you than of any other comrade in arms, but I fear that I may not be able to fulfil my duty as your protector' – his eyes glinted – 'as my lord abbot requested. As well,' he added swiftly, 'for purely personal reasons I should not like you to be injured in the coming affray. Those servants are there for a purpose and the sound of crossbows in preparation is unmistakable. There will be retaliation.'

'It may pass off peacefully.'

'I doubt it. Only the prior seems to believe he can persuade Hertilpole to be reasonable, and where is he?'

No-one knew.

Egbert grimaced. 'I'm beginning to feel something for Allerton, poor devil. Spineless he is but his heart's in the right place. He's clearly not in support of a confrontation. Come on, Greg. We won't stand by.'

'I'll stay here where I can see what's happening,' Hildegard offered as a concession to Gregory's plea. 'I would hate to cause Hubert to be disappointed in you, dear brother.'

The three of them set off towards the gatehouse.

As it took place the approach of the procession was reported back to those inside the walls by a young monk standing on the mound beside Hildegard. They could just see enough over the wall to watch what was happening.

The harbingers were the mummers in their usual masks and motley, accompanied by their hurdy-gurdy man, and they were followed by what seemed like the whole town with folk still wearing their own extravagant inventions from St Stephen's Day. And then came the pipers, more disciplined than anyone expected, followed by the bagpipers, skirling with dauntless purpose as they strode up the steep bank, and after them the drummers driving everyone on with a relentless beat, and the children, and the old fishermen now divorced from the sea, hobbling bravely on sticks, and their wives, and more children than anyone could believe. And then something massive, dark, almost human, as big as a giant.

'They have an effigy!'

'They've dragged it all the way from the town!'

'It's taking ten men to heave it up!'

'What is it?'

'It's a monk. See? See his head with the tonsure? What are they going to do?'

Excited speculation followed. The procession began to fill the foregate.

'Their spokesman's banging on the doors, asking for a word with the lord abbot,' the young monk informed everyone. 'To whom he sends his kindest and most reverential greetings. Hear that?'

'You can't say fairer.'

'Where is Abbot Richmond?'

'Alone in the church on his knees.'

'Can't someone fetch him?'

'He says he's not to be disturbed until everyone has come to their senses.'

'Never, then. Look!'

The entire procession had spread out now as more and more people reached the top of the cliff. They were standing in silence in a half circle like onlookers at a public hanging.

A few words were heard from the spokesman and some of the optimists inside the enclave expected Hertilpole to emerge from the porter's lodge to invite the man within the walls.

Nothing happened.

The spokesman tried again.

Still nothing.

The silence from inside the abbey drew catcalls from a lone voice outside. At once the jeers of the crowd started up. The drummers thumped the skins in time then abruptly stopped.

Into the silence the same voice shouted, 'Keep your promise, Abbot!'

'Promise! Promise!' thundered back from a hundred throats. The drums began to pound in time.

Without warning Hertilpole did appear. He erupted from the lodge, arms waving, screaming, 'Now, men, *now!*'

At once the abbey servants, who had only looked like an emergency holding force, showed that they were armed. Missiles hurtled over the walls and the mercenaries from the height of the turrets started loosing bolts from their crossbows randomly on to the foregate.

A roar of hurt rose up. The wounded screamed.

People scattered. Children howled. Women picked them up and ran to find shelter. The mummers jeered and raised their shields and threw the missiles back.

Someone put a torch to the effigy and in a rage of flame it ignited. With something in it that fed the fire, it blazed wildly. Flames leaped as high as the gatehouse roof. Sparks were swept over the walls on to the garth. The monks scattered with cries of alarm. Small fires sprang up and were stamped out.

Back on the foregate the crowd, knowing they had time before the crossbows could be rewound, flocked back with jeers and hoots of derision as the effigy burned. Some had weapons of their own. A few arrows arced over the walls and pierced the grass in the garth. Missiles continued to fly back and forth.

Slowly, as if making the decision itself, the burning effigy toppled towards the gatehouse and leaned there in a mantle of flames and coiling smoke. Its head began to melt. Its black robes gave off an acrid stench. The monk twisted in his coils. Burning pieces of his garments fluttered in the flames and broke off. Men on the foregate went round kicking the burning pieces back into the fire.

Hertilpole was demented. He ordered the gates open so that his men could confront the town folk with steel, but the porter had the key that would have unlocked the chain that held the beam in place. He made a theatrical search of his sleeves, his pouch, his pants. He went back inside the lodge but came out empty-handed.

Hertilpole cursed and shouted to God and fell to his knees and got up again. Meanwhile the burning effigy raged and sparks flew into the night sky like small, turning stars of gold.

Some monks started to sing.

Hildegard noticed a particular face in the crowd, drenched for a moment in the lurid light from the fire as he turned to look up at the bowmen in the turrets. When he started towards the church she watched him push through the west door.

And then she followed.

*The nave.*

The noise outside was cut off with finality when the great doors slammed shut. It left Hildegard in a pool of silence.

One tall candelabra shed a quivering light into the darkness, but any illumination was quenched before it reached the soaring vault overhead. Deep shadows below the scaffolding along the walls concealed whatever lay underneath. The wind, as before, rattled the loose planking, and lifted the covers on the walkways. Outside, distantly, like the drawn breath of a waking monster, came a sound of thunder.

A shape detached itself from the darkness and passed in front of the light.

He wore a cloak, his own this time, she supposed, and it trailed from one shoulder, in order to keep free the hand that held his writing desk. Instead of making for the inner sanctum where the abbot must be at prayer, he went to the tower steps.

Fearing to lose her chance, Hildegard ran forward. 'Magister!'

He jerked to a stop, swivelled to peer through the gloom then, recognizing her, began to laugh, the sound echoing from stone to stone. 'Well met, domina. Were you enjoying the show out there?'

'Did you know Hertilpole was going to order the crossbows to be fired on the crowd?'

'Hertilpole? I think it might be in order to show more respect to our lord bursar, my lady nun.'

Frowning, he stepped away from the tower door and stood for a moment staring at her with narrowed eyes. Until lightning flashed across his features through one of the tall lancets his face was a blur, but when they were doused in darkness once again she could still make out the two black sockets where his eyes must be and it gave her a sense that they were crawling over her flesh while he considered things.

'Are you here for sanctuary?' he eventually asked.

'No. I want to speak to you, magister. If you remember I asked you a question.'

'And I will answer it, despite your manner and for whatever the answer has to do with you. Yes, it was I who persuaded my lord and master that force is the best solution to our little local problem. Satisfied?'

She moved closer to get a better view of his expression. It was suspicious, arrogant, hard. There was a strong smell of beeswax, which she supposed came from the seals he used.

'I have other questions, magister. They concern your little local difficulty but will reach to Heaven if justice prevails as it should.' She saw him jerk up his head. Not waiting to hear him argue with her, she pulled the iron dagger-shaped seal from her scrip and held it up. 'Is this yours?'

'You must be a witch.'

Plainly shocked, his sneer was more chilling because he did not move. It revealed a cold control that seemed the more dangerous because it damped down his rage and allowed it to fester until such time as it might burst forth, monstrously. So he must have sat many a time when challenged or demeaned by his superiors.

She took a step towards him. 'I have your answer?'

'You'll get more than an answer from me, nun. I don't want you to tell me how you got hold of it. What's your price?'

'For keeping quiet?'

'Well?'

'Do you mean you have access to the allegedly depleted coffers of the abbey – like your master Hertilpole?'

His sneering laughter held a brief note of admiration. 'You have an inflated idea of the worth of your suspicions. What are they without evidence? I can take that seal from you freely—'

'I have evidence of your presence in the apple store.'

'You can't have . . .' He bit back the rest of his response.

'I possess a thread of gold which came from the piece of fabric you use to wipe your quill. I

323

saw it earlier, out in the yard. I'd make a good guess that they'll match.'

'Who sent you? Are you in league with Master Ake? We all know about him. We feed him tit-bits from time to time to pass on to King Richard in order to keep them happy.' He gave a sneering laugh. 'I can tell you now, you're wasting your time going after me. I am protected. This is disputed country, but be certain of one thing: the king's writ does not run here. They tell me you were in conversation with the friar we put out of town? You'll have to apply to Lancaster or Northumberland if you want to get anywhere. See what joy they give you if you think to accuse *me*!' He stopped abruptly.

It was the most she had ever heard him say. It was enough. Everything fell into place.

'This is nothing to do with the king's business,' she replied. 'It's local, as you've just said. You took a child's father from him. You took a good husband from his wife and family. You murdered two good and innocent men.'

'Why on earth would I do that? What are they to me?'

'They were something to your master and his hope of making money from a fake relic. That's one thing. You hoped to shut them up, satisfy him, and keep your position as his right-hand man—'

'So you want to make something of that little game?' His eyes, at first hooded, seemed to ignite with the outrage of being confronted by a woman who was not going to back down. His face was set in an expression of petulance and menace.

In the next flash of lightning his eyes shone as red as wolves' eyes in the night.

Opening his writing case with deliberation he first took from it a piece of thickly embroidered cloth with its ragged edges and pulled threads from the many times it had been used. He held it up like an exhibit so that she could see it glint in the filtered light.

Putting it on one side he then took out a pen knife used for sharpening his quills. He held that up too. His eyes never left her face. In the rapid succession of lightning flashes as the storm began to rage overhead they blazed in their dark pits with the hatred of revenge. His message was clear. Holding the knife like a quill he took a step forward and bared his teeth in a smile.

Hurriedly moving back out of range, she thought to escape outside but he was quick, slithering between herself and the doors at once. Recalling how the turret steps on the other side of the nave only led to the small watchtower where the guard was on duty, she decided she would make a break for it.

Grasping her only weapon, the heavy iron seal, she made a move but, with predatory foresight, he lunged towards her, snatching out for it, and her only recourse was to ram it back into her bag and scramble up the nearest ladder.

Halfway up she risked a glance down to see if he was following, but he was merely watching with the intent gaze of a bird of prey to see what she would do next.

Neither of them moved.

He said, 'There's no escape that way, no matter how high you climb. Do you want me to follow you and do it there?' The knife caught the sudden light. It was steady in his hand and left no doubt about what he intended.

'I made a mistake about you,' she said, surreptitiously climbing a little higher. 'I thought the way you contrived their murders the way you did was because you couldn't stand the sight of blood.'

'But as you see' – he flourished the knife – 'I do like it. I like the look of it. I like the smell of it. And best of all I like the way it drains from the body leaving nothing but a filthy corpse behind.' He tilted his head on one side to try to see her more clearly in the shadow cast by the platform. 'But you're right in one respect,' he continued. 'It is rather too gross a method to make it my preferred choice. It has no skill. It's a brutish and dirty thing to stick a knife into another human being. How much cleverer and puzzling to the ignoramuses who find the body to let a man die of asphyxiation in an apple store. How that had them scratching their heads! How could he die for no reason, they were asking like fools. They seriously considered devils and the evil eye. I must congratulate you on working that one out, domina. Come down now and receive your reward, I beg you.'

One hand went to his pouch and he produced an apple. He held it up. 'You deserve this, to add to your already impressive knowledge of the fruit.'

The lightning flashed again and everything was

blanched for a second before being inked to black.

'See it? Even God sends his light to show it to you. And why not? It's the apple of knowledge, forbidden to such as you. Look on it. And repent. And then prepare for punishment.'

For one brief moment it crossed her mind that this must be the penance Hubert wanted to exact from her for her grievous sin against the Rule and himself.

Rousing herself to fight back, she asked, 'Tell me magister. Are you afraid of heights? Why don't you bring it to me?'

He preened. 'I'm afraid of nothing.'

'Then come up and give it to me,' she coaxed.

'I prefer my victims to come to me. Like Edred that night. He thought he had me on his side and that I'd invited him up to the pond in that blizzard to tell him so. In fact I offered him payment to keep his mouth shut, but he refused. High up on his horse. Daring to look down on me.'

'Satisfy my curiosity then. I think you owe me that. How could you have not been seen when you fixed things for Aelwyn in the store?'

He held up the apple again. 'They know I'm often up there. To take my pick. Nothing strange about that. If you mean the surplices, that was easy, they were just hanging there in the laundry waiting to be taken and stuffed into place.'

'So how could you have been unseen when you returned from killing Edred? No-one was out that night without good reason. You must have been the only one to enter the building covered in snow.'

While he considered his answer she moved a little higher, thankful for the shadows that concealed her movements. She was almost out of his reach now. If he followed her she would have the advantage.

'People see only what they want to see,' he eventually explained, as if to a child. 'You're fools. I'm about the place all the time, the insignificant shadow of the lord bursar. Nobody notices me.'

'That's true. I hardly noticed you sitting in the corner of the abbot's chamber when I came to meet him.' With the candlelight shining briefly on his face as he came to the bottom of the ladder, she saw in his expression a thwarted desire to be noticed. Had she found his weakness? She asked, 'Does the lord abbot know what you've done?'

'Heaven forfend! He doesn't know anything. He's an incompetent fool. What do you imagine he would do with such knowledge, apart from run amok? He'd have me scourged from here to Rome!'

With one hand on the ladder he took a large bite from his apple and began to chew.

'You'd certainly be noticed then. Imagine!' She moved higher. 'Is that what you're hoping for? Notoriety? Your name on everyone's lips at last?' The difficulty was that she could not reach her knife because she needed both hands to climb the ladder. In a moment she would be able to swing on to the first platform on the scaffolding. And then what? Fear of the next move forced her attention back to the clerk.

She called down. 'It's strange, isn't it, magister, how hardly anyone mentions your name?' She took a surreptitious step upwards. 'I've only heard it once. I believe they call you Cuthred. *"Cuthred, take some notes . . . Cuthred, write this down."'*

There was no response from him. She took another step, her movements invisible in the darkness. 'Now would that be Anglian or Saxon?' she asked. 'It's certainly not Norman. Your Norman overlords have French names. Were your forebears bonded labourers who managed to buy their freedom? Or did they simply abscond and earn their freedom in a year and a day?'

'Hold your tongue!'

'Why don't you come up?' How long was he going to prolong this game? For sure he would not let her escape to freedom. He had to come up. 'You must know how to climb, Cuthred. You must have worked hard to weasel your way up from the stigma of your lowly birth to this height. Climbing must be second nature.'

He gave an angry jerk of his head but continued biting his way through the apple to the very core.

'I admit I'm surprised you don't support the mariners. Or would that be to acknowledge your origins?'

'I'll tell you once more—'

'It must be almost impossible to ascend the church hierarchy without any useful strings to pull. I assume that's why a man of your ability is so far from real power. How frustrating to have to suffer fools ruling the roost over you!'

His voice grated with menace. 'Are you coming

down or do I have to come up and fetch you down?'

'Come up, if you dare, Cuthred . . . *magister*.' Her laughter annoyed him as she hoped it would. It drew him on.

His temper flared. 'You've asked for it!'

Hurling the apple core into the darkness, he gripped the ladder with one hand, realized that he had to hold it with both hands in addition to the knife in order to climb up and so, pushing the knife into his belt, he set foot on the first rung.

In a trice Hildegard scrambled to the top and climbed on to the walkway. Careful to tread over the gaps between the planks, she dashed to the farthest end where another ladder led up to the next level. The rattling of planks below told her that he was following. The scaffolding shook. When she reached the top she began to untie the twine that held the ladder in place. Working quickly and helped by the darkness of the vault she pulled it loose, but to her dismay the ladder would not shake free.

Feeling along the edge in the darkness she discovered another tie, but no amount of pulling would undo the knot. She reached for her knife and began to saw at the rope.

The clerk was grovelling somewhere down below and, with a freezing of her blood, she realized that he had the same idea. It was not, however, the ladder he was trying to free, but the scaffolding itself. He was trying to release the ropes that held the struts in place. The entire edifice would crash to the ground if he succeeded.

Feverishly she looked round for some way of stopping him.

What one of the mason's men had said when he came up to make everything fast in the high winds a couple of days ago came back to her now. Searching along the platform for something she could use, she found a bucket lashed to one of the uprights. Quickly freeing it, she edged along the planks until she was kneeling directly above the clerk. Then she let it fall.

A curse came from below, but he grabbed at one of the struts and must have looked upwards because she saw a pale blur below. From it came a venomous snarl. 'You'll suffer for that, nun!'

Leaving his attempt to collapse the supports he hurled himself with outstretched hands towards a dangling rope she had disregarded. Its other end was tied to the main beam near her feet. It was a complicated knot and the weight of the man climbing up the rope pulled it even tighter.

*If he gets up here, I'm trapped!* She glanced frantically round for a means of escape.

The platform was incomplete and ended where the planks had not yet been laid. The main supporting joist had been positioned to reach the opposite side and was inserted into a hole in the wall of the tower. She judged the possibility of walking out along it, but then what? It led to the loop allowing access to the tower with the crossbowman on guard, or down the steps back into the nave where the clerk would be able to cut off her escape as before. Otherwise it was a long drop to the floor of the nave, an escape route that was out of the question.

Meanwhile he had hauled himself up the rope and was treading towards her along the platform with hands outstretched as if he found it difficult to see where he was going. It occurred to her that his night vision was poor.

Step by slow step, careful of where to put his feet, he came towards her. The scrape of his knife every time it scored into the stone wall next to the platform was guiding him through the darkness across the planks to where she stood.

Scarcely able to breathe for fear, she placed one foot on the wide supporting joist and paused for a moment to get her balance. Taking several slow and deliberate steps along it she warned herself not to look down. Another couple of steps took her further out until there was a frightening gap between the edge of the platform and where she was balanced.

Meanwhile the clerk was looming closer with muttered threats, intent on reaching her. Now he would have to step on to the joist, if he dare, in order to use his knife. She was prepared. It would be both of them. But she would not yield.

'Cuthred,' she called when he hesitated, 'you're a fraud and no matter how clever you are, you have no nobility of soul. It was a terrible thing you did. Repent now, before it's too late.'

'Be quiet! Respect me, you bitch! When I get to you I'll make you show respect!'

His reluctance to own the heinousness of his

actions aroused her contempt. 'I thought you said you had a reward for me? When are you going to let me have it?'

'Now. Don't doubt it! Hiding in the dark won't save you!' Concentrating on where he was putting his feet, he groped his way towards her. 'Where the devil are you?'

'Closer to heaven than you, Cuthred. I'm here, before your eyes. See me?'

She stretched out both arms to maintain her balance just as another sudden lightning flash illuminated her with a hiss of phosphorus that for one second blanched the colour from everything around.

He glanced across and saw her shining form in the unearthly light.

Darkness engulfed them as thunder crashed overhead. Dazzled but drawn by rage towards her he blundered forward.

When he came to the edge of the platform, not noticing that it had ended, he took one fatal step.

His yelp of surprise turned to cursing rage and finally to a scream of fear. It was abruptly cut off. A horrifying silence welled up from the floor of the nave.

At the speed of someone pursued by devils, Hildegard took a breath, ran back a few paces along the joist and jumped back across the gap to safety. She stumbled to her knees. Her legs would not hold her up. She was shaking with relief. The scaffolding rocked and groaned. Gasping with the fear that had been held in check during every slow step he had taken towards her, she gave way to sobs of relief. Tears scalded her cheeks. He was gone. She was safe. She had not fallen. Something had saved her.

Near at hand came a voice and a hand gripped her by one shoulder. Out of the darkness came a man's laughter.

She turned. And screamed. Almost fainting with terror, she gripped his hauberk so tightly the steel links bit into her fingers.

Through the intermittent flashes of lightning as the storm raged directly overhead, the scarred and battered face of the mercenary from the slype the previous night grinned grotesquely within inches of her face.

He grasped her hands, pressing them roughly on to his coat of mail to stop her escape until she was gasping with pain.

He grunted, 'What happened to Cuthred? Did he fall?'

Gaping and trying to struggle from his grasp she asked, 'How d–did you get here?'

'Out of the tower where I was on duty. I saw you standing on the joist and decided to follow you. It was easy but you have some nerve for a woman!' He chuckled. 'When you stood there lit by lightning he must've thought you were an avenging angel!'

He was still chuckling as he pulled at her to bring her close against him.

The shock was leaving her as she guessed his intention and her anger returned. 'Did you hear what he was saying? He confessed to murdering both of them.'

'He was a blundering sot-wit, thought too

much of his own cleverness. I'd have simply rammed a knife in his guts if he'd threatened me, and in theirs. Too much learning, that was his trouble. Reckon any fool can learn to read and write if they want to. Frankly, I've never seen the need . . . Not saying much?' he admonished when she did not respond to such brutality. 'Are you remembering what I said before?' He put his lips close to her ear. 'About never having had a nun?'

'We're in church—'

'So near to Heaven? I can't think of anywhere better.'

'I don't understand what you have to do with Hertilpole's clerk.' Weakly, she tried to play for time. 'Why do you call him a sot-wit?'

'Him and Hertilpole thought they ran me, but it's the other way about, that's why. I let them plot and plan then I go in and make sure it all happens the way it should. How do you think they get anybody to do what they want? By bleating about it? By prayers? By threatening hellfire? It's because I enforce it. Me! I'm for hire, lady. I work for Dickson, the abbey or anybody who wants me enough to pay my fee. I could work for you and your priory if you think you can afford me.'

'He admitted he murdered Aelwyn himself.'

'Of course he did. And who was behind that? Same as wanted that Edred out of the game. Old Blabbermouth. What a mess he made of it with his clever-clever plans. My knife would have done just as well. But no – and his creature agreed. I'll do it, said I. No, he said, no blood,

335

leave it to me, he said. All that about liking blood! He ran from it like the clerk he was.'

She rounded her eyes. 'So he was telling the truth?' By 'Blabbermouth' it was obvious whom he meant. 'And Lord Hertilpole is the power behind it all?'

'He thinks he is – cash for a fake relic – what a plan! With nobody letting on it isn't the real thing until Aelwyn has a pang of conscience and remembers in time he's supposed to be holier than thou! Edred in deeper than he realizes with his wheeling and dealing. And Hertilpole, wanting the moon but not prepared for the blood he would have to shed to get it! Fools to think it! How else could they get what they wanted without bloodshed? . . . And maybe more to come.'

'Bloodshed?'

'Yours?'

A silence fell.

'In a little while. No hurry,' he said easily. 'First things first.'

Eventually Hildegard said, 'And everything they did was only possible because of you?'

'Now you understand.'

'I hope they paid you well.'

'There's more than the relic and a paltry chest of gold at stake.' He lowered his voice a fraction to impart a secret. 'The abbey knows they don't run everything. Richmond knows. I'm sure you've cottoned on to it yourself.'

'Do you mean what I think you mean?' she bluffed.

He nodded. 'They're one small link in the

chain of power stretching from the Scottish border down to the palace of Westminster. I reckon the old fellow knows more than he lets on, despite what our friend lying on the cold tiles below thought about him. Abbot or not, he doesn't fool me with his praying.' He shook his head. 'How can you clever folk with all your reading not know what's really at stake?'

'What *is* at stake?'

'What do you think?'

He was gripping her so tightly against him that she had to lean back a little to look into his smug face. 'I don't know.'

He gave the grimace that was intended to be a smile. 'You're as sot-witted as all the rest then. It's the Crown of England, what else?'

She eased back a little but could not loosen his grasp. 'King Richard would never give up the crown.'

'He won't have a choice. He has no army of his own and they make sure he has no means to buy one. Gloucester, Arundel, Lancaster and the others are well armed. They can do what they want. They have the wealth and they have their armed men who owe them scutage. They're sitting pretty and they know it. As soon as they stop their bickering and decide which of them will wear the crown they'll make their move.'

She nodded as if this was all new to her. 'But why are you here?'

'To punish a bunch of mariners and their allies? I don't think so. That's only a sideshow. I'm here to summon an array when the call comes. I'm amazed at you! All you folk. Are you living in a dream world of angels and virgins? Sin and penance? Heaven and Hell? It's about power. Money. Steel. Nobody's exempt.'

The thought brought him back to the present, to the feast of virgin flesh as he imagined it, the joy of venery awaiting him. He pressed himself hard against her and she could feel his arousal.

'Now,' he was saying with a smug smile on his distorted features, 'we've prattled long enough!'

He automatically lowered his glance for a fraction of a second in order to lift the hem of his hauberk – it was amazing that he had not learned his lesson the first time. Hildegard took an immediate chance to swing the iron seal from within her bag and hit him hard under his jaw. There was a crunch as they connected.

He had no time to curse because she pushed him full in the chest with both hands, making him stumble backwards. When he came at her again she fell against the stone wall and had to dodge away out of reach. As he pursued her his steel-shod boots skidded on the edge of the platform. He grabbed for one of the uprights. Missed. And pitched backwards into the void.

He fell silently.

Then a sickening crack came as he hit the tiles forty feet below.

*What have I done? No, no!* Hildegard peered down into the nave. A group of people were looking up. She could see the pale blur of their faces. In the forgiving glow of the candlelight she could make out a shape spread-eagled on the tiles with a dark ooze spreading from it.

A hand came down on her shoulder just as it had already done and she flinched away in horror. But it was Gregory.

He took her in his arms while she kept repeating, 'I've killed a man! I've killed him!'

He steadied her, murmuring words she did not understand, confirming that it was over, all over, and only after a time was she able to return to herself and speak more steadily. 'Gregory? What have I done?'

'It's over. It's finished, Hildegard.'

'Did you see what happened?'

'We heard everything. He was going to violate you and then kill you. It was either you or him.'

She was unable to stop shaking.

'Come, are you able to climb down unaided?'

'Did you see?'

'We saw and heard everything,' he repeated.

'Is he dead?' she queried, disbelief persisting.

'As dead as the many men he has murdered with cold-blooded deliberation in the life he chose.'

He held her firmly until she could take a step without falling. Slowly, handling her like glass, he guided her down to safety.

A group of people clustered at the foot of the ladder. Torold and his silent friend, and Miggy, restraining Duke with both hands, were bathed in the glow from the candle flames. Thunder rumbled faintly in the distance as the storm receded. The boys gave a subdued cheer as she reached them and the silent boy touched her on the sleeve with the gentleness of a caress.

Miggy said, 'We saw you coming in here

339

following that clerk of Hertilpole's and thought we'd better find out what was up—'

'But you'd disappeared when we came inside and it was just him, talking to himself we thought, until we saw a pale blur up high—' Torold continued.

'We thought it was the ghost of St Hild. But then we saw the clerk looming out of the shadows and when we looked up again there was a flash of lightning and we saw the ghost was you—'

'But you vanished and there was that noise and we thought the whole scaffolding was coming down on our heads. But he stepped off the platform as if he hadn't seen it end—'

'And that armed guard appeared from out of the tower. We thought you were finished – until Brother Gregory appeared and started up the ladder—'

Gregory was still holding her. 'My gratitude for alerting us, lads. Well done. Not that we were in time to do anything.'

Egbert came over and pushed Gregory aside. 'Enough now.' Putting an arm round Hildegard and shielding her eyes with the other hand he said, 'Let the abbey servants deal with everything, Hildegard. It was not your fault.'

Torold had the last word. 'And now our lord God has revealed his true power. My father is avenged.'

Two days later, on the morning of the Eve of Epiphany, Prior Allerton ushered Hildegard into the abbot's private chamber where, as before, Richmond, old, frail, as ambiguous as ever, was sitting on his usual pile of cushions in front of a lusty fire. He waved to his servant to bring forward something comfortable for Hildegard to sit on and poured her a glass of blood-red wine with his own hand. The prior went back to his place on his right.

After a few pleasantries and an assurance that – after the townsfolk were beaten back down the cliff by the abbey servants who 'overstepped the mark in their zeal to protect the abbey', as Richmond put it – talks with the leader of the mariners, convened by the lord prior, were about to begin, 'with the hope of a more acceptable outcome to both sides than heretofore.'

The prior rumbled his agreement.

'Peter Hertilpole,' remarked the abbot blandly, 'has regained his wits after the scare he suffered when a candelabra accidentally fell on him. Fortunately for him, as you've probably heard, the infirmarer, our beloved Brother Dunstan, happened to be passing by the open door of the muniments room with a couple of stalwart assistants at the time and they were able to save him and all our documents from greater harm. His subsequent ill-advised response to the mariners was an understandable reaction to the shock of what had befallen him.' His pale eyes showed no inclination to hear her object to this interpretation of events.

'Now,' he settled back and took another sip of wine, 'I have asked you here, domina, to make amends for the fright you must have suffered when one of the abbey clerks, ascending the tower to give instructions to the guards, fell from the scaffolding and the guard, unable to see clearly in the darkness and having heard the cry as the clerk fell, missed his footing and fell also. Two falls in quick succession! And you, I hear, have witnessed both! I have therefore asked Master Buckingham to make his scaffolding safer in future. We want no more accidents.'

He leaned forward to take something from the stool beside him. 'Before you leave, briefly to re-enter the outside world in all its tumult and rumour in order to regain your sanctuary at Swyne, I have a gift for your priory. I trust that it will suffice to make amends for all that has transpired. You will find, inside this plain wooden box, the very thing that brought you to Whitby.' He handed it to her and when she was about to open it he stretched out his bejeweled fingers. 'No, later, in the presence of your prioress. I believe she will appreciate my donation.'

Hildegard could barely speak for astonishment. 'Is it the sacred object she hoped to obtain?'

'All things under Heaven are sacred and it gives me great joy to donate to her and her nuns this most holy work of God, this purported lock of hair from the head of our beloved Abbess, St Hild.' He took another sip of wine. 'Depart with my blessing, domina. *Pax vale atque*.'

Unable for once to think of anything to say, Hildegard, clutching the box, took her leave.

They were in the stables having their horses saddled up and Egbert was still in the sort of daze that verged on outright, unashamed mirth. He kept shaking his head and punching Gregory on the shoulder like a fellow accomplice in some jape that has confounded everyone's expectations and, to his astonishment, turned out rather well.

When Hildegard had emerged from her interview with Abbot Richmond, clutching something the size of a man's hand, they had decided there and then that they would leave at once and ride hard, changing horses as many times as was needed, in order to reach Meaux before the Feast of Epiphany ended on the morrow.

Luke was smiling with relief. 'I can't wait until I see the gatehouse of dearly beloved Meaux!' he exclaimed. 'And I have good news, too, to set us on our way.'

'Go on.' Egbert folded his arms.

'When I went down to Selby's house to return the little bursa belonging to Sabine, I discovered that our dear sister has removed herself from that malign household to the house of Anna, Edred's widow, where she'll help with her children. Better still, together they intend to set up as net-makers for the mariners. Master Dickson decided she wasn't happy as she was and that she would be better running a team making nets – to supply the fishing fleets up and down the coast. He has promised to give her the monopoly against any competitors within the town bounds for a small share in their profit. We may not approve of him, but he deals fairly with those he favours.'

'That's good news. What else?'

'She thought it might be due to something we had said that led him to the idea . . . She asked if she might kiss me for it.'

343

Hildegard smiled. 'I hope you said yes. It's kind to accept gratitude from those one has helped.' Luke blushed.

'All's well, then!' Grinning, Egbert geed his horse and they set off after him.

This time there was no hail or snow as they turned to have one last look at the magnificent edifice of the abbey. It stood in all its grandeur on the headland and behind it the sky was a pure, winter blue, as delicate and full of promise as a new-laid egg.

It suggested fresh beginnings: for the King himself after his calamitous year of betrayals and bloodshed and, perhaps, also for Prior Allerton now he had eventually roused himself sufficiently to look like the abbot he might one day become when Richmond's span was over.

As for the bursar, although still haggard and with feverish eyes, he already had the aspect of a man with a new plot in mind and the best that could be hoped was that the abbey would prosper from it and no harm would occur. The Cistercians exchanged ironic smiles when his brief memory loss was mentioned, when he had temporarily forgotten where he had hidden the year's rents for safe-keeping. It was considered to be something that could happen to anyone with so much on their minds. The town was mostly to blame for causing him stress and strain with their demands. Now all was to rights again.

Not forgetting that it was the King's twenty-second birthday, the Cistercians celebrated briefly and quietly on the ride back at a little wayside chapel before continuing with all speed to their beloved sanctuary at Meaux.

When they clattered into the yard as the Feast Day was drawing to a close the place was alight with festal candles. Cressets flared from the wall sconces and the sound of monks singing inside their austere church floated hauntingly across the yard as they dismounted and wearily discussed whether they should go into the midnight service or collapse on to their beds.

On the morrow Hildegard would ride on to Swyne, her mission complete, her penance duly paid, with the triple-locked pouch, the plainly carved reliquary, and one other object, a gift no bigger than a man's hand, containing something that later might give rise to speculation.

'Let's go into Matins,' she suggested. 'Let's give praise for our safe arrival home.'

A figure watching from the steps of the church counted them in.

Four of them.

His two reliable monks militant. His youngest priest. And his nun.

With a sigh of relief, Abbot Hubert de Courcy turned to go inside to conduct the midnight Office.

*Penitent or not, she was back!*